POLICE NAVIDAD

MYSTERY WRITER'S MYSTERY #4

BECKY CLARK

Cover design by Steven Novak

ISBN: 978-1-954385-01-6 (paperback)
ISBN: 978-1-954385-00-9 (ebook)

www.BeckyClarkBooks.com

This book is dedicated to everyone who likes Christmas, dogs, senior centers, kids, and/or punny book titles.

ONE

"**P**eter can be baby Jesus in the pageant!" Barb bounced excitedly in her armchair. The action made her look more like an eight-year-old than an eighty-year-old.

I glanced over at Peter O'Drool, her pug, who raised his wheezy face at the mention of his name, then wagged the tip of his curly tail.

"I'm sure baby Jesus drooled and got gassy, but nothing like Pete. And I'm pretty sure that crosses the line into sacrilegious. If I'm going to write a Christmas play, it's going to be secular." I shrugged at Peter in his doggy bed. "Sorry."

In an effort certainly meant to snub me, Peter jumped on to Barb's lap, stood on her thighs and before she could stop him, licked her nose. Then he turned around three times as he snuggled down. Two seconds later, she made a face, and lifted him back to the floor. "Peter! Excuse yourself."

The odor crashed across the room like a tidal wave, first toward Don sitting at the end of the couch closest to his wife, then to me. Even though the December temperature had barely reached freezing, Don jumped up to open the front door of their apartment and gave it a couple of good flutters. I fanned a hand in front of my face.

"See? Pretty sure baby Jesus never did that."

Peter O'Drool took umbrage and curled back in his bed, making a point of turning his back on me.

"Be that as it may, Pete would make an adorable addition to any play," Barb said, holding her nose.

"I bet I can write a part for a doggy elf," I mused. "How much does this gig pay anyway?"

"What's that?" Don cupped a hand behind his ear.

Barb leaned closer to me. "He dropped his hearing aid—"

"Again?" I turned to Don and shouted, "What were you doing this time? Juggling with them?"

He stuck out his tongue at me. He gave the door a couple more swings, then closed it and sat back down, the worst of the stench dissipated. He made sure to sit with his working ear toward us.

"Darn hearing aid is out of warranty and I can't get an appointment with the audiologist until after Christmas. I still have one ear that mostly works. Everything's just in mono instead of stereo these days." We sat there in silence for a moment, until he asked, "What were we talking about?"

"I was asking how much I'd get paid for writing this Christmas play."

"Nothing. Sorry, Charlee. It's a fundraising event between our Leetsdale Senior Center and the elementary school nearby."

"It's a low-income school," Barb said. "The principal came by a few months ago and made a presentation to the board. We all thought it sounded like a great idea. Kind of a *unite the generations* thing as well as a fundraiser. During their winter break, the parents will have the option of bringing their kids to the senior center for daycare. The kids and the seniors will all hang out together. There will be a store, the kids can sit on Santa's lap, stuff like that." Barb grinned, pleased as punch, leaning closer to me. "We got a great Santa who volunteers all over town playing Santa at homeless shelters and local events. It was quite the coup, if I do say so myself."

Don made a particularly grumpy noise, sort of a cross between a *harumph* and a louder *harumph*.

"Don really wanted the job, though."

"I'll live," he said, tacking on an even grumpier *harumph* at the end.

Barb narrowed her eyes at her husband. "Donald David Singer, that is not in keeping with the Christmas spirit. If you keep acting like that, people will think … well, I don't know what they'll think. But it won't reflect kindly on you." She sighed then turned to me and continued, "The culmination will be the play. Which we really hope you'll agree to write."

Barb's face was so hopeful it hurt my spleen. As much as I hated to disappoint them, I really didn't have time to write a play. My bank balance was screaming at me every day, accusing me of slow and steady strangulation. It was on its last gasp. I needed the next installment of my publisher's advance for the romantic suspense novel I was struggling with, and the only way to do that was to finish the draft of the darn thing and get it to my editor. Then and only then would I have time to write a Christmas play for kids and seniors to perform. Of course, the kids might be seniors by then.

"Barb, I can't. I just can't." Her face crumpled so I added, "Besides, you don't want me anyway. I have no idea how to write a play. Nor do I know anything about writing for kids." I looked toward Don for help.

Don reached over and patted Barb's knee. "It's okay, dear. Charlee's right. Just because Mavis crapped out on us and decided to book that cruise because Denver was suddenly too cold isn't Charlee's problem. Charlee needs to live her best life, and that clearly doesn't include poor children, Peter's star turn, or a bunch of futzy old folks." He leaned back against the couch and winked at me.

I shook my finger at him. "You are evil, Donald David Singer."

"Let me get us all some tea, while we talk this over," Barb said.

She scooched forward in her chair, but I waved her back down. "No, you sit. I'll do it. It'll give me time to plot my revenge against Don." At the kitchen doorway I looked back at Don, grinning at me. "I bet you expect me to bring you something to eat, too."

"There's carrot cake already sliced in the fridge," Barb sang out.

"Don't forget to warm the teapot!" Don called.

I shook my finger at him again and tried not to let him see me smile. I loved these two people, and pretty much adopted them as my grandparents. But they sure knew how to manipulate me. There was no way I could refuse them, especially since they never really asked me for anything. I sighed while I filled the kettle. While it heated, I ran the hot tap to warm Barb's favorite china pot. I knew exactly where to find it because their kitchen was exactly like mine, since my apartment was directly underneath theirs. I've made tea in Barb and Don's kitchen as often as I have in my own. Maybe more, actually.

I heard the soft murmur of their voices in the living room and wondered what else they were plotting for me. I chose some chamomile, hoping it might relax them enough that I could hypnotize them or something so they wouldn't remember asking me about writing a holiday play. As I gathered everything on the tea tray and carried it to the living room, I tried another tactic.

"You guys have read my books. They're not at all kid-friendly. I'd be a terrible choice to do this. Maybe I can help you find someone—" When I looked up after setting down the tray, I saw them both smiling hopefully at me. I stared back at them, trying my hardest to keep a neutral look on my face. It didn't take long before I was laughing. "You guys! How do you *do* that? I'm like putty in your hands."

Don patted Barb's knee again. "Our work here is done, dear."

The smile slid off Barb's face. "We don't want to pressure you, Charlee. Really we don't. But you're the only person we can turn to. We know you'll keep your word and get it done in time. And we truly believe you have the talent to write a Christmas play."

"We know you always worry about your career, ever since the … um … unfortunate incident with your agent—"

"Oh, the one where I was accused of her murder? I'd almost forgotten." I handed Don a slice of cake.

"Yes, that one." Don chuckled. "You worry too much about money."

"Says everyone who has money." I handed a plate to Barb.

Don raised his hands in surrender. "Fine. Worry about money and your career all you want. But think about this. This will give you tons of publicity."

"Tons? A rinky-dink Christmas play at a senior center with child actors? Color me dubious."

"I'm serious. We'll get you all kinds of publicity." Don forked a big bite of carrot cake. "I'll get the marketing department on it."

"The Leetsdale Senior Center has a marketing department?" I asked, mid-bite.

"They will on Monday."

I whooshed out a breath. "You're incorrigible."

"Please say yes, Charlee," Barb said. "Please?" She poured us all tea.

Neon lights flashed in my brain reminding me of everything I needed to do this month. Writing a play for kids wasn't on the list. Was never on the list. But then the neon was replaced with something much more somber and muted. Guilt. Selfishness. The Ghost of Christmas Present. What kind of horrible person was I that I couldn't even spare a couple of days to write, what, thirty pages or so? I was a Scrooge. A Grinch. A Bad Santa.

I took a deep breath. "I will write a holiday play for your event." I sipped my tea, trying not to smile, while they clinked cups in victory.

"Thank you, dear," Barb said.

I waved her off.

"No, I mean it. We know you're busy with other things—"

"Other things that make you money," Don interrupted.

"And we really, really appreciate it. Really."

"I know." I set my teacup on the coffee table. "I shouldn't have made such a fuss. I feel so selfish. I want to do it, really I do, but I also want to get my manuscript finished. But I also want to help those kids and the senior center." I slumped against the back of the couch. "I don't know what I want."

"People want what they want, Charlee," Barb said. "Even when it makes them feel guilty and selfish. It doesn't make you a bad person. It just makes you a person."

"It just doesn't seem like the Christmas spirit for me to have my nose stuck in a suspense manuscript that's decidedly not Christmas-y. Plus, I'm cranky because my mom says she's not coming to Denver for Christmas because her friend Doris is having hip replacement the week before and can't get anyone else to stay and take care of her. So, Mom to the rescue. Which also makes me feel guilty and selfish." I shook my head in defiance. "Writing a Christmas play is exactly what I need right now to morph me from Scrooge to Santa." I took another big bite of my cake. "I'm all in. When do you need it?"

"Could we get it next Saturday, the eighth?" Barb looked at Don for agreement. He nodded.

"One week from today you will have a holiday play in

your hands." I glanced over at Peter. "It will not have a gassy little pug in it, however."

Don stuck out his hand. "Deal."

Barb tapped one fingernail on the edge of her cup. Probably plotting how to make a star out of Peter yet.

TWO

As I tried to negotiate room in my freezer for Barb's gift of two loaves of banana bread and umpteen dozen Christmas cookies, courtesy of the senior center cookie exchange party, I reminded myself there were worse ways to get paid for writing. "Besides," I said to the ice tray I was forced to remove, "It's only twenty or thirty pages, right? How hard could it be?"

Never having written a play, much less a play for children, I went to the only know-it-all I appreciated, my computer browser. I searched "how to write a children's play" and began scanning blogs and articles. I jotted notes as I read. *Write what you love. Write what kids love. Know your market. Know your cast. Use the right words. Offer lessons but don't preach.*

I numbered my list. "Great. Zero for six."

I gleaned everything I could from the articles I read, until they began to sound repetitious. Then I closed my laptop and turned to a clean sheet on my yellow legal pad to brainstorm ideas. "What will this play be about?" I mused, tapping my pen on the page.

I wrote my ideas without editing. No ideas were bad ideas when brainstorming, after all.

I wrote, *Someone stole Santa's sleigh and tomorrow is Christmas Eve!* Tapped my pen some more. *But really Rudolph took it for a joy ride and got stuck in a snowdrift because he doesn't have thumbs and can't hold the reins. And who will lead it? The other reindeer? Can he boss them around? Is he in charge of Dasher and Dancer and the gang? And if Santa found out, Rudolph would probably get demoted — maybe even fired — red nose or not.*

Rereading what I'd written, I inserted an editor's caret after "joy" and added between the lines "to the world." Even with the pun, the idea couldn't be salvaged.

The entire paragraph got crossed out with an angry X. Many of them, actually.

I tapped my pen some more then wrote, *All the cookies Mrs Claus baked disappeared and tomorrow is Christmas Eve! She accused Santa, but really it was one of the elves who took them because while he was busy playing World of Warcraft, his cookies burned and he had nothing to take to the office party.*

I quit writing but wondered what kind of drama that accusation would bring to the Claus' relationship. Could they mend a rift like that? Wasn't that pretty unfair of her to bring it up right before the busiest, most stressful night of his entire year? And why was she baking cookies anyway? Santa was destined to get a ton as soon as he left the North Pole. Too many, probably. And what's an elf doing playing computer games when it's crunch time at work? They should have their office party in February when everyone can relax and let their hair down for a while.

I tore the paper from the pad, wadded it up, and tossed it toward the trash can.

Thirty minutes later, I had eight more wadded up balls of yellow paper on the floor near the trash can. And who knows how many more that had miraculously landed inside.

I made an emergency conference call to my critique group.

When they all clicked on, I explained my dilemma. "So I need you guys to help me get some ideas."

"Right now?" Jenica asked. "I'm in the middle of—"

"No can do," Kell said.

"Oh dear," Cordelia said.

"Can't now," AmyJo said. "I'm at work."

"Why'd you answer, then?" I asked.

"Because you sent us a 911!"

That dual feeling of selfishness and guilt roared back at me. I'd done it again.

Everyone started talking at once, the bane of every conference call. "Hold it!" I shouted. "It wasn't fair for me to ask you guys to drop everything and help me."

"Damn straight," Einstein said.

I heard Heinrich laugh, thus kicking off his loud, phlegmy cough. I waited for him to stop. "I guess I deserved that."

"Damn straight," Einstein said again.

"I said I was sorry."

"No you didn't," he said.

"Well, I am. Let me try again. Would it be possible for any of you to join me at Espresso Yourself tomorrow morning for a brainstorming session?"

"You buying the coffee?" Jenica asked.

"Absolutely. And some butter braids, if we get there early enough."

"Damn straight," Einstein said.

THREE

The next morning, I woke and showered early. When I stepped into the kitchen, Ozzi was reading the Sunday funnies in the *Denver Post*.

I leaned over his shoulder. "Did Dagwood get a sandwich? Dennis the Menace repeat some gossip his parents had no business sharing with him? Was Garfield in bed? I'm dying to know." I gave him a long, lingering kiss on the mouth.

Ozzi's eyes rolled into the back of his head. "I don't remember."

I topped off his coffee.

"None for you?" he asked.

"I'm off to Espresso's to meet my critique group. They're going to help me brainstorm something."

He tried to hide a smile.

"What?" He didn't answer. "You know it makes me nervous when my boyfriend smirks."

Ozzi stood and started gyrating his hips. Then he bent and bopped his butt around. "What does it do for you when your boyfriend twerks?"

I stared, trying not to laugh. "Absolutely nothing."

He grabbed me around the waist and performed a sexy bump-and-grind. "When will you be home?"

"I don't know. When you're done twerking?"

"Fair enough."

He was still twerking when I closed the front door.

The walk across our apartment complex was wintry, but blessedly devoid of snow. Maybe that bodes well for an uneventful holiday. Christmas was several weeks away, but some people were already going on and on about the magic of a white Christmas. I suspected these people lived where there was no snow, because everyone else knew what a hassle snow could be, especially at the holidays. Airport delays. Dangerous travel. Slip-and-falls. Cancelled parties and events. The only time a white Christmas was magical was when all your loved ones were tucked inside a cozy and well-stocked house with you, and nobody had to go anywhere. Then, for sure, let it snow, let it snow, let it snow.

I gave my scarf another wrap around my neck and wondered if Ozzi would still be tucked inside my cozy kitchen when I got home. His apartment was technically in a different building than mine and Don and Barb's, in the back of the complex. Our friends and families have finally quit asking us when we're going to move in together, accepting our answer that we like the together-yet-apart aspect of our living situation. Our motto was *a little elbow room is good for a relationship*.

But I wouldn't mind having him warm up my elbows when I finished at Espresso Yourself.

While I waited for traffic to clear so I could cross the street, I smiled at the wooden, hand-lettered sign inviting everyone to "Espresso Yourself — Coffee and Books" with the tagline *for when you have a latte on your mind*. While I did have a lot on my mind, I wasn't much of a fan of lattes, instead preferring Lavar and Tuttle's plain 'ol bottomless cup of strong, black coffee. I snorted, realizing they were both strong and black too. Two gay ex-Marines who loved each other only a little bit more than they loved their free weights. And by the looks of their arms, they loved their free weights an awful lot.

I pulled open the door expecting to be assaulted by the compatible aromas of coffee and pastry. Instead, I was assaulted by competing music, about four notches too loud. From the café side blasted "Angels We Have Heard on High" and from the used bookstore side blasted "Grandma Got Run Over By a Reindeer."

I had to shout to be heard. "Lavar! Tut! What's going on here?"

Tuttle leaned close to my ear and shouted, "Cheese and rice, Charlee! Lavar is trying to kill me!"

"With noise?" I shouted back.

"With dogma!"

"Go turn that down," I scolded. "I can't hear myself think!"

Tuttle strode behind the counter and silenced the angels, then walked over to an old boombox sitting on one of the bookshelves and quieted Grandma and her reindeer.

Lavar hurried out of the kitchen, drying his hands on a towel. "What did you do?" he demanded of Tuttle.

Tuttle showed him his palms. "Don't look at me! Charlee said she couldn't hear herself think."

"Hey! Don't throw me under your Christmas bus!" I'd been looking around the place. A few days ago, Ozzi and I were at the hardware store and he said it looked like someone's garage threw up all over it. I laughed at the mild clutter, because I hadn't seen Espresso Yourself yet. Now I could honestly say that Espresso Yourself looked like Christmas threw up all over it.

I figured out fairly quickly what the turf war was all

about. Lavar was a devout Christian and Tuttle was a devout atheist. The blue painter's tape dividing the two halves of the business clued me in. Oh, and the fact that the café side had every surface covered with religious Christmas symbols. Lavar's domain. Tiny gold twinkle lights draped and drooped, crisscrossing the ceiling so you could barely see it. Gold stars, advent wreaths, and shimmery angels filled the rest of the surfaces. Enormous poinsettias sat in the middle of each café table.

Tuttle obviously had claimed the bookstore side and it was decorated with all the secular trappings of the holiday. Wherever my eyes landed, they took in an inflatable *something* wearing a Santa outfit: cartoon characters, animals, snowmen, even a Christmas tree which seemed like overkill to me, even though its Santa hat topper was pretty cute. The brown door to the restroom was decorated with the facial features and buttons of an enormous gingerbread man, complete with fabric arms and legs attached on either side.

Lavar yanked open the restroom door, and stood with one exasperated arm outstretched. "And look what he did in here!"

A bit hesitant to view what someone had done in a restroom, I tentatively leaned forward to see Santa's cheery face on the closed seat of the toilet. The rug on the floor in front of it depicted Santa's red coat down to his black belt.

"That's ... something," I finally said.

Tuttle pointed indignantly at a three-foot tall angel figurine standing in the corner of the café, and stood tapping his foot while I took in the sight he presented to me. I tried to maintain some control over my face, but felt my eyes widen. The sweet-faced angel wore a wreath encircling her head, around which were placed four candles. If Lavar had never lit the wicks, I could honestly say it was the least objectionable decoration in the place, despite its size. But the fact was, he *had* lit them and now that poor angel had hard wax rivulets dried on her cherubic little face. Like she'd wept tears of concrete.

I stood for a long time taking it all in until I felt a wet nose nudge my hand. Looking down, I saw their sweet mid-sized rescue dog, Nova, gazing up with eyes that again begged me to rescue her. She wore reindeer antlers along with an angel outfit made of starched layers of tulle complete with a set of wings. She sat at my side with a doleful expression, also taking in the sights. She shook her head slightly, antlers wobbling. After a bit, she sighed and began weaving her way among the café tables to the corner where her dog bed permanently resided. When her wings got stuck between two chairs, she glanced wearily back at me as if to say, "Can you believe this?"

I don't know how I missed it, but an almost-life-sized creche lined the wall near Nova's bed, making her an anachronistic addition to the tableau.

I hurried to her, removing both her outfit and her antlers. She offered me bemused gratitude. A lesser dog would have stuck out her tongue at Lavar and Tuttle. But Nova was patient in the extreme, allowing her people to be who they were.

I pressed Nova's items into Lavar's hands and stared up at his Pikes Peak physique. "How serious is this?" I asked him.

He glared at Tuttle who glared back. I watched their staring contest with growing trepidation. Not only were they my friends, but they were my butter braid dealers. What would I do if they broke up and closed the business?

Lavar's stony expression wavered. He crossed his arms with more purpose, biceps bulging.

Tuttle reached over and poked his index finger into Lavar's cheek. Then he did it again. And again.

The third time was more than Lavar could stand and he busted out with a laugh that would make Santa jealous.

Lavar pulled Tuttle into a bear hug. "I'll get you next time!"

"So what exactly is going on here?" I asked while they shared a sweet kiss.

"King Tut didn't appreciate my Christmas decorations—"

"You mean winter holidays," Tuttle interrupted.

"Christmas decorations," he said pointedly, "so I challenged him to a Decorating Contest." Lavar waved a hand around. "Clearly, he lost."

A customer piped up from one of the far tables, "You both lost. And so did I. I think I've been blinded."

"Ha!" Lavar snapped his towel in the customer's general direction. "Would a bear claw bring your vision back?"

"Yes, it would, my man. Yes, it would."

Lavar slapped the towel over his shoulder and went behind the counter. I followed him, ready to order. Two big plastic jars, one labeled "Christmas" and one labeled "Winter Holiday" sat near the register. Propped against them was a notecard that read, "Decorating Contest—One Penny One Vote."

When Lavar delivered the guy's bear claw I said, "These look pretty even to me."

"Who're you voting for, dollface?" He leaned across the counter at me.

"Hm. I'm not sure. Who is getting my coffee and a couple butter braids?"

Lavar raced to fill a cup, but not before Tuttle had a blueberry butter bread heating in the microwave.

"Actually, I'll need at least two. I'm treating my critique group."

Tuttle and Lavar reached for another butter braid at the same time, then turned to me to settle the dispute. I reached into my wallet and pulled out a penny which I dropped in Tuttle's jar. "I do love the hustle on the butter braid. But I also love how you thrust that cup of coffee at me and didn't even slosh any out." I dropped a penny in Lavar's jar. "Now, how 'bout you two nuts push a couple tables together. And there'll be another penny in it for both of you if you keep the music off so we can work."

"Here, here!" said a voice from the bookstore side.

"Aw, you guys are no fun," Tuttle said with a playful smile as he and Lavar pushed two tables together and rearranged the chairs. Tuttle removed the poinsettias with slow, exaggerated movements so I'd be sure to see. I flipped him an entire nickel, much to Lavar's protestations.

As I settled in and opened a blank document on my laptop, my critique group joined me. I sat at the end of the table. Heinrich gave me a peck on the cheek and took the chair to my right. Einstein dropped his ancient backpack, held together with duct tape and presumption, and sat next to him, grabbing for the coffee cup in front of me. I rescued it just in time and called to Lavar to please bring more coffee and mugs for everyone.

"You're paying, right? You said you would." Einstein squinted at me.

"Yes. Even though I'm under the impression the college pays you to teach physics to future Einsteins."

"True. But free coffee tastes better."

I had to agree.

AmyJo McFarland came in next, unraveling about three miles of scarf before she sat to my left. Cordelia Hollister-Fiske sat next to her. Kell Mooney came in while Jenica Jahns was taking off her dramatic black cape. It matched her lipstick perfectly and I told her so.

"I know, right?" She fluttered her fingers. "Perfect with my nail polish too." Jenica had ragged fingernails, bitten to the quick, but she wasn't ashamed of them. Drew as much attention to them as possible, in fact. Today each finger sported a black coating, with a small red dot right in the center. "In honor of Christmas," she explained.

Tuttle hooted from behind the counter. "Gurl!"

Lavar *tsk-tsked* her, like an old fishwife.

Jenica looked questioningly at me. "Don't ask."

She and Kell each reached for the seat at the other end of the table. Kell dragged a chair for himself and they both sat at the end, one at either corner.

After Lavar and Tuttle served everyone coffee and butter braid slices, I explained our mission. "I have to write this Christmas, er, holiday play for a bunch of kids and seniors to perform, but I don't have any good ideas."

"Do you even know how to write a play?" Einstein asked with his mouth full.

"Nope. I'm hoping that part comes later."

Heinrich said, "I can send you a bunch of plays for research." The word, like so many of Heinrich's words, came out coated in phlegm. "I teach a unit about plays."

"For kids?" I asked hopefully.

"If kids like Eugene O'Neill and Edward Albee."

"Well, anyway … remember, we're brainstorming so there are no bad ideas. Ready?" I positioned my hands above my keyboard. "Go!"

Nobody said anything so I lowered my hands.

Eventually Kell said, "There's a hostile takeover of the North Pole *and* Santa's brand by Hanukkah Harry."

Kell was a gazillionaire businessman. This is how he thinks. I dutifully typed it. "Anyone else?"

AmyJo helped herself to another slice of blueberry butter braid. "Santa gets too fat to fly."

As I was typing, Heinrich said, "I've got a bunch of ideas."

"Shoot."

"Three ghosts come on Christmas Eve to change a terrible person into a good person."

"You mean like *A Christmas Carol*?"

"No. This one will be a racecar driver."

"Why a racecar driver?" I asked.

"Because I like racecar drivers." All of Heinrich's S's were extra phlegmy today.

"What else you got?"

"Human gets adopted by elves and goes on a search to find his real parents."

"That's *Elf*," Jenica said.

"Everyone bullies Rudolph for being different until they realize he can save Christmas."

"That's *Rudolph the Red-Nosed Reindeer*," Cordelia said.

"And a really bad lesson," I added, but dutifully typed because there were no bad ideas when brainstorming.

"Okay," Heinrich said. "Kid wants a BB gun—"

"*A Christmas Story*," everyone shouted.

Heinrich shrugged. "I guess all the good stories have been told."

"That can't be true," I said. "Anyone else?"

"I got one," Einstein said. "Make it a play about kids and old people writing a Christmas play about kids and old people writing a Christmas play. You could call it Schrodinger's Christmas."

I assumed it was stuff like this that made Einstein stick to writing physics textbooks, but I typed it anyway.

Cordelia fingered the pearl necklace hanging in front of the scoop neck of her sweater set and said quietly, "You know, Charlee, I'd love to hear the story of the angel who directs the Magi to the manger. How they knew to follow the star, how they came up with the gifts, did they ask to hold the baby Jesus, that sort of thing."

Cordelia was a constant source of delight to me. She was such a prim and proper socialite, who wanted to know if the Magi asked to hold baby Jesus, but I knew she was probably going home after this to work on one of her erotica manuscripts, each one making me blush more crimson than the last. I typed her idea while nodding at her.

"I've got one, too," Jenica said.

I watched her as I typed.

"Kids today are interested in social issues, right? They're all tiny little activists raising their tiny little fists. So, make it about an issue. Like global warming. All this global warming is wreaking havoc on the North Pole, which means they need to pack up the toy shop and bug outta there. Like, to the Caribbean. But once they get to the Caribbean, it's so nice and relaxing that none of the elves want to work anymore. They all become Rastafarians, change Christmas to April, and smoke weed all day."

We all stared at Jenica while she stabbed at her pastry in a self-satisfied manner. She shoved the bite in her smug mouth then noticed everyone staring at her.

"What?" she said, spitting out a couple of crumbs.

"I know I said there were no bad ideas, but Jenica, my friend … *that* was a bad idea."

Everyone, including Jenica, laughed.

I turned back to my laptop. "So, let's see what we've—uh oh." My notes were gibberish. "My fingers slipped. Moved over one key."

Wondering how to decipher everything, I stared at the screen for a minute. Suddenly I leaped up, thrust a couple of twenty-dollar bills in Lavar's hand. "You guys stay and enjoy the coffee and the"— I waved my arm around at the decorations— "ambiance. But I've figured out the plot." Stuffing my arms into my coat and my computer into my messenger bag, I hurried back to my apartment.

~

Ozzie had showered and smelled delicious, but I sent him home anyway. "Gotta work," I said, pushing him out the door.

In a couple of hours, I had pounded out the rough—very rough—story about Figgy the Elf who has wanted to work in

Santa's Information Technology Department forever. He's very shy, barely speaks above a whisper, and truly doesn't like talking or dealing with people, so he figures working with computers is the answer. Unfortunately, he's really bad at it. His boss, Cranberry, has moved him to data entry, but he has screwed that up also. When he was working on the Naughty and Nice List, his fingers moved over one key and he ruined it … right before Christmas! The other elves were able to get most of the data back, except for the village of Middling. Figgy is beyond distraught, but his friend Elfy agrees to go to Middling with him to try and fix everything. They borrow Santa's magic to get there, but when they start trying to sort people back to the appropriate lists, they find it's harder than it looks. On top of that, some evil genius whizbang kid has devised a plan to be the only one on the Nice List—forever—using a high tech forcefield to ground Santa in Middling, so she can steal all the presents on the sleigh to boot.

I wasn't sure of the ending yet, but had the rest of the week to figure it out.

Late Thursday night I finished. The play was formatted properly with a complete plot and a satisfying ending. At least it was satisfying to me, and not simply because I was finished with it on December sixth, leaving plenty of time for the school and senior center to put it on.

It also meant I could get back to my romantic suspense manuscript. But not tonight. First, I had to get Santa, his elves, and the townspeople of Middling scrubbed from my brain.

I called Ozzi. "You want to come over and watch something not Christmasy that might lead to—"

"Give me three seconds."

~

F riday morning, after I saw Don take Peter O'Drool to the patch of grass next to our building, I got dressed and marched up the stairs to their apartment.

"I did it!" I told Barb triumphantly when she opened the door.

"That's marvelous, dear! Don ... Charlee got the play written!"

Don came to the door holding Peter. "Your talent knows no bounds."

"I don't know about that. It seems to me that a twenty-five-page play shouldn't have taken five days to write."

Don snorted. "You know what they say about Rome."

"That it was invaded by Barbarians leading to its downfall?"

"I was thinking that it wasn't built in a day, but regardless. You got it done. Good for you." He looked at the packet of papers in my hand. "Is it any good?" Don said with a wink.

Barb smacked him on the arm. "Of course it is! Our Charlee wrote it."

There was absolutely nothing better than having a fan club for your writing. Especially one that had actually read all your books and claimed to be captivated by each one. *If only I could capture that feeling and bottle it. I'd make a fortune.* There wasn't a writer in the world who didn't chase that high.

"You're too sweet, Barb." I handed her the play.

She took it from me, saying, "I'll get busy and make some calls. You be sure to bring the copies to the senior center tomorrow morning by nine o'clock. Enough copies for the entire cast and maybe a few extras too. I'm so glad you finished it before Saturday so we could gather everyone easily. See you tomorrow!"

Barb's nest of curls bounced excitedly as she closed the door in my face.

I chuckled as I headed back to my apartment. "I guess I'm going to the print shop before I get back to my manuscript."

FOUR

The next morning, about fifteen minutes before nine, I turned into the parking lot of the Leetsdale Senior Center. Most of the close-in parking was designated handicapped so I followed the parking lot around the side of the building. I was backing into a spot when someone darted behind me and hurried to the back of the building. I slammed on my brakes, but they never even turned around or gave an apologetic *my bad!* wave. *Geez, if they were doing some illegal dumping or chasing a stray cat, they should still watch out for traffic.*

I parked and popped my trunk. I heaved out the box of scripts—I figured fifty would be more than enough—and set it on the ground. Smudging the grime with my glove when I closed the hatch, I again rolled my eyes at the ridiculous color of my car, a combination of red and green, maybe a little brown, which was, I suppose, what Christmas would look like all mixed together. When anyone asked, I told them the color was "olive red" but now maybe I'll start calling it "Christmas barf."

When I passed through the automatic doors into the building, Don and Barb were already there, waiting for me.

Barb pointed to a table across the lobby. "You can put that there, dear. Did you find us okay?"

I set the box where she indicated. "I did, but I almost hit some idiot in the parking lot." I pulled off my sunglasses and dropped them in my purse. When I turned around, a tall Black woman stood with us.

"That idiot was me."

Unlike me, she wasn't acting embarrassed and still wore her sunglasses, so I didn't quite know how to react. It occurred to me I was grinning, since I do that when I'm embarrassed, so I changed my expression. But I went too far the other direction and felt myself scowling. "I'm so sorry."

The woman moved her hand, so I thrust out mine to shake.

"I'm Charlee Russo. I didn't mean to ..." I trailed off because she ignored my hand, having raised her hand to remove her sunglasses.

I looked to Barb and Don for help, but neither of them seemed involved in this display of human drama.

Instead, Barb asked, "I can't remember if either of you have ever been here before." She turned toward me. "Is this where you judged the pie contest that time?"

"No, that was at—"

The woman said, "I came by a couple weeks ago, just to see if the space would work. I'd like a more in-depth tour, though, if you wouldn't mind."

"We'd be delighted. You can drop your coats and purses over there." Barb pointed to the same table where I deposited the scripts. "Charlee, this is Leona McFalls, the principal at the school. Leona, Charlee is our playwright."

We both shrugged out of our coats, but the woman held on to her handbag. "I'll hold on to this," she said, with a pointed look at me.

Barb and Don led us through the lobby and stopped at a

hallway. Don pointed to the right and said, a little too loudly, "There are offices thataway, and stairs to the basement."

Making sure she was speaking into his good ear, Barb said, "Oh, that reminds me, Don. We need to get that bin of ice melt filled. I'm not even sure there's enough for one more snowstorm."

He nodded.

Barb continued the tour, pointing to the left. "Restrooms thataway."

We walked on and Barb led us a few steps into a large room. "We call this our multi-purpose room. We'll have the play in here." She pointed to the stage along the far wall. I saw three stairsteps leading up to it. There was a heavy black curtain hanging as a backdrop across the back of the stage and another partially drawn about halfway across the stage. It curved along the left side, reminding me of emergency room partitions.

"I can't remember ever having a play here, but we do have quite a few bands perform for us. We like to move the chairs and tables out of the way and have a nice dance every so often." Barb pointed to the curving curtain. "I was thinking that one could be drawn across the side to make kind of a backstage area for the play."

Don waved his hand around the large open area where we stood. "There are usually tables and chairs set up around here. During the week we play cards or bunko, or bingo—"

"Or work on jigsaw puzzles or just sit and have coffee with folks," Barb said.

"Nice." I climbed the three steps to the stage, walking toward the left side. "What's back here?"

"Mostly a place where the bands stow their stuff," Barb called. "All the way back is a door leading to the dumpster in back of the building."

Leona nodded. "I think this will do just fine."

Barb and Don beamed proudly at the benediction of their home-away-from-home.

We moved back into the hallway and traveled a bit further before stepping through a large doorway on the opposite side from the multi-purpose room. Again, we stepped into a large open room.

"We call this the dining room, but it too has many purposes," Don said.

Barb pointed toward the back of the room, probably at the same place the stage was located in the multi-purpose room, I thought. "But the kitchen is back there, so it's where we serve lunch every day." There were lots of round tables set up, much too close to each other, it seemed to me. As if reading my mind, Barb said, "Normally those round tables are spread throughout the entire room, but this is also where we'll set up the store, so we cleared out half the space for that."

Don patted his belly. "Still gotta eat!"

"What's in the basement?" I asked.

"Classrooms, an exercise room, and a lending library," Don said.

"Wow, I didn't realize how big this place was. It's nice," I said.

Voices sounded in the lobby, and Barb motioned us back to the multi-purpose room, calling down the hallway, "We're in here, everyone!" She pointed to some chairs near the stage placed side by side in a row of six. Like a panel of judges for a reality show. "You two sit there, while I go gather up the rest of the board members."

I was ready to leave them to their planning meeting, but couldn't figure out a polite way to say my goodbyes. It was uncomfortable sitting next to this woman I called an idiot. Small talk seemed impossible. I sat in awkward silence, waiting for Barb and Don to come back so I could excuse myself.

They returned to the multi-purpose room followed by

eight seniors, all laughing and talking at once. Everyone took seats in some scattered chairs facing me and Leona. One man in a wheelchair rolled next to the others. I expected Don and Barb to sit next to me, but they didn't. Barb sat with her friends. Don stood where everyone could see him. *This must be how Salem's witches must have felt.*

"Thanks to everyone for coming this morning to hear about what's going to be happening here at the Center over the next two weeks—"

"Speaking of hearing, Don," the man in the wheelchair interrupted. "Did you really break another hearing aid?"

The other seniors laughed.

"I did. I should start buying them in bulk at Costco." He laughed. "Anyway, I'm going to turn this over to Leona McFalls, Principal of the 56th Avenue School."

Everyone clapped politely while Leona walked to where Don had addressed everyone. Don took a seat next to Barb.

"First, I really want to thank everyone on the Leetsdale Senior Center Executive Board for allowing this partnership between you and my school." Leona's stiff posture revealed her nervousness. I thought maybe that could be the reason for her testiness with me. "This event is our annual fundraiser. We've been searching for a community event that benefits the neighborhood as well as the school. As you probably know, many of our parents struggle economically so we wanted to find a partner for a larger project, since it's in everyone's best interest to have fully funded, functioning neighborhood schools. We don't need anyone to rescue us, but I've been looking to form a long-lasting productive partnership within our community. I'm hoping the Leetsdale Senior Center will be that entity."

The man in the wheelchair raised his hand. "Hello, I'm Winston, the board president. We've talked on the phone." Leona nodded. "But don't our taxes fund schools here in Colorado?"

"Good to meet you, Winston." Leona smiled, more at ease now. "And, yes, historically, property taxes have funded schools, but years and years of politicians pandering to voters about cutting their taxes have gutted funding for everything, from emergency services to infrastructure projects to, sadly, education. Eventually the state had to step in, but because of revenue and spending limits written into the state constitution—also in an effort to pander to voters—funding has fallen tragically short year after year, and worse for already struggling schools. Individual schools are left to pick up the pieces." Leona's voice took on an edgier tone. "Some districts in wealthier neighborhoods don't feel the pinch as much as we do here at 56th. So we're forced to go into the community to beg people to be able to educate their children. Hence, this fundraising effort."

I looked out at the others and realized I wasn't the only one feeling guilty and uncomfortable about not wanting to pay taxes. But there was the other side of the coin to think about ... how would society pay for the things we need, if not for taxes?

"Well, that's enough preaching from me," Leona said briskly. "Let's talk about this event. School is out for winter break, and I have a couple of different goals. First, I want to alleviate any daycare costs for our parents. Most of them work, but all of their wages would be spent on daycare until we're back in school in January. You all have been gracious enough to open your doors to our kids. I understand you have a long list of volunteers among your members to come every day and spend time with them, reading, playing, doing crafts, and such. I don't know exactly how many kids will be here every day. Some might go to work with their parents. Some have older siblings or *abuelas* to watch them. But I assure you, the ones who come here will be on their very best behavior, and I think they are some of the most wonderful kids on the planet, even if I do say so myself. Most of them are very excited to know they get to be in the play, which will culminate the event on Saturday, December twenty-second, which is just two short weeks from today."

Don stood again. "Now that we have a script"—Don nodded in my direction—"we need to redouble our efforts to sell tickets to the play. Leona mentioned needing this event to do double-duty—provide daycare during winter break and raise money. The other way we're going to raise money is by having our very own Christmas Shoppe."

"This is the part I don't understand," Winston said. "Won't the kids see their parents shopping here for their toys?"

"You must have missed that meeting, Win. The store isn't for parents to buy toys. It's for the kids to buy gifts for their parents. We thought it would be nice for the kids, who otherwise might not get a chance to give their families something to show their Christmas spirit."

Barb said, "We've been gathering donations for months, Winston. Haven't you noticed all that stuff piled in the dining room?"

A woman sitting next to Winston laughed. "He doesn't even notice when Felix starts doing the foxtrot with him!" Everyone enjoyed a good laugh at Winston's expense, even Winston, who threw his head back and guffawed.

I watched while a man, presumably Felix, pulled a woman in leggings and sneakers to her feet and gracefully took her for a spin around the room.

"What's going on?" a woman asked. I recognized her as Barb's friend Lorraine from the pie contest I judged last summer. Her macular degeneration must have progressed.

The man sitting next to her said, "Felix and Gloria Mae are dancing."

"Figures," she said, settling back into her chair.

While I watched them foxtrot or waltz or polka or what-

29

ever they were doing, I wondered if I had something to contribute to their Christmas store.

I had been tinkering with some crafts made of sheet metal whenever I needed to step away from my writing. I could donate some of the ear cuffs, jewelry holders, and table-top candle sconces I've been making.

Felix and Gloria Mae returned to their seats and Leona continued with her presentation. "I understand that much of the merchandise has been donated by your members here or by the community. The Board and I had a long discussion about the store. I am adamant that the kids pay something for the merchandise—" Leona was interrupted by murmuring but she used her Teacher Look and everyone piped down. "Even though the merchandise has been donated, the kids must pay for it. I've been telling them this for a couple of months now, so it won't be a surprise to them. I want them to learn about pride. Pride that they can delay their own gratification and save their money. Pride that they chose something of value to show their parents how much they love them. Pride in their money-management skills. Now, that said, this merchandise will only cost them their valuable nickels, dimes, and quarters. Nothing will be priced more than a dollar."

"Fifty cents," Don corrected.

"Even better," she said with a smile. "Mrs Perez, one of our parents, will oversee the store. She will probably need some of the seniors to lend her a hand with it."

Don jumped up. "Before I forget, I want to introduce Charlee Russo who wrote and will direct our play. Let's give her a big hand. I know she won't take an impromptu cruise to the Caribbean!"

I would if I could afford it, I almost said.

Everyone clapped enthusiastically for me, except Leona, who was more restrained. I stared out at them, dumbstruck, as Don's words sunk in. *When did I agree to direct the play?* I scanned my memory for that part of the conversation and came up short.

Leona turned toward me. "I'm assuming there are plenty of roles for everyone? Kids and seniors alike?"

I shook myself from the shock of being the director and said, "Yes, as many elves, townspeople, and dogs as we want."

Barb piped up. "I've got all the major roles cast already." There was noise in the back of the room and everyone turned. Barb clapped her hands like a little kid. "In fact, here comes Santa and two of your elves right now!"

Two men and a twenty-something girl walked in. I could feel the girl's apprehension—perhaps dread—all the way up in the front of the room. There was absolutely no mistaking which one would be playing Santa, though. One of the men was fat and had a majestic more-salt-than-pepper beard and a long wavy mane of matching hair. That left the other two—a balding middle-aged white guy, and the girl—to play the main elf characters, Figgy and Elfy. The balding guy was a bit old for my vision of an elf, but he was gregarious and smiling, so it might work. I wondered about the girl. She was barely visible, hunched into her teal parka. When she used the backs of both hands to flip her hood down, I saw the whitest person I'd ever seen. Pale, almost translucent skin, hair the color of grubby athletic socks, even her lips were devoid of color. She'd better be careful not to fall in a snowbank because without her brightly-colored parka, she'd disappear until spring thaw.

I sighed. Those two playing elf BFFs was quite a stretch. The magic of theatre, indeed.

As I was processing all this information, I was surprised to see Ozzi walk in behind them and wave at me.

"Okay," Don said. "Unless you have anything else, Leona?" She shook her head. "Then everyone is excused. You can go, unless you're involved with the play. Thanks for coming, everyone!"

All the seniors dispersed, but I hurried over to Barb before she disappeared too.

"Um … I'm directing?"

"Of course you are, dear. Who else could do it?"

"Anyone?"

She laughed. "You're so silly. We'll start the read-through when everyone gets here." She bustled away, pecking Ozzi on the cheek as he walked past her.

"Surprise!" he said.

"What are you doing here?"

"My company is one of the sponsors."

"The hack factory is altruistic? That's a bolt from the blue. You want to know another?" Without waiting for him to answer I said, "Apparently I'm directing this thing also. I thought I was only writing it, but I think Don and Barb hoodwinked me somehow."

Ozzi wrinkled his nose. "Actually … I'm the one who hoodwinked you. It was my idea to have Don and Barb ask you to write and direct because I know you can't say no to them." He grabbed me around the waist and pulled me close. "Don't be mad. I thought it would be a fun way to get to spend more time together while we work on this project."

"I'm not mad, just … surprised, and a bit worried. I expected to get back to work on my manuscript. I got my bank statement a couple days ago and yeesh." The silly face I made belied the quiver in the pit of my stomach. "I thought my only job today was delivering the copies of the script. What will you be doing?"

He shrugged. "Whatever they need me for." Ozzi pointed at Santa and the two elves. "Ernesto, Doug, and Daisy work with me. We all get comp time to volunteer for this."

I tilted my head at my altruistic but sneaky boyfriend and raked my fingernails through his wavy hair. "I love your hack factory," I said with a kiss that gave me a different kind of quiver in my stomach.

Ozzi backed away sooner than I expected with a guilty look on his face.

"I do have to tell you something else, though."

"Uh oh."

"Ernesto Santiago is a huge know-it-all." Ozzi rushed forward before I could say anything. "I know how much you hate that, but Don and Barb asked if I knew anyone who could play Santa for them. Ernesto already has that beard and he plays Santa all over town, so I passed on his information. Plus, his name is almost Santa!" He finished in a rush.

"You don't have to convince me, but I do appreciate the heads-up. Besides, now that the shock has started to wear off about having to direct this thing, I'm kind of looking forward to it. I think I can set aside my pet peeves for the holidays."

He cocked his head and squinted at me. "Really?"

"I guess we'll see, won't we?"

Don motioned to Ozzi that he was needed elsewhere so I took the opportunity to hit the restroom before I had to begin any official duties. And I sincerely hoped someone would let me know exactly what those duties might be.

As I walked toward Ernesto sitting alone on a folding chair, I watched him lift a phone to his ear and a flask to his lips. Most flasks were fairly discreet, but this one was emblazoned with the Mexican flag. He raised it in acknowledgment as I walked by.

I felt confident that Don's Santa wouldn't have carried a flask. But while I had to agree that Don was better suited temperamentally than Ernesto, Don was clean-shaven, had very little hair on his head, and when he laughed, his belly didn't shake like a bowl full of jelly.

Ernesto was gone when I walked back in the multi-purpose room, but I saw Leona by herself, pouring a cup of coffee from the big urn on a table in the back. I was thrilled to know others enjoyed their coffee as much as I did. This might be a good time to try to reset her first impression of me, maybe get us back on less testy footing. We could bond over caffeine.

As I veered toward her, the furnace rattled on and a hot blast blew behind me like a marching band made solely of sousaphones, alpen horns, and Tibetan dungchens. Stumbling with surprise when my long hair flew forward, completely covering my face, I swear I felt my waistband turn forty-five degrees. I let out a loud shriek and smoothed my clothes. Using my entire forearm, I relocated my hair back into place.

When I could see again, I was greeted with the sight of Leona scowling at me with pity and annoyance. So much for our reset.

"Hey, Leona," I called as she turned to walk away. "I wanted to apologize for that idiot comment earlier." Her icy stare made me lose any sense of what I was going to say. "I didn't know it was you."

She arranged her regular face into her principal face, and it scared me. "And what would you have called me if you did know it was me?"

"I … uh … I wouldn't have called you anything?"

She turned again, but I grabbed her arm, sloshing her coffee. Luckily, the only drips ended up on my shoe, and not on her. "Listen, I wanted to tell you about what I'll be donating to the store. I've been making these metal crafts— candle sconce thingies, jewelry holders, and ear cuffs—and I thought they'd be a great addition."

"Yes," she said dryly. "Everyone needs more … thingies."

"I'm also donating a couple of complete sets of all my books. I'm actually a mystery author." I don't know why I felt so strongly that she like me at this moment, but I did. I probably reeked of desperation and I hated myself for it. Why did I care if this woman took an instant dislike to me?

"I'm sure *someone* might like that," she said in a way that made clear that someone was not her. "Now if you'll excuse me, I have to take this call."

Her phone was nowhere to be seen and she walked away sipping her coffee, probably plotting how to get me fired from this job I'd been shanghaied into.

Well, the joke's on you, Leona …. Hm. Suddenly I wasn't at all clear what the joke might be or who it was on.

Luckily at that moment Peter O'Drool pitter-pattered nearby wearing a green striped elf costume. I scooped him up and nuzzled his wheezy little snout. "At least you love me, right, Pete?" He sneezed in my face. "Dude. Pretty sure that will get you on the Naughty List." I used my other arm to wipe my face.

"Charlee, come here. I want to introduce you."

Barb stood nearby with an elderly woman. When she turned around, I recognized Barb's nemesis from the pie-baking contest last summer. She had a face you couldn't forget, especially if you've seen the Wizard of Oz. She bore a scary and uncanny resemblance to Miss Gulch. I instinctively held Pete tighter.

"Charlee, this is Thelma, your Mrs Claus and our costumer for the play. She can work miracles with fabric and thread."

Those gnarled arthritic hands seemed to suggest otherwise, but what did I know? I juggled Peter a bit so I could shake her hand, but she backed away.

"I hope I'm not expected to work with a … dog."

The way she said it left no mistaking how she felt about pooches, even adorable ones like Peter. I vowed then and there to put Peter O'Drool in the play. And to rise above any bad juju Thelma was putting out into the world.

"It's nice to see you again, Thelma. Thanks for agreeing to wrangle the costumes for the play."

"You're welcome." She abruptly turned and led Barb away by the elbow, talking about her costume budget, leaving me and Peter alone. He wiggled and I set him on his feet where he waddled off in his jaunty manner. Thelma's words certainly hadn't penetrated his mood.

Coffee sounded important at this moment, but the two elves beat me to it. I waited my turn at the spigot several steps behind them, idly listening to their conversation, as one does.

The nervous ghost-girl Daisy said, "This is pathetic." I assumed she meant the non-artisanal coffee from non-sustainable urns, but she continued. "Whoever heard of a Mexican Santa?"

Oh, great. Angsty and racist. Just what a Christmas play needs.

"It reminds me when I did Shakespeare in the Park," Doug said.

"In New York?"

"No, Longmont. But they wanted to do an all-girl version of The Tempest. So stupid. Only one gal in there originally. Clearly not what the Bard intended."

They wandered away with their coffee and I wondered if this play truly needed elves. Maybe I could teach Peter O'Drool and Nova the lines and get rid of these two completely. I thought about yelling after Doug that I would pay good money to see an all-female version of The Tempest. In my fantasy I blew him a noisy raspberry for good measure. In real life, I crossed the room to where Don and Ozzi stood, sipping my coffee while Don spoke.

"—can't believe I don't get to be Santa. Just because some corporate fat cat wanted to pretend to be altruistic and threw a bunch of money to get their own guy in as Santa. A travesty."

Ozzi chuckled. "That fat cat travesty is my company, Net Software."

Don frowned. "Of course I knew Net Software was involved, but I thought you worked for some outfit called The Hack Factory. Could have sworn that's what Charlee said."

Barb and Leona walked over. Barb said, "Let's go ahead and get started. We'll sit at those tables on the stage. We're just waiting for our set designer."

Leona checked her watch. "I'm sure he'll be along any minute now." Leona looped her arms through both of Don and Barb's and began walking away, saying, "Are you sure about this Ernesto playing Santa? I'm already terrified this event won't pull in the money we need. I will do everything in my power to have this event succeed." She stopped walking and all three of them glanced at Ernesto taking a swig from his flask. "Everything. You mark my words."

Ozzi and I followed them to the stage where I saw a couple of long tables pushed together. They had three plates of frosted sugar cookies in every conceivable holiday shape evenly spaced along them.

Barb pointed me to the head of the table and we all took seats. Ozzi sat on my left, Ernesto was at the other end. When Leona saw him down there, she hurried to sit next to Ozzi, but Barb and Don beat her to those seats. She started for the seat on my right, but Daisy quickly slid in before her. Doug sat next to Daisy. The only two seats left were on either side of Ernesto. He missed all the seating drama, happily stuffing cookies in his mouth.

It made me weirdly happy that Leona was willing to sit next to me to avoid sitting next to Ernesto. At least she liked me better than him.

"I can always tell when artificial vanilla is used in baking," Ernesto said, waving a green frosted Christmas tree in the air. He bit off the trunk and speaking with his mouth full, added, "I make my own vanilla by soaking very expensive vanilla beans in very expensive vodka. Makes exquisite cookies."

Thelma muttered under her breath, "Sure didn't stop him from eating six already."

"Let's get to know each other a little—"

Barb was interrupted by a man and a young boy. They were loaded down with large sheets of thick Styrofoam and some cans of paint and brushes. "I'm so sorry I'm late," the man said. "It took forever at the hardware store."

I stared at the Styrofoam, thinking how heavy it looked. I didn't know you could buy it in such thicknesses. But the sum of my Styrofoam knowledge certainly weighed less than a piece of Styrofoam.

"You must be our set designer. We were just getting started," Barb said with a welcoming smile. She gestured the two of them on the stage. Ozzi retrieved another chair and made room next to Thelma. The boy sat there. Thelma scooted her chair closer to Doug, as if the boy might have rabies. The man sat at Ernesto's left, across from Leona.

As they were getting settled, the man said, "I hope it's okay I brought Bobby with me. I know this is mostly for daycare during the week when the parents are working, but I'll watch him while his mom is—"

"Working," Leona interrupted.

From the looks on the faces of Bobby and his dad, I didn't think that's what he was going to say.

Barb said, "Bobby, you help yourself to some of those yummy cookies Thelma made." Bobby received a nod of permission from his father and dove in.

"I guess I'll introduce everyone." Barb turned back to the table. "First and foremost, this is Charlee Russo, our playwright and director." I gave a little wave. "Next to her is her boyfriend Ozzi, and of course you all know me and Don and Peter O'Drool."

Don doffed an imaginary hat while Peter wiggled frantically to get down from Barb's arms when he saw Bobby eating cookies. Peter insinuated himself between Bobby's shoes under the table.

Barb continued. "Leona McFalls is the principal at the 56th

Avenue School. Ernesto Santiago there at the end is our Santa Claus."

Don gave a little huff, then pretended he'd been clearing his throat. I remembered Barb scolding him about being gracious, even though he really wanted to play Santa.

"Mexican Santa," Daisy said quietly to Doug sitting next to her. "His sleigh must be a low-rider. Instead of cookies and milk, kids can leave out tacos and *cervezas*." Doug chuckled. "On Dasher, on Dancer, on *Chollo, Pendejo*," she added.

I glanced around, but it seemed I was the only one who heard them. I always believed myself to be the type of person who would stand up to racism when I heard it, but I was too shocked. *What would I say, anyway? How do I reprimand full-grown adults? Is that my job here? Was this the time and place?* My mind raced, trying to land on a course of action.

It finally did. I shushed them, dying a bit inside that I didn't have the courage or quick thinking to do anything else.

By the time I returned my attention to the introductions, Leona was saying, "Carlos Morales is our construction pro in charge of building our sets and scenery. And this is his son Bobby, one of our best students."

"How old are you, dear?" Barb asked him.

"Twelve, ma'am."

I glanced back toward Carlos just in time to see Daisy roll her eyes at Doug.

Abruptly pushing my chair back, I stood, gesturing at Doug and Daisy. "Excuse me for a sec. Can you two come with me for a minute?" The shock of their racism had worn off and I had to say something or else I wouldn't be able to live with myself.

While I waited for them to join me on the other side of the stage, I heard Carlos say, "I've worked on Habitat for Humanity houses and helped reconstruct trails on a bunch of fourteeners."

"In the winter? Oh my!" Barb gave little shiver.

When Doug and Daisy joined me, Doug asked, "What's up?"

I took a deep breath. Confrontation was difficult and I didn't want to make it even more so by saying something stupid. "Those things you were saying earlier. They were really offensive. That's not the kind of environment I want to foster here, especially when we're going to have a bunch of impressionable kids around."

"Geez, it was just a joke," Daisy said. "You people are so sensitive and politically correct these days." She walked back to the table with a dismissive wave of her hand.

You people? I stared at her with barely contained fury. I watched a romantic comedy once where Meg Ryan's character pronounced daisies the friendliest flowers. At the time, I hadn't thought to personify flowers, so it seemed a charming observation. But now as I put myself back at my childhood bedroom windowsill, chin resting on my stacked fists, I remembered the confident mass of daisies my dad had planted in the flowerbed in our front yard. An army of perfectly cheery clones. Looking through the lens of time, though, I see those bright flowers on their spindly stems, bobbing and weaving in the slightest of breezes, bent completely to the ground pummeled by hail and rain, white petals scattered in the dirt, never quite the same afterward. Not tough, not resilient. Simply replicas of each other. No character of their own. Put a single daisy in a rose bed and it wouldn't survive. Daisies needed a mob to thrive.

Was that true of this Daisy too?

Doug at least had the decency to look uncomfortable. But was it because he knew what he and Daisy were saying was wrong? Or because I called them out on their behavior?

"Is that all you wanted?" he asked, walking backward away from me. "I'll try to be more woke."

That didn't go at all how I wanted, but I guess getting an apology from one of them was better than nothing. But by the time I reached the table and pulled my chair out, I wondered if he had been mocking me.

Ernesto was droning on about fourteeners and presumably had been the entire time. "You probably didn't know that Colorado has fifty-eight mountains over 14,000 feet, but they're not all considered fourteeners. To be an official fourteener the peak must be three hundred feet higher than the saddle of an adjacent peak." Ernesto was exactly the kind of know-it-all I hated. He took a swig from his flask, and Carlos snuck a glance at Bobby.

It was clear by looking at him that Ernesto had never climbed one, certainly not recently. If he had, he'd have to be careful someone didn't shove him over the edge.

Barb continued with the introductions. "Thelma here is our Mrs Claus, and in charge of costumes. Doug Beesley and Daisy Dolan are our elves, and they both work together with Ozzi and Ernesto at Net Software."

I turned to Doug and Daisy. "What do you two do there? Are you hackers like Ozzi?"

Before either of them could answer, Ernesto said, "I'm head of HR. Love it. The only way they'll get me out of there is to tie a chain around me and drag me out." He laughed and shot some cookie crumbs across the table.

Thelma made a point of plucking a paper napkin and with delicacy and slow-motion precision, wiping up the crumbs and depositing the napkin in front of Ernesto. He didn't even notice.

Doug said, "Not a hacker. I work in HR too, and Daisy here is our intern. She just graduated from college. We volunteered. I used to do quite a bit of acting, so when Ernesto mentioned it, I jumped at the chance."

"Are you an actor too, Daisy?" I really wanted to get a bead on this girl.

"I was voluntold," she said with a smirk. "Ernesto's intern, remember?"

She didn't seem nervous now. Did I misjudge her, or did she already find her comfort zone?

Bobby looked at Ozzi with awe. "Are you really a hacker?"

"No, I'm not. Charlee was just making a joke. Mostly I code software for other companies. If somebody has a great idea but doesn't know how to make it happen, I make it happen for them."

"I'd like to go to college and maybe work with computers," Bobby said.

I feigned shock. "You mean you don't want to be a writer, like me?"

Bobby shook his head. "I want to be rich."

"Fair enough," I said.

"Let me give you and your dad some advice," Doug said. "If you want to go to college, start saving your money." He took a long appraising look at Bobby. "Although you'll probably get a scholarship. Not many scholarships available to boring white kids like my twins, even though their mother died. Usually, colleges eat up those kinds of sad stories, but not in our case."

Did Doug really think college acceptance was a competition between ethnicity and dead mothers? I was shocked again at his casual racism, but more shocked that Ozzi didn't call him out on it. When I turned to look at him, my loving, socially conscious boyfriend merely smiled at me. Doug was oblivious as well.

Were the next two weeks going to be like this?

FIVE

B arb must have seen the look on my face while I stared back and forth at these two men who may as well have been from Mars, for as much as I understood them.

"How 'bout we start the read-through of the play now, Charlee?" she prodded.

I blinked twice and her face swam into focus. "Yes. The read-through. Good idea." I passed out a copy of the script to everyone. When I sat down again, I explained the basic premise of the play while they flipped through the pages. "So, Santa will be played by Ernesto. Figgy is an elf played by Doug. Elfy is Figgy's friend, played by Daisy. Thelma, you are Mrs Claus, and please make notes on your script about costume needs while we go along. You and me and Barb can go over those afterward. Barb, I know you're not going to be in the play, but will you read Figgy's mom's part today? And Don, will you read the part of Cranberry, Figgy's boss?" They both nodded. I turned to Bobby. "There's a part for you if you want it."

Bobby shook his head. "No thank you."

I turned to Ozzi. "Will you read any other part we haven't assigned?"

"Love to."

"Perfect." I flipped to the first page of my script. "The basic premise is that Figgy is incredibly socially awkward and very shy. Unless he's talking to his friends, he barely speaks above a whisper and must be told to repeat himself all the time. Because he doesn't like dealing with people, he wants to work with computers and finds himself on Santa's IT team." Everyone laughed. "Problem is, he's really bad at computers too and has lost Santa's Naughty and Nice List."

"Uh oh," Don said with a wink at Bobby.

Bobby smiled back.

"Carlos, you can follow along and make any notes for any sets you'll need to make," I said.

"Be sure to save your receipts," Don told him. "We'll reimburse you as soon as you turn them in. We don't want you to have any out-of-pocket costs." Don pointed at the Styrofoam and paint he and Bobby walked in with. "Like that stuff. Give me the receipt."

Carlos pulled out his wallet. While he was locating the receipt, he said, "I went ahead and got this Styrofoam to make stars to hang from the ceiling."

Ernesto barked out a guffaw. "Why stars? The play isn't all set outside at night."

"Because glittery stars seem Christmas-y? And will catch the lights nicely?" Carlos glanced at the pile of Styrofoam uneasily, suddenly looking not at all sure of himself.

Barb said, "Put some stars out over the audience too. Maybe with twinkle lights. It'll be pretty."

Carlos relaxed a bit and nodded at her while he stood and reached across the table to hand the receipt to Don.

Ernesto pointed at the Styrofoam. "You shouldn't use that stuff. You should have bought corrugated plastic. Like that stuff front yard election signs are made from. It's heavier than Styrofoam, more body, less likely to break."

"I think the Styrofoam will work just fine," Don said. "Look how thick it is."

I tried to veer Ernesto away from his pompous know-it-all opinions about Styrofoam. "Carlos, have you given any thought to the rest of the scenery? I know you just got the script, but I mean the basic framework?"

"I have. I'll make the flats with a plywood frame and canvas stretched across. I was thinking—"

"What you *should* do—" Ernesto waited until he had everyone's attention, then took a big swig from his flask before continuing. "What you *should* do is make periaktos. Those are three-sided scenery pieces used in theatre design for millennia. You just need to give them a tiny turn to have new scenery."

"That sounds much more complicated, and I want to be able to allow any kids or seniors the opportunity to help build the flats and paint the scenery on the canvas," Carlos said.

"Oh, that's a good idea," I said. "It'll look—"

"It'll look like crap," Ernesto said with a hearty laugh.

"The kids and seniors will be the stage crew, too," Carlos said.

Ernesto barked out another laugh.

Everyone tried to ignore Ernesto and listen to Carlos' ideas. For everything Carlos proposed, Ernesto had a derisive comment or some way he thought would be a better way to do something.

I could see Carlos turning red and his fists clenching and unclenching. The tension in the air crackled. Everyone must have been feeling as much anxiety as I was. I wondered why someone didn't take charge and stop this. I glanced at Barb who raised her eyebrows at me.

Oh yeah. I was the one in charge.

I stared across the table at Ernesto, then shifted my eyes to Carlos next to him. "Carlos, I agree with *every single thing* you just said." I emphasized the phrase for Ernesto's benefit. "It sounds like you have it all completely under control. But can you explain to me what a flat is?"

Carlos nodded, grateful. "It's all the scenery we'll need—trees, the front of the houses in the village, Santa's office. Basically, anything that needs to be moved on and off the stage."

Ernesto started to say something, but he must have seen the look on my face that said Santa might not have long for this world. He cleverly decided to swig from his flask instead.

I shifted my eyes to Carlos. "So everything is on wheels?" After he nodded, I added, with a pointed glance at Ernesto. "I'm glad we have a professional on the team."

Carlos blushed.

"I mean, if Carlos is willing to take on this job, he should do it the way it makes sense to him."

"If you don't mind, I think I'll go and let you guys do your read-through without me." He stood and gathered his script and pen. "Unless you change the script drastically, I can go make my notes and my shopping list and get started."

I laughed. "There will be absolutely no changes. This script is locked down. We don't have time to make any changes."

Bobby pushed back his chair to go with his father.

Thelma pushed a plate of cookies toward him. "You may as well take them. They'll just get stale."

Bobby looked up at Carlos who simply shrugged. Bobby picked up the plate. "Thank you, Miss Thelma."

Thelma watched them walk away. "Not many children have manners these days."

I tried to hide my smile, but Barb noticed and did the same. Seems Thelma's bark might be a tad worse than her bite.

Thelma turned toward Ernesto and said crossly, "Not many adults do either," and pulled the plate of cookies away from him, out of his reach.

But her bark was still pretty bad.

I picked up my script and read, "Santa's Middling List—a short Christmas play." I glanced up from my script and explained, "The other IT elves were able to get the Naughty and Nice List fixed for everywhere except the village of Middling." We started in on the read-through and got all the way to page three before Ernesto interrupted the progress.

Doug's Figgy character had just said the line, "I said, I'm not sure, but I think your algorithm protocol user interface might have a syntax spreadsheet storage error in the server. Maybe even in the mainframe."

Everyone around the table had giggled at the nonsense phrases, because Figgy clearly had no idea what was wrong and was talking gibberish about computers.

The next stage direction was that Santa had to repeat what Figgy had just said. Ernesto tried three times to say the tongue-twister gibberish and couldn't.

Don said it perfectly on his first try.

"See? Don can do it and I'm sure you can too," I said.

Ernesto began arguing with me but I held up my hand. "If you can change the dialogue and still make it nonsense and funny, then be my guest."

We made it through three more lines.

Ernesto read from the script. "I need to get that sleigh in the air no later than six p.m. tomorrow." He then dropped the script and began a long-winded, droning monologue about what time the sun might set at the North Pole in December and how long it would take him to deliver all those toys. "If you add in wind velocity and direction, the health and age of the reindeer and the weight of the toys, minus the tare weight of the sleigh, of course—"

He kept talking and even drew a diagram on the back of his script to illustrate something. I didn't know what because I quit listening while rewinding through the highlights of my life to see what I'd done that was so terrible that the Universe needed to pay me back in this manner.

My eyes wandered from the stage to where Carlos and Bobby were cutting Styrofoam stars. The Styrofoam was so thick that Carlos had to use a saw. He had put Bobby to work painting the stars and dribbling glitter on the wet paint. Bobby globbed too much paint and way too much neon-orange glitter on. Bobby's posture crumpled when he realized what he'd done, but Carlos set down his saw and dropped to one knee next to him. He had his hand on Bobby's shoulder. I couldn't hear what he was saying to him, but it must have been gentle and instructional since Bobby worked much more carefully and methodically afterward.

I interrupted. "Ernesto. Ernesto. *Ernesto!*" When he finally stopped talking, I said, "I can guarantee there will be no North Pole scholar" —*except you*, I wanted to add— "at our performance. Santa needs to get his sleigh in the air no later than six p.m. Nobody will be doing the math." I picked up my script again. "Okay, Santa hurries off, Figgy bangs away at his computer some more, realizes it's hopeless, begins sobbing and the stage goes dark. End of scene one." I looked around the room. "Anyone need a break?" Nobody did so I continued. "Okay, scene two puts us in Santa's corporate office conference room. Santa is sitting on his throne at the head of a long table and he says …" I nodded at Ernesto to begin the dialogue.

"What did you do, Figgy?" Ernesto's Santa said. He dropped the script, shaking his head. "No, no, no. Santa wouldn't say something so gruffly! He's a right jolly old elf!"

I quickly read over the section, and as much as I hated to admit it, Ernesto was right. "I'll soften it. Everyone change that line to *Figgy, tell me again—slowly—what happened.*"

While everyone was writing in their script, I snuck a glance at Ernesto who was smiling at me with a smug little look on his face. Santa certainly wouldn't do that!

The furnace wheezed on just then. The force of the sudden gust of hot air caused the pages of the scripts on the table to flutter and sail to the floor. Ozzi scooped them up and placed a plate of cookies on top of them. I heard Carlos and Bobby laugh and turned to see them chasing Styrofoam stars skittering across the multi-purpose room.

We returned our attention to the read-through and made it to the bottom of the next page where Ernesto's Santa said, "Of course you are, Middling is a tough case. It took me over three hundred years to get that list right. Very tough. It's not a cut-and-dried, black-and-white kind of place. It's a gray area. It's in the middle of everything. Not too cold and not too hot. Not too rainy and not too sunny. Not too urban and not too rural. Equal number of old people and young people. Same number of cats and dogs." Ernesto dropped his script and eyed me across the length of the table. "That sounds like everywhere in the world to me."

"Well, it's not," I snapped. I honestly didn't know if I could take one more interruption. This was just a cute little Christmas play and he was making it into a Broadway extravaganza. I slapped my script hard against my hand. "Can we just move on?" I spoke low and put extra space and subtext between my words.

Ernesto raised his hands in surrender at my outburst. I knew everyone was exchanging glances around the table.

"Should we take a break, Charlee?" Barb asked gently.

"No. Let's just get this over with." I snapped at her too, but felt bad about it.

"Merry Christmas to us," Doug muttered.

We got another half page read, but this time it was Doug who interrupted with a laugh at the stage direction that had his character Figgy "oozing from his chair" in embarrassment. "I can't do that. I'm a middle-aged elf. Can I just get up instead?" He laughed and everyone joined in, the tension broken.

Doug continued with Figgy's lines. "I wanted to do a good job, really I did. I didn't want to let them down. But just wanting isn't enough, I guess … there has to be something backing it up. Skill or training or even Santa's magic snow—"

Ernesto said, "That sounds like Santa does cocaine."

"Maybe change it to holly?" Barb suggested.

"Or cookies?" Thelma said, helping herself to one.

"That sounds like they're spiked with weed." Daisy laughed.

"What about tinsel?" Don asked.

"Tinsel it is. Change your scripts, everyone." I made a note to tell Carlos we need a chest filled with tinsel next to Santa's throne.

We made it all the way to the end of scene five interruption-free. But then the stage direction had Figgy and Elfy throwing tinsel on each other for the magic teleportation to the village of Middling. I'd written that fog would swirl around them so they could run offstage and "disappear" while the new set for the village gets wheeled on stage, ending the scene.

Ernesto guffawed again. "You bringing the fog machine?"

As much as it pained me to have to agree with him, I had to agree with him. When I was writing the play, it never occurred to me that I'd be responsible for turning the stage directions into actual reality. We agreed to have Figgy and Elfy just turn in circles doing the "Wayne's World" thing with their fingers while the stagehands moved the scenery in front of them so they could disappear.

We made it almost a paragraph further before Ernesto interrupted. Figgy had written the name of a townsperson on his Naughty List.

"How do the elves know everyone's name in Middling?"

As I was forming my answer and trying to keep the expletives out, Don said, "You didn't ask how throwing tinsel on someone could transport them through space. It's just how it is. Now hush up. I want to see what's going to happen next."

I wanted to kiss him on the mouth. But not really. Just a figure of speech.

Another page and a half was read without editorial comment. Then Ernesto said, "A lump of coal? Kids don't know what that is. How many kids have ever seen a lump of coal? Change it to socks or underwear. The threat of those gifts will strike fear into the heart of a child."

I glared at him. "Kids are smart. They've never seen a unicorn either, but I bet they'd want one of those."

Ernesto and I had a stare-down.

Don said, "Personally, I'd like socks and underwear from Santa. Means the missus here doesn't have to drag me all over town shopping with her."

Leona spoke for the first time during the read-though. I'd almost forgotten she was there. "I'm pretty sure Charlee is right." I flashed a smug smile at Ernesto. "Not about the unicorn, of course." The smile slid off my face and reappeared on Ernesto's. "But about kids being smart. Part of education is expanding someone's world. I'm sure they've all heard the story about Santa leaving chunks of coal for the naughty kids, but if they haven't, then now they have. And if it prompts them to find out what a lump of coal is, then even better."

Ernesto shrugged. "You're the professional. I guess."

Leona cut her eyes at him. Like me, she must have wondered if that was an intentional dig or not.

We made it six more pages through the script and I wondered if Ernesto getting reprimanded by a principal was what he needed all along.

But then Leona interrupted after hearing the line from one of the children of Middling who said, "Oh please. You think I haven't done that? Grown-ups don't listen. They make stupid zero tolerance rules when tolerance is the thing we need the most!" Leona looked me in the eye. "I'm not sure that's a good lesson."

"Agreed. It's a terrible lesson. Adults always punt the ball away when they should hunker down and do the hard work to solve problems," I said.

"That's not the lesson—"

"Remember that time a principal suspended some poor kid for bringing a butter knife in her lunchbox to cut her apple? Were they threatening anyone with the knife? No. Were they a danger to themselves? No. But some lazy principal didn't want to have to think through each individual situation so just created arbitrary zero tolerance rules about knives, saying there was never a reason for a kid to touch one. That's just stupid." My voice had ratcheted up and I took a deep breath.

Leona was quiet for a minute. "Yes, it is."

"I'm just trying to give kids some agency in this play," I said. "Figgy and Elfy are stand-ins for kids in real life. I want them to be able to solve their own problems without the help of parents." My voice was modulated a tad better now. I hoped Leona understood this wasn't directed at her, exactly. But I was frustrated by all the interruptions and worried that the one thing I wanted to do with this play had missed the mark. "And for the record, I'm sure you're not like this."

"I should say not."

Leona looked back at her script and I waited for her to keep arguing with me. When she didn't, I hurried the read-through along and—saints be praised—we actually made it all the way to the end.

Everyone began murmuring comments about the script.

"Funny."

"Nice lesson."

"Lots of parts for kids and seniors."

"Blessedly short."

I didn't respond to any of them because I was digging for one of the bottles of ibuprofen I kept in my purse. I popped two pills into my mouth and washed them down with cold coffee. "Tell you what. Let's finish this tomorrow, starting at one o'clock. We can do the blocking and deal with costumes when we're not so … tired." I almost said *cranky*, but then I realized I was probably the only cranky one. "We don't have long to put this all together, but this all went … great. Take your scripts with you and start trying to memorize your lines. Then the next day, Monday when the kids and seniors are here, we won't have to backtrack to loop them into the other roles."

Everyone began pushing back their chairs, standing and stretching.

Bobby had wandered in about thirty minutes before the rehearsal ended, sitting on the floor to listen.

Ernesto called to him. "You like fishing?" When Bobby replied he did, Ernesto said, "I know all the secret fishing spots in Colorado. I can show some of them to you and your dad, if you like."

"That would be great!"

Ernesto launched into a series of fishing facts that seemed more self-aggrandizing than factual to me, but Bobby seemed enthralled.

Ozzi and I walked into the hallway between the multipurpose room and the dining room. I looked around then grabbed Ozzi's hand and dragged him further away to have some privacy. "What is *with* that guy?" I asked him, incredulously. "Just when I think he's hopelessly annoying, he invites Bobby and his dad on a tour of his favorite fishing holes."

"Ernesto?" Ozzi laughed. "Yeah, he's kind of a piece of work."

"How in the world did he get to be the head of Human Resources?"

Ozzi shrugged. "He's good at his job. Everyone likes him. We get along well."

"You're a better person than I am, then."

"But I don't smell as good."

Ozzi nuzzled my neck and I melted into his embrace. If the ibuprofen didn't cure my headache, maybe this would.

As I stood there, letting my boyfriend nuzzle me, I heard Daisy say, "I thought we were going to have a dead Santa on our hands." I opened one eye to see Daisy and Doug putting on their coats. We were far enough away they didn't seem to notice us.

"Yeah, I was trying to figure out how we'd break it to the kids that somebody wrung Santa's neck," Doug said with a laugh.

"There's still time. I don't think he's going to get any less annoying. This play might be fun after all." I watched them walk away and Daisy did seem to have a little energetic pep to her walk now.

"Can I hitch a ride?" Doug asked Daisy.

"Are you asking because I'm the intern or because I'm your Elfy pal?" Daisy joked as they moved out of earshot.

I pulled away from Ozzi and looked after them. "Those two are a couple of Grade A racists."

Ozzi frowned. "Doug and Daisy? I don't think so. What makes you say that?"

I frowned back. "You were there. You heard Doug say that because Bobby was Latino he'd probably get a scholarship when his boring white twins probably wouldn't."

"I don't think he meant it like that."

"Why do you say that?"

"Because I've met his kids. They *are* boring."

I decided against telling Ozzi the other things that Doug and Daisy said during the read-through. He had to work with them and he seemed to have a good relationship with them. I didn't want to color his thinking. But I vowed to myself that if any more racist claptrap oozed from their mouths, I would definitely call them out on it.

SIX

The next day when Ozzi and I got to the senior center, Carlos and Bobby's glittery stars were already hung above the stage and out across where the audience will sit for the performance. They wafted gently, catching the light just like Carlos said they would.

"Ooh, pretty!" I saw the globby neon-orange one and smiled. "I hope the furnace won't blow them back to the North Pole."

Nobody else was around yet because I wanted to get there a bit early. Barb must have known I'd be nervous because when I left yesterday she pressed a key to the senior center into my palm.

I was taking off my coat when my phone rang. "My brother," I said to Ozzi while I answered. "Hey, Lance."

"Hey, Space Case. Mom wanted me to call you to make sure you're okay with her not coming for Christmas."

I hopped up and sat on the edge of the stage, my feet dangling. "I still think she'll show up."

"She won't."

"I know." I sighed. "I hope Doris and her hip appreciate my sacrifice."

"That's right. It's all about you." He paused. "So did I do my duty? Can I tell her we had a heart-to-heart, hugged it out, and sang *Kumbaya*?"

"Sure, why not? She'll believe that."

We were quiet for a minute.

"Seriously. Are you okay?"

"Yeah, I'm a big girl. I know Doris doesn't have anyone else to help her after the surgery. And I guess I don't really have a choice, do I? Besides, Barb says I can want what I want and it doesn't make me a bad person."

"Little bit."

"I was actually thinking of calling you to drive to Santa Fe with me to surprise her, but now I'm up to my eyeballs in a Christmas pageant." I told Lance all about it while I stared up at the glittery stars, leaving out the racist parts and the part about Leona hating me. I did, however, tell him all about Ernesto. The furnace came on and sent the stars fluttering wildly. When the whoosh died down, I told him about that too. "So I guess I'm staying here. Oh, are you coming to Barb and Don's for Christmas Eve? She asked me to pin you down."

"I'll be there."

We hung up and I rubbed my neck. I felt another headache coming on, but didn't know if it was from looking up at the stars or because I had just heard Ernesto's know-it-all voice telling someone about the history of Christmas trees. I hoped he had gotten all his nonsense out of the way yesterday.

Thelma came in with her arms piled high with fabric. I hurried to give her a hand and we set up a little costume station for her in the center of the multi-purpose room. Ozzi and I hauled in her sewing machine, iron, ironing board, more fabric, and some ready-made clothes from her car.

I held up some of the clothing. "Did you already make all these?"

She rolled her eyes so hard at me I feared she'd burst a blood vessel somewhere. "Don't be a ninny. I pulled them from our closet."

I tried to keep from smiling as I sorted through trousers, vests, dresses, skirts, and blouses which would be right at home in a period piece. The townspeople of the village of Middling will all look remarkably like Thelma and her husband over the past sixty years.

The furnace blasted off and sent my hair into a tornado. When I had sorted myself, she gave me instructions to label this, iron that, and organize these, which I happily did. I was much better at following directions than giving them.

Daisy and Doug arrived and Thelma called them over. She handed them each a pair of white cotton gloves, pointy elf ears, and spats that went over their regular shoes, turning them into pointy elf shoes. It made me wonder why elf stuff was always so pointy. I snickered when I thought, *I should ask Ernesto. He probably knows.*

Daisy and Doug started to walk away but Thelma called them back sternly. "This is not my first rodeo. You need to put those on and keep them on to get used to wearing them. I'll get the kids and seniors fitted tomorrow, but I know you two and our Santa have to go to work tomorrow."

"Actually, we get some comp time tomorrow since we're doing this," Daisy said smugly.

"I don't care if you're going rock climbing like a couple of ninnies tomorrow. *Today* you're going to wear your costumes." Thelma waited until they donned their gloves, ears, and spats. Then she handed them each a strip of fabric in the same color as the spats that had bells attached. "Right ankle," she instructed. They wrapped them around their right legs and secured the Velcro she'd sewn on.

The slightest movement had the bells ringing merrily. Doug and Daisy did a couple a do-si-dos while laughing at the noise. The do-si-dos turned into some inappropriate twerking so I shouted, "Okay everyone. Up on stage. Let's get this show on the road."

We started at the beginning, but this time through we weren't saying any of the lines, just dealing with the blocking. I wanted to figure out where everyone would be on the stage or backstage at any given time.

"Ernesto, I need Santa over here for this part." I plucked a roll of masking tape from a nearby table.

"Why would he be over there?" he said. "It makes much more sense for Santa—the star of the show—to be over here." Ernesto walked in the opposite direction from where I had pointed.

I concentrated on modulating my voice and keeping my cool while being large and in charge. But I did not want a replay of yesterday. "First, Santa is *not* the star of the show. Figgy the elf is." I waved vaguely in Doug's direction. "Second, just do it!" My modulation and cool evaporated and I think I might even have stamped my foot like a petulant preschooler. I took a deep breath and walked to where I stashed my purse. I dug through until I found some ibuprofen, then popped a couple.

After I dry-swallowed them, I turned, fully expecting Ernesto to be exactly where I left him. I was surprised to see that he moved closer to where I wanted him. Not exactly where I had pointed, but decidedly closer. I walked over to the exact spot I wished him to be and pointed again. "Here. Right here." I tore two pieces of tape from the roll I clutched and created an X on the floor. "X marks the spot, Santa."

Ernesto sauntered over like it was his idea all along. He purposely stood six inches from the X.

I pointed at the X.

He moved three inches closer.

I pointed at the X.

He moved one inch closer.

I pointed at the X.

He made a big show of straddling the X and making his shoes touch either side of it.

"Perfect." I shot him an *I win this round* smile.

I walked away looking at my script as the furnace blasted on. A loud noise and an OUCH caused me to whirl around. One of the stars had fallen on Ernesto who stood, holding both sides of his head. I wasn't worried since I knew it was just Styrofoam, but I did feel a twinge of remorse that my first thought was, "Good. Maybe now he'll shut up." I felt a much bigger twinge of remorse when I realized I'd muttered it out loud which I only learned when I saw Doug and Daisy staring at me with their mouths open. *How dare they, of all people, judge me. At least I didn't add a racist insult like they would.*

Everyone else had rushed to Ernesto, asking if he was hurt, if he needed anything, bringing him a chair.

For heaven's sake...it was just a piece of Styrofoam. He was being kind of a baby. I walked closer to him and saw a glob of neon-orange glitter stuck to his temple with a red lump forming under it. The point of the star must have just pegged him perfectly.

Ernesto stared at the Styrofoam star that hit him and then reached down to pick up a bent paperclip. "Was that thing held up by *this*?" He shook the paperclip at everyone standing around him.

We all looked up. I pulled a folding chair over and stood on it to get a better look at the stars still hanging. I had to agree with Ernesto that those puny paperclips didn't look like they'd do the job. But I didn't agree with him out loud.

Carlos walked toward us from backstage. "What happened? I was at the hardware store."

"I'll tell you what happened!" Ernesto said. "That ugly Styrofoam star just fell and hit me in the head."

"Oh no! I'm so sorry."

I cocked my head at Carlos. Why did he feel the need to

tell us he was at the hardware store? And why wasn't he carrying anything? I suppose he could have set his purchases down somewhere, but he still wore his coat. "You were where?" I asked him.

"Hardware store," he said quickly, but didn't meet my eye. "I knew the furnace blew hard in here from when I came the other day to scope the place out. That's why I bought the thicker Styrofoam so it wouldn't blow so easily when the furnace kicked on." He walked over to Ernesto and placed a hand on his shoulder. "I'm so sorry, Ernesto."

I stared as people bustled around Ernesto. If Carlos came here earlier in the week, and we'd all been feeling the blast of the furnace all day yesterday, did he really think that bent paperclips would hold those stars?

Carlos dropped his chin to his chest and closed his eyes. I realized he was saying a prayer. He clearly felt awful about Ernesto getting injured.

I walked over to him. "Ernesto, I think we should get you to the hospital, get you checked out." What I didn't point out was the fact he was overweight, didn't eat right, drank too much, and he was pretty old.

"Damn hospitals don't care about me. Just want to pump me full of expensive drugs, run up the bill." He took a long swig from his flask.

"Then we'll call 911," I said. "I really think you need to be checked out."

"I don't need anything of the kind." Ernesto waved everyone away, like we were a black cloud of pesky gnats.

Carlos apologized again then kicked the neon-orange glitter star that had fallen. It skittered easily across the stage, almost to the curtain hanging across the back of the stage. Carlos was clearly angry with himself, but it all seemed like such an overreaction. I mean, that star would not have skittered so easily across the stage if it was heavy enough to hurt Ernesto.

Despite the bump, it seemed like Ernesto was making a big deal about not much of anything. He probably liked all the attention, even though he made a big production of waving everyone away.

I picked up my ibuprofen bottle and shook three tablets into my palm. "Here, Ernesto. Have a couple of painkillers." I held them out, but before Ernesto could take them from me, Ozzi covered my palm with his hand.

"Wait. Didn't you tell me you have atrial fibrillation? Are you on blood thinners? I don't think you're supposed to take ibuprofen, Ernesto. My mom has that and she was told not to mix over-the-counter drugs with her prescription."

I dropped the pills back into the bottle and set it on the arm of Santa's throne.

Ernesto shrugged and took another swig from his flask.

"Whew, that was a close one." Barb looked with concern toward Ernesto then back toward the bottle of pills.

Don nodded. "Medicine isn't something to goof around with. You should sit back down. I'll get you some more water."

"Get on with your business, all of you," Ernesto said gruffly. "I thought it was all-fired important to get through this rehearsal. Quit your mollycoddling and get on with things. It's just a little bump. Hardly feel it."

"That's not what you said a minute ago," I said.

Doug had been staring and scrolling on his phone, but now looked up. "Yeah, ibuprofen is bad if you're on blood thinners because it's a blood thinner too." In his jingle shoes he walked over to pick up the bottle of ibuprofen and studied it. "These are 500 milligrams each." He checked his phone again. "This says 800 milligrams could be harmful." Doug looked hard at me. "You were going to give him 1500. You almost killed Santa."

"Well, not on purpose." I saw how everyone was looking at me. "Wait. That came out wrong. Not what I meant." I scanned each face, making sure they knew I wasn't a potential Santa killer. "You know what? Let's call it a day." I looked at Ernesto, Doug, and Daisy. "Can you three come in and finish your costume fittings before you go to work tomorrow?"

"I'm the boss," Ernesto said. "We can be late if I say so."

"We have a staff meeting first thing Monday, boss." Doug shook his head and laughed. "I can't believe you make twice the money I make but you can't be bothered to remember the meetings that you schedule."

"That's why I pay you, to remember stuff like that," Ernesto said. "Are you two willing to stop by here on the way in?"

"Are you willing to buy doughnuts and coffee?" Daisy asked.

"If I remember." Ernesto winked then winced.

"What about you, Thelma? Can you come in early?" I asked.

Barb said, "Remember that tomorrow is the first day the kids will be here and you'll need to start in on costumes for anyone who wants a part in the play."

"Ugh, kids." Thelma wrinkled her nose. "May as well get it over with then. Yeah, I'll be here bright and early." She pointed a gnarled finger at Ernesto, Doug, and Daisy. "Do not make me wait."

Ernesto dragged a folding chair closer to him and sat, rubbing his temples.

Ozzi followed him and took a knee so they were eye to eye. "I think I should drive you home."

Ernesto waved him away, but thought better of it and gave a tiny nod.

Ozzi called to me. "Charlee, if I drive Ernesto's car, can you follow and bring me back here for my car?"

"Ernesto lives way over near Greenwood Village. Isn't that out of your way?" Doug asked.

"Is that on our way, Dad?" Bobby asked Carlos. Carlos shushed him without answering.

Barb asked, "Do you have anyone at home, Ernesto? Could they come get you?"

Ernesto shook his head.

"It's not far out of our way," I said. "It wouldn't be a—"

Doug interrupted me. "Let's make this easy. I'll just drive Ernesto's car."

"Then how will you get home?" Ozzi asked.

"My twins borrowed my car so they were picking me up anyway. I'll just have them pick me up at Ernesto's instead. No big deal."

Transportation got arranged and everyone said their goodbyes and shuffled out the doors. Ozzi was the last to leave.

"Are you sure you don't want me to stay and help?"

I shook my head. "Nope. I need to go through this entire play, figure out the blocking, make a list of all the sets and costumes we need, see how many extras we can accommodate. I said I'd give a part to anyone who wanted one, but now I'm worried I won't be able to. I just want to make sure I'm ready for Monday morning. I really thought we'd get more done this weekend."

Ozzi laughed. "Did you really? A bunch of amateurs who've never put on a play before? And you didn't even know you were involved until yesterday morning." He wrapped me in a hug and kissed the tip of my nose. "I think you've done a remarkable job already. I can't believe you didn't kill Ernesto for all the—" Ozzi's eyes widened. "Oh, I didn't mean that. You couldn't have known about the ibuprofen. I only remembered it because Ernesto and my mom both got diagnosed around the same time so I was interested, trying to gather as much information as I could."

"Frankly, I can't believe I didn't kill him either. But I would have used my hands, right around his neck. He's so odious. How do you get along with him so well? It's all very strange to me."

"Well, he did come on pretty strong this weekend. Maybe he was showing off. I don't know. He's not really like that at work. He's funny and nice to everyone. Knows his job like nobody's business," Ozzi said.

"Does he drink like that at work?"

"I've never actually seen him drink."

"What about that flask he was nursing all day today?"

"Maybe it was water."

"Yeah, and maybe Peter O'Drool can roast chestnuts over an open fire."

Ozzi laughed. "I can see why you didn't take to Ernesto— I warned you though, remember?" I nodded. "But I've known him a long time. I guess I'm just used to him. And I know you don't believe me, but he's a huge asset to the company. He worries about everyone, gets people out of jams. Pulled some strings with our health insurance broker and got one of our coders medical coverage for her pregnancy before the new employee waiting period was up. She told me it was a miracle. I think he's just one of those softies who doesn't want you to know he's a softie."

"I'll have to take your word for that." I handed Ozzi his coat. "Now get out of here. The sooner I start, the sooner I finish." I guided him toward the front doors of the senior center.

"Lock this door when I leave."

"As soon as it hits you in the butt."

I sent him off with a kiss and a wave into the twilight, making an elaborate show of locking the door.

A deep breath settled my nerves and I strolled calmly through the now quiet and peaceful space. I hadn't seen what they were up to in the dining room so I peeked in there. They'd created a clothesline-type of contraption across part of the ceiling with a multi-colored fabric curtain dividing the room between the dining area and the Christmas store area. When I looked closer, I saw the "fabric" was actually flat bedsheets, some with flowers, some with thin stripes, some with tiny geometric designs. The dining room half had a bit more open space, with fewer of the large, round banquet tables set up. That's where Chef Joe would feed all the kids and seniors who showed up every day. Barb told me that it would all be on a drop-in basis, since nobody knew who would attend any given day. The senior center board put out the word that depending on the number of kids, they might not have room for the seniors to have their regularly scheduled card games or quiet meetings. Many of the more curmudgeonly types said they'd be back in the middle of January when everything was back to normal. I was a bit surprised that Thelma had volunteered, as much as it sounded like she disliked kids.

On the store side, empty six-foot tables were arranged in a tight U formation, ready to display all the merchandise on them. The table arrangement would allow shoppers to maneuver on both sides of the tables without too much crowding as they browsed. A card table was set up against the wall, probably where the cashier would be.

Boxes were stacked all along the wall. If they were full of the merchandise to be sold, it would be a well-stocked store.

I made a mental note to bring in some of my metal crafts to donate to the cause. They weren't great works of art or anything, but they were useful and mostly on the attractive side. Writing books took so long that the endeavor didn't always feed my creative side. But these crafts I could do start to finish in just a few hours. I found it a great creative outlet and it was a welcome diversion—or procrastination—from working on my manuscript.

I returned to the multi-purpose room, grabbed my notebook and script, snuggled into Santa's throne, and began making lists and reminders to myself.

While I was sitting there, the furnace kicked on and scared the bejeebers out of me. It was dramatically louder when the center was empty. I shoved my script under the notebook so the pages wouldn't whip around but couldn't do anything about the stars dancing above my head. It was mesmerizing watching them up there, bobbing and weaving like so many glittery boxers.

One fell, and then another. They skittered across the stage. While I waited for the furnace to blow them all down, I went in search of some twine or something to anchor the stars better. I was pleased when the furnace eventually shut off and those were the only two casualties. Picking them up, I was a bit surprised by their heft. With that thick Styrofoam and the large size of the stars, they probably weighed a couple of pounds each. I felt bad that I thought Ernesto was being a baby. It probably did hurt when it hit him.

I dragged a folding chair over and, standing on tiptoes, reached as high as I dared. It wasn't high enough.

I hauled out the step ladder I'd spied when I was back-stage searching for twine and scissors. I replaced the fallen stars and began to reinforce the rest. As I worked, I mentally blocked the scenes and hoped the scenery would be easy for kids and seniors to move.

It took me a couple of hours to anchor all the stars in the sky, both above the stage and above where the theoretical audience will sit. I had a momentary wave of panic. What if nobody came? I'd have to remember to ask Barb if there actually was a publicity committee or something like Don had promised. At the very least, I could get Lavar and Tuttle at Espresso Yourself to put up flyers and talk it up to their customers.

As I stowed the step ladder and twine where I found it, I saw the multi-purpose room was kind of a mess. I took a few minutes to pick up stray coffee cups, organize the chairs more logically, and straighten up Thelma's costume area.

I reached for what I thought was a dropped napkin on the floor, but when I got closer, I saw it was a man's wallet. I opened it up and saw a fifty-dollar bill poking out. The driver's license inside said it belonged to Ernesto. "Must have lost it during all the hoopla." I debated what to do with it. *I could just take it to Ozzi tonight and have him give it to Ernesto tomorrow. Or I could come in early when Ernesto will be here for his costume fitting.* I glanced at the clock. *Or I could take it to him tonight.*

Ernesto said there was nobody at home with him. *Maybe I should go check on him, just in case.* I typed Ernesto's address from his ID into the map on my phone. Only twenty minutes away. I debated whether it was too late or not. By the time I'd get there it would be almost ten. Ultimately, I decided I'd drive over there and if it looked like he was still awake, I'd knock. If not, I'd just bring the wallet to Ozzi to deliver it to Ernesto at work.

I followed the directions the nice lady living in my phone spelled out for me and got to his house with no trouble. The porch light was on and it looked like the living room light was on too. Maybe he was watching TV, as the lights flickered and danced in muted tones behind the curtains.

I knocked softly on the door, not wanting to startle him. There was no answer so I knocked a bit louder. Still nothing. I could hear the TV so the third time I knocked quite loudly.

The door flung open. Ernesto stood in front of me scowling, wearing only a t-shirt and boxers. "Whatdoyouwant?" His words came out in a slur. I smelled the whiskey on his breath.

Making sure my eyes stayed on his face and didn't accidentally drift down toward underwear territory, I held out the wallet. "You dropped this at the senior center. Thought you'd need it."

He tried to snatch it from my hand but missed. He grabbed it on his second try. "Thanksh."

Because I'd only just met him, I didn't know if this was normal behavior or not. Was something wrong or was he simply a weekend lush?

"Ernesto, I really think you should go to the emergency room and get checked out."

"Go 'way. Quit bothering me so I can get some sleep." He slammed the door in my face and turned off the porch light.

"Or just stay here and drink yourself into a stupor. What do I care?" I muttered and began to walk back to my car. I took a deep breath, turned, and knocked loudly on the door again.

Ernesto yanked it open again. "What? Ihavework-tomorrow."

"Are you *sure* you're okay?"

"I'm fine. If you'd jush leave me alone, I could get some shleep."

I narrowed my eyes at him, squinting from the dark porch. "Are you going to be able to be my Santa in this play? Will you actually be at the costume fitting at seven tomorrow morning?"

"Said I will, so I will."

I didn't move from the threshold.

"I'm fine. I'll be fine." He waved me off. "Get outta here so I can shleep."

I shrugged. "If you're sure. I'll see you—"

He slammed the door again.

"—tomorrow."

SEVEN

I wasn't planning on being at the senior center so early the next morning, but I didn't sleep well, with all the worries about this play poking me in the brain all night. I decided to get up and get over there. Maybe that would calm my nerves. Besides, what was I going to do at home on a Monday morning? Something boring like eat a leisurely breakfast? Work on my manuscript? Have a snuggle session with Ozzi?

The cupboards were bare, my muse took a vacation, and Ozzi was snoring in his own bed. At least there might be doughnuts and coffee at the senior center.

It was surprising to see so many cars in the senior center parking lot. I thought I'd be unlocking the doors and making the coffee. Luckily, the aroma of strong coffee swirled around me as I dropped my coat into a chair in the multi-purpose room. Someone already had the big urn set up on a table in the corner.

Barb and Don walked up while I was filling my cup.

"We normally have the coffee in the dining room, but with a bunch of kids running around, we thought it might be safer back here," Barb said.

"Were you worried they'd drink it all?" I joked.

"No, so they wouldn't knock it over and—" She saw me smiling at her over my cup. "Oh you. Between you and Don, I don't know who teases me more."

The three of us stood, sipping our coffee, gearing up for who-knows-what to happen. Most of my days were fairly straightforward: eating, writing, Netflixing. Not always in that order. But for the next couple of weeks, I suspected nothing would be predictable about my days. I decided to embrace the unknown and revel in it. Or at least do my best not to ruin Christmas for any kids.

We took in the activity around us. I was happy to see Ernesto, Doug, and Daisy already here for their costume fitting. It looked to me like Doug had been first in line because he was elfed out completely: pointy ears, pointy shoes, jingle bells around one ankle, white gloves, and a truly adorable set of clothes. Red-and-white striped knee socks. Green culottes. Red-and-white striped long-sleeved shirt under a matching green vest adorned with applique snowflakes.

Daisy still wore her office attire. She slumped in a chair, nose buried in her phone, but looked up and laughed at Doug when he walked over to her and did a little jig.

Doug walked away from her and toward us, calling over his shoulder, "You want some coffee?"

She jumped up. "I'll get my own. You don't do it right."

Thelma hollered. "You spill coffee on that costume and there will be H-E-double toothpicks to pay!"

"Yes, ma'am!" Doug smiled at her and gave her a jaunty little elf jig.

I laughed. "You're in a good mood so early in the day."

"I'm better off than Santa, that's for sure." Doug dipped his chin in Thelma's direction where she tried wrangling a Santa suit that looked a tad too small over Ernesto's tad too large belly.

"He's drunk anyway. Won't even notice," Daisy said nonchalantly while she filled her cup.

"I'm sure that's not true, dear," Barb said gently.

Daisy shrugged. "He's sure slurring his words. That's all I know."

Doug frowned. "Are you sure? That doesn't sound like him."

We all turned to watch Thelma tugging the Santa jacket this way and that to see if it was workable or not. It looked like "not" was winning. Suddenly Ernesto enveloped Thelma in a bear hug. *Maybe he is drunk*, I thought. But he slumped to the floor, almost pulling Thelma down with him. A bottle crashed from her table to the floor, sending glass shards and brown liquid across the linoleum. She shrieked and we all set our cups down and rushed over.

"Oh my gosh!" Doug dropped down next to Ernesto and patted his cheeks. "Hey, buddy, wake up. C'mon, wake up!"

I dialed 911.

"What happened?" Don asked.

"I don't know!" Thelma's eyes were saucers. "One minute I'm trying to get him to suck in his belly, and the next he's on the floor. It was like he completely lost power. Deflated like a balloon!" Thelma accepted Barb's comforting embrace.

After I hung up, I sniffed the air. "What was in that bottle that broke?"

Don hurried for the mop to start cleaning the mess.

"Ernesto brought me some of his homemade vanilla. Vodka and vanilla beans. That was so thoughtful of him," she wailed.

I helped Don corral the broken glass and vanilla beans, then he took some quick swabs of the floor. The floor would remain sticky, but nobody would slip and fall in any puddles.

Two paramedics came before we barely finished, with two police officers right after them. The EMTs both went to work on Ernesto and the cops moved everyone out of the way, back in the corner with the coffee table, so the paramedics could work.

"He's our Santa," I said to one of the officers. "Yesterday he got hit with a star, but it was light. Didn't even break the skin." By the way the officer stared at me, I realized I was rambling. I took a breath and started over. "We're getting ready for a Christmas play. Ernesto Santiago, the man there in the Santa suit, is our Santa and was getting fitted for his outfit when he just dropped. Yesterday one of those stars" —I pointed up— "fell and conked him on the head. There was no blood or anything."

The officer glanced toward the ceiling. "Those look like Styrofoam."

"They are."

"That's not going to hurt anyone." He turned toward his partner. "Robinson. Think one of those could hurt someone?"

Robinson followed his finger to one of the stars. "Nah. That's just Styrofoam."

Carlos and Bobby walked in. "What's going on?" Carlos asked.

Thelma sprang in front of Bobby, grabbed his hand, and pulled him out of the room. She looked back at us over his head. "The kids are coming! C'mon!"

Barb and Don hurried after her, but it took a bit longer for the rest of us to realize they were forming a human shield across the doorway so the kids wouldn't be traumatized by seeing paramedics working on Santa Claus. Daisy and Doug joined Thelma, Barb, and Don trying to block the view into the multi-purpose room.

I pulled Carlos with me, whispering, "Something happened to Ernesto. He just collapsed during his costume fitting."

We stood shoulder to shoulder shielding anyone who walked past.

Carlos crossed himself and mouthed a prayer.

It didn't seem possible, but Daisy looked even more pallid than normal. She flinched as a large contingent of children, their parents, and seniors shuffled down the hallway.

I heard the sharpness of Thelma's voice as she snapped, "No, Winston, you can't go in there. You can just wait for your coffee." She took half a step into the hall and looked back to inspect the blockade. It seemed she was satisfied we could hold it without her, so she shooed everyone streaming in the senior center down the hall and into the dining room. The kids began peppering her with questions.

"What's going on?"

"Is it a Christmas surprise?"

"Do you want to see my doll? I brought her from home so she wouldn't be lonely."

"Are you the principal of this school?"

"My mom said I'm eating lunch here today and I want pizza. Is there pizza for lunch?"

"Why are there police cars here?"

"It's just an inspection, nothing to worry about," Thelma said.

"Can we see the police car?"

"I'm going out to sit in the ambulance."

Thelma grabbed a boy by the hood of his parka. "Not if you know what's good for you."

The boy saw her face and scrambled away from her to clutch his mother's hand.

Thelma stuck two fingers in her mouth and a shrill whistle sounded. The noise immediately abated. She announced in a loud, clear voice, "Parents, there's a sign-in sheet on a clip board in the dining room, just ahead and to the right. Get your children signed in and then please leave through the kitchen door. It will take you right into the parking lot. Children, you go in and find a chair. Sit in it and await further instructions. Do not move from your chair once you sit in it." She paused. "As soon as you sit in a chair, the floor becomes hot lava." The children squealed with delight at an impromptu game of Hot Lava so early in the morning. "Seniors, you go in and claim a child. Clamp your hand on their shoulder and also await further instructions."

"But they'll be in hot lava!" a little girl said in a worried voice.

Thelma said, "Old people wear special shoes. Absolutely immune to hot lava. Now all of you … do as I say! Chop chop!" She clapped her hands and everyone cleared the hallway and moved into the dining room.

"That was impressive," I said.

The crush of arrivals slowed to a trickle. Thelma had deputized one of the seniors and stationed them at the front door to direct any newly arriving parents and children around to the kitchen door to bypass the hallway altogether. We were just about to dismantle our blockade of the doorway when one of the seniors hurried down the hallway with one of the children.

"Potty time!" she sang out.

We reassembled our blockade.

I looked over my shoulder in time to see one of the paramedics shake his head at the cops. Their flurry of activity slowed down. I rotated completely so I faced into the multipurpose room. The paramedic's monitor had a flat line across it. "He's … dead?" I whispered. "Because of Styrofoam?"

Doug turned too. "It must not be from the star hitting him. Last night I ran him to the ER—"

"What? When? Did he call you or something? When I was there he just wanted to go to bed."

"He called me around midnight. Said his head was killing him. They observed him for a while, gave him something for his headache, and released him a couple of hours later. I drove him back home and put him to bed. The nurse told me everything was fine, but he'd have a headache for a day or two because of his age and poor health."

Doug and I watched the scene swirling around Ernesto.

Suddenly he took a big shuddery breath. "He was my mentor, taught me everything I know." I looked at Doug and his eyes were red. Tears rolled down his face. "This is terrible." He began choking out deep, racking sobs.

I put my arm around his shoulder. "You guys hold the fort here. Doug and I are going to sit down." Don nodded at me and everyone shifted position to fill in the void we left.

I led Doug to a folding chair near the coffee station in the corner. I didn't know what else to do, so I poured him a cup which he automatically accepted with shaky hands. I pulled another chair close to his, but positioned it in such a manner to block his view of Ernesto. Doug set his coffee on the floor under his chair, placed his elbows on his knees, and dropped his head. I rubbed his upper back until he stopped crying.

Officer Robinson asked, "Who's in charge here?"

Don stepped forward. The officer led him out of earshot.

I watched their pantomime, trying to figure out what they might be saying. Robinson spoke. Don shook his head and replied to him. Don's look of anguish was evident even way across the room where I sat. Robinson sighed and walked over to the paramedics, leaving Don where he was. The officer spoke to one of the paramedics. The paramedic shook his head. Robinson said something else. The paramedic spoke to his partner. She shook her head too. Robinson squatted down and spoke to them both. The paramedics looked at each other for a long time before one of them shrugged. Robinson nodded at them, then at Don.

The paramedics lifted Ernesto on to their stretcher and began gathering their equipment. It looked to me like they were getting ready to leave. Don and I hurried over to the doorway to help the human blockade. We shuffled from the doorway to block the way if anyone left the dining room. The way was clear for the emergency workers to take Ernesto through the front door.

After they did, I pulled Don aside. "What was all that about with you and the cop?"

Don whispered. "Paramedics don't transport dead bodies, so he was telling me we'd have to wait for someone from the coroner's office. I told him we had fifty elementary school-aged kids and at least that many seniors across the hall and we couldn't wait for someone from the coroner's office. He agreed with me that this place was too public for what needed to be done."

Doug hadn't moved from where he sat in the corner.

I called Ozzi to tell him what happened. He said he'd come right away.

Daisy and I sat with Doug near the coffee corner. We were silent until Doug straightened his back, looked me straight in the eye, and quietly said, "You made Ernesto move immediately before that star hit him. You put him directly underneath it."

It took me a minute to process what he was saying. "You think I had something to do with the furnace coming on and dropping that star on him? You heard the cop. There's no way a piece of Styrofoam would kill someone. Not even if they were unhealthy."

"Plus, you tried to give him that ibuprofen." Daisy cocked her head at me, studying my face.

I stood, pushing my chair away. I spoke quietly, gently, peering down at the two of them. "You guys are in shock. You don't know what you're saying. But I want you to know I had nothing to do with this. It was just a tragic accident. Probably didn't even have anything to do with that star."

As I walked away, I knew that couldn't be true. And yet, how *could* it be true?

I found Don and Barb in the hallway near the kitchen. I cornered them and said, "We have to cancel this play."

"You will do nothing of the sort."

Leona's voice behind me made me jump.

"The show must go on. Don here was lobbying to play Santa the other day so he's your new Santa." She suddenly looked stricken. "Did the Santa coat leave with him or do we still have it?" Barb and Don must have looked as shocked as I was that she was more worried about the Santa costume than the man who had been wearing it. Leona softened her tone a bit. "The kids and community are relying on this event. You can take a day or two to regroup, but this play will be performed on December twenty-second. That gives you twelve days. Ha!" she said without humor. "Like the Twelve Days of Christmas." She swooshed into the kitchen and I heard her giving instructions to Chef Joe.

"Did you guys call her? Why is she here?" I asked them.

Don shrugged but Barb said, "It's the first day the kids are here. She probably just popped in to make sure everything was okay."

Chef Joe hurried out and saw Don and Barb. "I need you!" He pulled them away.

I guess I was glad Leona came and took control. We were all a bit discombobulated and there were children to take care of, after all. The word got around to most of the seniors, but everyone agreed it was best that the children not hear anything about Ernesto. I hoped we could get back on an even keel soon, though, so Leona won't have to be here every day.

Wait.

Just two days ago Leona said she'd do everything in her power to have this event succeed. She had even added the clincher, "You mark my words." It was obvious Leona didn't want Ernesto as the Santa in the play.

I shook off the thought Leona could be involved in any of this. It was just my imagination acting up. *Ernesto died because he was unhealthy. Nobody killed him.*

EIGHT

The rest of Monday passed in a blur. I had been only vaguely aware of Ozzi talking to me, telling me he'd take Doug and Daisy with him. It didn't occur to me until after he left that he also had a long relationship with Ernesto, just like Doug and Daisy did, and was probably mourning his friend. Daisy hadn't worked at Net Software very long, though, so she couldn't have developed any kind of deep friendship with Ernesto. She did seem quite shocked and disturbed, maybe even more than the rest of us. Perhaps she'd never known anyone who died.

The more I thought about it the next day, however, the more I wondered what her relationship was with Ernesto. She felt comfortable telling everyone that Ernesto was drunk, and had made all those racist jokes during the read-through. Was she ... could she ...? "Stop it, Charlee. You're acting crazy."

"Who are you talking to?" Bobby asked.

"Myself. Don't pay any attention to me. What can I do for you?"

"I was just wondering who was going to play Santa now that Ernesto is dead."

He said it so matter-of-factly I couldn't help but stare at him.

"Ernesto *is* dead, isn't he?" Bobby asked.

"I don't know what you're talking about." I bent down, pretending to brush a thread off the leg of my jeans so he wouldn't see my face. But he didn't need to see my face.

"That was no inspection. I know he's dead," he said quietly. "Don't worry, I won't tell the other kids. Could be traumatizing."

"Why do you want to know about Santa?"

"I just heard some grown-ups talking about how Don really wanted to play Santa and was totally bummed when he couldn't. But now they say he's happy." Bobby shrugged. "At least that's what I think they meant when they said he was floating on air. I don't think anyone can really do that, so I used context clues to figure it out." He looked up at me. "Is that what it means?"

"Yes, but Don is as upset as anyone about Ernesto."

"That's what I figured, but those grown-ups made it sound like—"

I took Bobby by the hand and told him to take me to the grown-ups who were so blithely accusing Don of murdering Ernesto. I used different words though.

"They were playing cards." He led me down the stairs to the rooms they'd set up with different activities for the kids. It was decided that the seniors should hang out down here too, in case the police came back to tie up any unfinished business. We poked our heads into all the rooms. I pointed out two different groups of card players, but after studying each one, he shook his head. After we scanned the last room he said, "I can't find them now."

"That's okay. Narrowing down the seniors who play cards is like narrowing down the fish that swim. You go on and do something fun."

Bobby ran back to the room where they were working on

jigsaw puzzles. Winston was letting the kids push him in his wheelchair while he explained the jet stream to them.

Halfway up the stairs I ran into Don. "I've been looking for you," he said.

"What now?" I asked wearily.

"I just wanted to make sure you knew I want to be Santa."

My hands flew to my ears. I leaned forward and grabbed his arm, whispering, "Do not say that out loud ever again!"

He rubbed his chin, puzzled. "Why not?"

"You sound just a tad too gleeful that those Santa boots are yours to fill now. People are talking."

Don blanched and reeled enough that he needed to grab the railing. "Oh my ... I didn't think ... I feel terrible. A man is dead..."

"Exactly. And it hasn't gone unnoticed how much you wanted Ernesto's job."

"Do you think people might think that I had something to do with his death?"

I thought about all the times lately that people thought I'd had something to do with someone's death, and all the times I had suspected other people. My entire critique group, for instance. "People think strange things, Don. Especially when there's a death involved. Ernesto died because he lived an extremely unhealthy lifestyle. But nobody wants to believe that because then they might realize that they live an extremely unhealthy lifestyle too, and they could be next. It's so much easier for them to speculate on you—or me—killing Ernesto."

Don raised his eyebrows.

"Both equally incorrect suppositions, of course. But please, don't act so ... so ... gleeful about getting to play Santa now.

Don looked devastated. "I can't believe anyone thought I was happy about a man's death."

I stepped up the staircase so I was even with him and gave him a hug. "Nobody who knows you would ever think that."

I released him from my embrace. "Maybe you'd like to say a few words before our next rehearsal? I'm not exactly sure when that will be because of Doug and Daisy, though."

He nodded then continued past me down the stairs.

I trudged the rest of the way up the stairs, hoping that whoever was talking about Don got it out of their system. I knew how bad it felt to be unjustly accused. But I also knew Don. He rarely talked about it, but the fact he and Barb didn't have grandkids has been an almost unbearable weight. When their daughter died in a skiing accident when she was in college in the 1980s, it just about crushed them both. One of the first things they asked me when I moved into the apartment complex was whether I skied. I had joked that I was the only native Coloradoan who'd never strapped skis to her feet. I didn't understand their interest until many months later, when they told me about her. They were leery of getting too close to me if they thought they might lose me too, but now I'm sure they think of me as their replacement daughter. We all realize it's not the same, but it's something. And now that I'd brought Ozzi into the fold, they had a surrogate son as well.

But nothing to fill the grandchildren-shaped hole in their hearts.

That's why I knew Don was so keen to play Santa, but others might not realize.

I wanted Don's name cleared, and I wanted it fast. "I want what I want," I murmured, heading for the dining room. "Maybe a sandwich, too." Barb said that was okay, for people to want what they want. *I definitely don't want to ruin Christmas, so the show will go on like everyone wants. But making everything merry isn't up to me.*

There was a line for lunch, so until everyone had been served, I plopped into a chair and mindlessly opened my phone and clicked on social media. I immediately wished I hadn't. I scrolled just far enough to see that people were once again talking about my "black touch" and how I "just happened to be around another death." I clicked off my phone and slapped it face down on the table in front of me.

How did that get out already? I glanced around the room and saw so many people on their phones, even Thelma. I thought about Don telling me this event would give me tons of publicity. "This is not the publicity I wanted!" I moaned.

A shadow loomed over me and I lifted my head to see Leona next to me. "I hear you're going to give up on these kids, on this play."

"I'm not!" As much as I wanted to just go home and scrub away my black touch, I promised. "The show must go on."

After lunch it seemed the kids and the seniors weren't so shy around each other any longer. I saw no seniors with their phones out. Quite the opposite, in fact. The oldsters and the youngsters seemed to be interacting like old friends in some cases, or at least studying each other like scientists and specimens.

Everywhere I went I almost got run over by kids acting like kids and seniors suddenly acting like kids. As I moved through the senior center, I heard snippets of conversations.

"I've wanted to teach kids magic forever."

"I've wanted to learn magic my whole life!"

"I've wanted to be a grandpa forever."

"Now I have a grandpa!"

"I love to read to kids."

"She's helping me read gooder."

"Finally, someone to eat my goodies who isn't watching their weight."

"Can I have another cookie?"

Winston, in his wheelchair, had a boy on his knee while

they pored over the newspaper. "It says here a polar vortex is on its way to Colorado next week."

The boy looked up, worried. "Will it keep Santa from coming?"

"Oh no, no, no." Winston said. "Don't you worry about that, Javier. A little weather won't bother Santa and those reindeer." The boy visibly relaxed. Winston pointed to the article. "Besides, it says here it should be gone by Christmas. But even if it's not, it's too cold to snow during a polar vortex. And Santa has that toasty warm jacket."

Javier got his worried look again. "But what about the reindeer? They don't wear coats."

"Ah, but those are magic reindeer. They never need coats."

I smiled as their voices faded behind me.

I'd brought some of the extra metal crafts I'd made and took the opportunity to go out to my car to collect them. I knew I wanted to give one of them to Barb for Christmas, but still hadn't decided which one. I saw her near the lobby doors talking to Gloria Mae so I veered around the building until I saw the dumpster. The back door should be around there someplace. I'd carry them into the store when Barb wasn't around, to keep her from peeking.

As I reached the door, I saw the area littered with cigarette butts. Gross. I juggled the box I carried. I must have made a bunch of noise because the door was opened for me from the inside. I wondered who was responsible for all the litter. As I struggled with my box through the door, I muttered, "Filthy habit."

My eyes adjusted after the door banged shut behind me. Leona stood with Carlos. "Thanks for getting the door," I said to her.

She simply stared at me so I hurried away to find somewhere to set down the heavy box. *What is her problem?* I wondered, as they resumed whatever conversation I'd interrupted.

After I shook out my arms, I checked for Barb, but the coast was clear. I carried the box into the half of the dining room where they were setting out the merchandise for the store. I was directed to put them out anywhere on the tables and then to check in with Mrs Perez to tell her what I'd brought so she could log it in and price it.

I didn't want to lump it all together, so I placed the ear cuffs on the display stand I'd brought, the jewelry holders on a different table, and the candle sconces on yet another. I studied each piece as I placed them on the table, trying to put them in some sort of hierarchy of desirability. Barb was the last person on my Christmas list, but I was afraid I'd be dithering up until Christmas Eve.

"I can't decide what to buy either," Bobby said.

"I'm not buying. I just brought some stuff I made. But I don't think they have everything displayed yet. You have plenty of time to shop."

"What did you make?"

I pointed them out. "These candle sconces, those jewelry holders, and on that far table those little ear cuffs." I pointed to the cartilage on the outside of my ear. "It's jewelry that goes here."

"What's a sconce?"

"It's something to hold candles or lamps. Sometimes sconces are attached to walls, but mine sit on a table. I buy this decorative sheet metal and use a bunch of tools and my superhuman strength to get it into that shape. Then I clamp it and rivet it and hope it holds together. When you put a candle in the middle of it, the light shines through the decorative holes and it looks really pretty."

"Cool."

"Who are you shopping for?"

"My mom."

I remembered how quickly Leona jumped in when talk turned to Bobby's mom that first day. In case he wanted to talk about her, I gave him the opportunity. "What kinds of things does she like? What does she like to do?"

Bobby fingered the tablecloth. "I don't know." He looked up at me. "People call her 'unreliable' but I'm pretty sure that's code for something they don't want me to know."

"Does she live with you and your dad?"

"Sometimes. Sometimes she makes me breakfast and walks me to school, and sometimes I do that on my own." He shrugged and jabbed the toe of his sneaker into the floor a few times.

I asked quietly, "Does she ever hurt you?"

"You mean my feelings or my body?"

"Both."

"I like when she's around, but it hurts my heart when she's not. Maybe if I'm better or I get her something really nice for Christmas, she'll stay around more."

My heart shattered. I had no words, so I just squeezed his shoulder.

Bobby picked up one of the sconces. "These are cool. Maybe I'll get her one of these."

Mrs Perez bustled by. "You'll have to wait until I get them priced. Come back tomorrow. We should have everything set out by then."

Bobby wandered slowly along the table, trailing his hand gently at the edge. I hurried out before he saw the tears in my eyes.

I shook my head as if that could erase the sadness and walked into the multi-purpose room to focus instead on something I could control—how I was going to wrangle all the kids and seniors who wanted to be in the play. I hoped Doug and Daisy would be back tomorrow for real rehearsals. If they weren't, I'd have to contact them to see if they were still interested in being involved, under the circumstances. But that was Future Charlee's problem.

The notepad filled with my notes and random thoughts

about the play still rested on the seat of Santa's throne where I'd left it. The throne, however, was pushed to the back of the stage, near the far curtain. I sat in it without moving it. It was kind of nice being so far from all the hubbub of the senior center. Not quite a day at the beach, but less like a day on Omaha Beach. It was middle ground I could live with.

As I read through my notes, I heard voices behind the curtain.

"You tell her to leave Bobby alone. My son already has a mother."

"Stephanie, what are you talking about?" Carlos sounded weary.

"She was just there in the store with him. I know they were talking about me."

"So what if they were? Bobby can talk to whoever he wants. And I'm pretty sure Charlee doesn't want to be Bobby's mother."

Charlee? They were talking about me?

"Well, you make sure she doesn't."

"And how am I supposed to do that?"

"I don't know, Carlos, but if you won't then I will."

Stephanie's voice sounded clipped, sharp. I tiptoed over to the far side of the curtain to see Bobby's mother. I peeked around the curtain and saw a leggy blond in a mini-skirt and purple sheepskin boots. Part of her long hair was up in a top-knot that cascaded in long curls down her neck and shoulders. Her hands were on her hips. When she turned toward me, I hurried off the stage and out of the multi-purpose room.

Halfway across I realized Bobby never answered definitively whether his mom hurt him.

NINE

L unchtime was chaotic. Chef Joe hadn't made enough spaghetti for fifty hungry children and seniors so he had to supplement with pancakes. I took the opportunity to grab a burger and fries at the drive-through and eat in the relative tranquility of a fast-food parking lot at lunchtime. By the time I got back to the senior center I had indigestion and a plan.

When everyone had their fill of basghetti and pancakes, I herded them into the multi-purpose room, even ushering Mrs Perez and her helpers out of the store for a minute to listen to me.

I stood on the stage so everyone could see me. "So … I want to … can you all just quiet down? This won't take very long. I just want to …" Nobody was listening. The noise, in fact, was growing like a snowball heading downhill.

Carlos had come to see what was going on and stood off to the side. I caught his eye but he looked as bewildered as I felt.

From the back of the room I heard someone clap their hands twice. All the children clapped back. The room went silent. Mrs Perez smiled at me and with a wave of her hand, encouraged me to begin talking.

"Wow. That's like magic. Thank you, Mrs Perez," I said.

Don started to speak but I clapped twice at him and he clammed up.

"Definitely magic."

The adults all laughed, but the children waited expectantly.

"As you know, in a couple of weeks we're going to put on a Christmas play!" Apparently I had enough excitement in my voice to raise a chorus of cheers from my audience. "And if you want to, you can be in it." I nervously shifted my weight back and forth, waiting to see how much cheering this would bring. If all these people wanted a part in the play, I honestly didn't know what we'd do. That many elves, townspeople, and dogs simply wouldn't fit on the stage.

There was a lot of cheering. A lot. Way too much.

I clapped twice and gained control of the room again. "This play has need of some kids to play Santa's elves, other kids to play dogs and cats, and some kids and adults to play townspeople. So raise your hand if you'd like to do any of that." About half the people raised their hands. "If you don't want to be in the play, but want to help Mr Morales with the scenery and stuff, go stand by that wall." I pointed, and Mrs Perez and her team took the opportunity to tiptoe out the doors, back to the safety of the Christmas store. "And if you just want to come to the performance, that's great too!"

The kids began shouting at once about the roles they wanted, running back and forth between their friends to see what *they* wanted to do. Opinions were changed—and verbalized—many times over. I caught Barb's eye and realized she and Don were laughing at me. I raised my palms, surrendering to the chaos, and began laughing too.

After a bit, I clapped twice and was rewarded once again with silence. I had to admit, Leona and the teachers at the 56th

Avenue School did a great job with their students. A group of four seniors standing near the back continued their conversation. At least, that is, until all the children turned and stared at them until they quieted.

"Okay, let's do this. Hey, Barb and Don, will you come up here and give me a hand?" When they climbed the stairs and stood next to me, I clapped again and said, "If you want to be an elf, please line up in front of Mr Singer here." Don waved and positioned himself at the far right of the stage.

Chaos erupted once again.

I clapped twice and yelled, "Freeze! Nobody move." Everyone froze in place. One foot in the air as if in mid-stride. Hands waving in the air. Walkers hovering off the floor. Giggles began quietly, then as a wave of helpless laughter when the silliness of the scene became apparent. Children fell to the floor in hysterical laughter. Adults helped them up.

"Okay let's try this again. Nobody move, but when I give the sign, line up in front of the role you want in the play. Mr Singer is for any elves. Mrs Singer is for any townspeople. And I am dogs and cats." I turned toward Carlos and pointed to the wall. "Mr Morales, will you go stand down there to meet your crew?" I turned back to the crowd. "Anyone who doesn't want to be IN the play but wants to work ON the play painting scenery and such can meet Mr Morales over there. Everyone else is excused to go play games and work on crafts in the basement." About half my audience disappeared, much to my relief.

After Barb had moved to the far left of the stage, I raised one hand in the air and almost said "*On your marks, get set, go!*" But then I remembered seeing a buffalo stampede one time and changed my mind. Most of the seniors here were fairly robust, but some were frail. I didn't want the paramedics to have to return. I thought fast. "When I clap, I want you to go to the line you want, but … and this is very important … you can only take tiny tiptoe steps, like you're all baby penguins." I waddled across the stage as an illustration, to hoots of laughter. "Ready?"

"Yes!" they roared.

I clapped twice and they all—kids and seniors alike—began waddling around like penguins. Most of them were having so much fun acting like penguins that they forgot they had an actual assignment. Soon enough they remembered why Don, Barb and I were standing at the edge of the stage, and Carlos near the wall. It wasn't long before the human dam broke. Friends wanted to be with friends so negotiations ensued as to which role would be better. "No! Come be an elf!" Adults tried to talk children into shorter lines. "Are you *sure* you wouldn't rather be a dog?" Kids began choosing their elf names. "I'm Snowflake!" … "I'm Pixie!" … "I dibs Mr McJingles!" … "I'm Pumpkin Spice Latte!"

I saw Thelma standing in the back shaking her head, probably trying to do mental calculations about how many costumes she'd need to get together in the next twelve days.

Just when I was tearing off sheets from my notepad for each of us to make a list of the people in front of us, Chef Joe stuck his head in the doorway and hollered, "I just baked cookies. Come and get them!"

The kids scattered and the adults followed behind them at a speedy clip. I looked at Don and Barb who both shrugged. "He makes really good cookies," Barb said.

Don was halfway down the stairs, calling over his shoulder, "I'll get you one if there are any left!"

After everyone was sated with cookies—and I had to admit, they were delicious—I tried again. This time, though, I did something a bit different. After I sent away anyone who didn't want to be involved in the play, I told the remaining adults to stay put while the kids waddled like penguins to their lines. Then I stole a move from Thelma's playbook and told every adult to line up next to a child and clamp one hand on their shoulder. "This will be your Christmas buddy. You will be in charge of getting them to Thelma for their costumes, and you will work with them on their scenes when we start rehearsing again." After a couple more trades, and some seniors clamping hands on two kids' shoulders, everything seemed like it might work.

Since it was getting late in the day I said, "Why don't you all take a little bit to get to know your Christmas Buddy. Then tomorrow we can start to work on the play."

Like the Grinch, my heart grew two sizes while I watched people of very different generations, races, and socioeconomic backgrounds laughing and talking together.

I tried to pretend I didn't see Stephanie peeking through the back curtain, staring daggers at me.

TEN

I got to the senior center the next morning before eight o'clock, but the place was already full of people—young and old—and much laughter. Buddies paired from yesterday, some still waddling like penguins.

A group was busy decorating a tree in the lobby with a colorful paper chain the children had made in one of the craft sessions yesterday. Each paper link was stained and grubby with excess paste and there was much more paper chain than tree, but the kids were proud of their creation and the adults made sure the glorious mess was visible to all.

I organized myself on the stage, and was relieved to see Doug and Daisy climb the stairs to join me. They both had their costumes draped over their arms.

"Are you here to rehearse or to quit?" I eyed the costumes nervously.

Doug smiled. Daisy did not.

"Rehearse," he said. "I thought about quitting, especially with all my new duties and the turmoil over at the office—"

"Doug got promoted to Ernesto's job," Daisy explained.

"Oh, that's great, Doug. Congratulations."

"Thanks. I wish it wasn't under these circumstances, though."

"Yes, I can only imagine." I picked up my notepad and script with all the random notes scribbled everywhere. "Can we work through the entire play today? Do you have time?"

"That's why we're here," Doug said with a smile. He elbowed Daisy. "Right, Elfy?"

"Right. It's a dream come true." Daisy spoke in a sarcastic monotone.

I described the funny scene to them of trying to organize everyone yesterday then explained how I ultimately paired up every kid who wanted to be in the play with an adult so they could help each other focus on the task at hand.

Doug laughed. "The kids must be a handful."

"The adults too." I grinned. "And this morning I had a brainstorm in the shower. I'm only going to put the extras in one scene so they don't have to focus for too long. Plus, it gives me a good way to cycle more people into the scenes."

"Seems like you have it all figured out." Doug nodded approvingly. "Good for you."

Thelma walked by, and with the not-at-all subtle pointing of an arthritic finger, reminded Doug and Daisy to wear their pointy ears and pointy spats, and their white gloves so they got used to wearing them.

The elves donned their finery while I went to start gathering up the rest of my actors and extras. Don wanted to wear his Santa outfit since Thelma had tailored it for him already, but I didn't want to distract all the kids.

It took us four hours to rehearse a forty-minute play, but we had a lot of interruptions and distractions. We worked on one scene at a time, and when we finished, I waddled my extras straight down to Thelma's costume area where she and her committee dealt with outfitting them into elves, dogs, cats, or townspeople.

They simplified things for themselves by handing

women long, one-size-fits all elastic waist skirts, and the men jaunty hats of all styles, telling them to embellish the rest of their costumes from their own closets or the nearby thrift store.

For the dogs and cats, most of them already in character on their hands and knees, she was going to make headbands with ears, a decorated piece of fabric to drape across their backs with a tail attached.

The kids clamored to design their own animal, so Thelma shrugged, and said, "Okay by me," and called over some of her committee members to help them with their designs and the cutting and sewing. Some kids wanted to be Dalmatians, some brown dogs, some poodles, some pit bulls, some black dogs— "And you have to call me Smokey, like my dog. Arf." The cats wanted to be Persians, calicos, Siamese, and one cheetah, so someone on the committee ran to the fabric store to get faux fur. The cat extras got into character by waiting and licking their paws. Their adult buddies sat in chairs and petted them on their heads.

Elf extras were a bit more elaborate, with their full costumes, pointy spats, and ears, so Thelma had to concentrate on those. She took measurements with her gnarled hands and wrote everything down in her shaky cursive.

After I left my charges with Thelma, I gathered up the next group I needed for the next scene. We were a well-oiled machine.

By the time lunch rolled around everyone was starving. Chef Joe had made enormous rectangular pizzas in sheet cake pans and the kids giggled at the idea of square pieces of pizza, which led to many conversations about what the seniors ate when they were kids. One boy wanted to know what hardtack tasted like, making the adults roar with laughter.

I stabbed my salad and smiled as I glanced around the room. This was working out much better than I expected.

Barb and Don acted like they knew everything would run smoothly from the start.

After lunch, I wandered into the store and was pleased to see it fully functional. Kids were browsing with their adult buddies, discussing the merits of one gift over another for their parents. They discussed the things their parents liked, and many of the seniors took the opportunity to offer gentle money management tips. But with even the most expensive items under a dollar, the lessons were lost on the kids.

I still hadn't decided which of my metal crafts to give Barb, and glanced at their positions on the tables. I was surprised and delighted that many of my donations had already been sold, but then I had a moment of panic. If they sold out before I chose one for Barb, I wouldn't have time to make any more.

Mrs Perez sat at the check-out table with the cash box. I picked up a jewelry holder and one of the sconces and carried them over to her.

"Checking out?" she asked cheerily.

"No, actually, these are two of the things I donated." I explained to her my dilemma and she waved me away.

"Just bring back the one you decide not to give her."

I thanked her and hurried to the basement, trying to shield the items from view in case Barb was nearby. I glanced around, trying to decide where I could stash these while I made up my mind. The classrooms were out because they were all taken over by craft areas, reading rooms, and play spaces. The exercise room was out because it was basically just a big open room with mats on the floor, a couple of fitness balls, and some yoga blocks and mats. No good hiding spots.

The lending library was much more promising. Tall wooden shelves held a zillion jumbled books of all genres. I passed one shelf labeled "Mysteries" and stopped to have a look. I was surprised to see a complete set of my books, but then realized Don and Barb probably bought them specifically for this senior center library. A closer look revealed that none of the spines had been cracked. I rubbed some dirt in my hurt feelings and shook it off, just like I was taught to do in softball.

Continuing to the end of the row of bookshelves, I saw a stack of thousand-piece jigsaw puzzles on the floor. Perfect. I reached over the top of them to drop my metal crafts between the stack and the wall, an excellent hiding place. When I leaned over further, I saw something already hidden in the space behind the puzzles.

The Styrofoam star that had hit Ernesto.

I left it where it was, but not before I had a pang, realizing someone had probably stashed it down here so nobody would be traumatized by seeing it again. I wondered why they hadn't just thrown it away, though.

My curiosity dissipated when I heard a familiar voice that seemed very much out of place.

I poked my head into doorways until I saw my brother Lance in one of the craft rooms, surrounded by kids of all ages.

"What are you doing here?" As the words were coming out of my mouth, I noticed all the paper airplanes in various states of construction and flight. I couldn't help but tear up. The room swam in front of me. "Just like Dad used to do with us."

Lance pushed up then pulled down both sleeves of his hoodie, a clear indication he was embarrassed. "Had a day off and some extra paper. Thought I'd grace these kids with my presence."

I swiped at my eyes and knew Lance didn't have several reams of neon-colored paper just laying around his house.

Kids began tugging on him, needing attention. I watched my childless big brother, amazed at how good he was with them. Patient. Spoke to them like peers. He was helpful, adjusting a fold here, giving a tip about flying there. He sat with the little ones on his lap at the table, their chubby fingers folding and pressing at his direction. The older ones received verbal help with their more complicated designs, along with joking, easy camaraderie.

One little girl, no more than four years old, twisted on his lap and looked into his face before asking, "Are you really a policeman?"

"I sure am."

She turned back to her paper airplane and asked, matter-of-factly, "Can you make the bad men stop shooting guns near my house? It scares me and my mom."

"I bet it does. I'll do my best."

She put her arms around his neck and hugged him.

Lance and I locked wide eyes. I placed one hand on my heart. Lance mouthed, "I know!"

I left them to their paper airplanes, so proud of my normally caustic big brother. I couldn't wait to tease him about his gooey marshmallow center.

I passed by a room where Leona was reading "Stuart Little" to a group of kids and three seniors. I climbed the stairs, realizing I could actually go home right now. Maybe even do a little writing.

I saw Barb heading into the Christmas store area and decided to spy on her to see if she was admiring anything in particular, like perhaps a jewelry holder or table-top candle sconce.

Peeking around the corner, I saw she was simply delivering a cup of coffee to Mrs Perez. Dang it. Maybe I should enlist Don to help me decide. I'd already wrapped up a gift for him, so I wouldn't be spoiling any surprise.

Mrs Perez walked away with Barb past the curtain separating the dining room from the store and I almost ducked out, but movement at the far side of the curtain caught my eye.

Nobody else was in the store so I watched Stephanie creep

around the tables, casting furtive glances the entire time. Her tall purple sheepskin boots brushed and tugged at the table-cloths with each step. I became nervous that she'd end up pulling them down completely. I saw her duck down a couple of times, and quickly move her hand above the merchandise.

Appalled she was stealing from a charitable organization set up to help her very own child, I hoped Bobby wouldn't learn of this. I watched until she ducked back behind the curtain. I sprinted after her just as Hazel came in the other way. I thought it was Hazel, anyway. She had styled her hair quite differently today.

"Oh, I wonder if you can help me?" she said, waving her cane at me. "Boyd hurt his back. Or at least he claims he did. Seems to happen a bunch when there's work to be done." She winked at me and adjusted today's wig.

I watched as the curtain quit moving, certain that Stephanie was long gone by now anyway.

Hazel needed help getting her donations out of her car, so I followed her to the parking lot. I carried in a big box for her and then handed her off to Mrs Perez who had returned to the store area.

I hurried off to find Barb or Don. I found them together, relaxing at one of the dining tables. "Did you guys see Stephanie run through here a little bit ago?"

"No, dear. Who's Stephanie?"

I pulled out a chair and sat next to Don. I leaned in close and spoke quietly. "She's Bobby's mom—Carlos' wife—and I think she's stealing from the store."

"Oh no, dear. That can't be." Barb shook her nest of blue-white curls.

"Why not?"

"Because this is a community fundraiser. A Christmas store. For children. Why would she do that?"

"Why indeed?" I mused.

"I'll keep my eyes open, but if you're asking me to call the police, I won't do that," Don said firmly.

"Why not?"

"Because I am not interested in getting anyone in trouble two weeks before Christmas. And I won't embarrass Carlos or Bobby like that." He peered over his glasses at me. "If it's even true."

I admitted it might not be true but I told them what I saw, and that it all looked very suspicious.

"Maybe she was buying something and wanted to keep it a surprise," Barb said.

"Maybe, but regardless, she didn't pay for it."

"Was Mrs Perez in there?" Don asked.

"No. I think she was in here."

"Well, that explains it. She'll probably pay Mrs Perez later." Don must have seen my skeptical look because he added, "It's possible."

"But not probable." I told them I wouldn't mention it to anyone, except Carlos.

"No, dear! Don't embarrass him."

"Barb, I promise I won't embarrass him." I knew full well this would embarrass him, but better to be a little embarrassed than to have your son find out his mother was a shoplifter. "I'll talk to him quietly about it. Nobody will hear, but he needs to know. For Bobby's sake."

During the entire conversation Don was fidgeting with a piece of paper. "What is that?" I asked.

He tried to wave me off, but I saw Barb's pinched mouth and Don's sad eyes. I grabbed the paper from him. As I read the words on the flyer, I began to breathe faster and felt my face get hot. "They're having a recall election for your board seat? Who did this?" Before he could answer, I remembered Bobby's and my search for the card players. "They think you had something to do with Ernesto's death?"

"It's terrible," Barb said softly.

Don simply nodded.

I tried to reign in my indignation because it would not help Don at this moment. I slid the flyer back to him. "Do you know who is behind this?" I asked again, quieter.

"No," Don said.

"Some coward, who should have come to Don directly if they had a problem with something."

Don covered Barb's hand with his. "Now, now. It'll be fine. You warned me about spouting off about wanting to be Santa, and you were right, as always. It's just politics, you'll see. Nobody thinks I really killed Ernesto. They just want to be on the executive board."

"Is there anything I can do?" I asked.

"Oh my goodness, no. You have enough on your plate."

"You'll tell me when you figure out who is behind this?" I asked.

His mouth crinkled into a smile. "Why? What will you do to them?"

"I'll make sure they get on Santa's Naughty List, for starters."

"Okay, you do that, and I'll handle the rest."

"You sure?"

"I'm sure. You focus on talking to Carlos—"

"Without embarrassing him," Barb added.

I left them with many more assurances I wouldn't embarrass anyone and went to find Carlos. He was helping Bobby and some of the older boys and girls attach the canvas to the two-by-fours for the scenery flats. I had to smile at their craftsmanship. Nails were bent and went every which way along the edge. The canvas was crooked; loose in some places, folded over in others. But the enthusiasm for their hammering and creating was contagious. Carlos explained some of what they'd been doing. The pride he had for these kids was obvious.

"Nice job, guys," I said. "Can I trust you not to nail each

other to the flats if I borrow Mr Morales here for a minute?" The kids giggled and doubled down on their efforts. "Can I talk to you?"

"Is something wrong? You know … with the scenery … or something?" Carlos looked worried.

"Why would anything be—no, it's completely unrelated." I walked over to a quiet area and explained what I saw with Stephanie.

Carlos looked at his work boots for a long time before he raised his head. The pride and swagger I saw when he talked about his crew was gone. "Stephanie has a drug problem."

"Does Bobby know?"

Carlos shrugged. "We've never told him, but he's a smart kid. He probably knows."

"So, do you think she might be stealing from the store?" I wondered how much money she could make from the donated trinkets on those tables. Although, there was that expensive looking necklace I saw earlier. I made a mental note to check to see if it was still there. But even so, would that be enough to score some drugs? I was woefully ignorant about the nitty-gritty of the drug trade.

Carlos shrugged again, but didn't say anything else.

It seemed I kept my promise to Barb. He didn't seem embarrassed, just very, very defeated.

I placed my hand on his forearm. "I'm not going to say anything more about this, Carlos. I just wanted you to be aware. I'd hate for Bobby to have seen what I saw."

He nodded and walked back to his crew. When he reached them he called out a cheery, "Way to go, kids! Nobody's shirt is nailed to the scenery!"

I returned to the store. Mrs Perez was just finishing displaying some pieces of intricate, probably handmade lace.

"That looks nice," I said. I quickly scanned the tables for the necklace. "Did you sell that pretty necklace with the fake pearls?"

Mrs Perez leaned in close. "Those aren't fake." She laughed at my wide eyes. "I know!" She walked over to where it was displayed. "I'm not advertising the fact it's real. Some mom or *abuela* is going to get a big surprise."

I wondered why nobody had bought it yet, but was more astonished that Stephanie hadn't swiped it. She obviously didn't know they were real pearls, but still, it was far and away the nicest thing in the room. If I was a drug addict looking to sell stolen goods to support my drug habit, I would have swiped this in a heartbeat.

Poor Bobby.

Poor Carlos.

Poor Stephanie.

ELEVEN

After a nice bit of time working on my manuscript Wednesday afternoon and evening, I was refreshed and excited to get back to rehearse the play today. Pulling open the door to the senior center, I wondered how many of my extras would remember their blocking and parts, now that it was Thursday.

I enthusiastically greeted everyone as I walked into the multi-purpose room, but the smile slid off my face when I saw Detective Ming standing with Leona. He wore his overcoat and black kidskin gloves. Neither of them looked pleased to see me, but believe me, the feeling was mutual.

Taking as long as humanly possible to remove my coat and scarf, I finally walked over to them.

"Hello, Detective Ming. Hi, Leona," I said, earning only a scowl from her in return. She stalked away from us. I watched her go and realized if she was a character in one of my books I'd have written, "She strode away with irritated, bristly deportment." But then I would have edited it to something less dramatic.

I took a breath and turned toward Detective Ming. "I'm

almost afraid to ask, but what brings you here?" I giggled nervously and really wished I hadn't.

"Actually, *you* do, Miss Russo."

"I do? I don't remember calling you." I pretended to laugh an airy little laugh at my own joke, but it turned into a coughing fit and I really wished I hadn't done that too.

Detective Ming stood there staring his inscrutable half-smile at me. After all this time I knew he did it to intimidate and make me nervous, but after all this time it still worked on me. *Cripes. Why was he here? Something about Ernesto?* I felt a trickle of sweat run down my back but knew it wasn't from the blast furnace in this place. He, of course, was cool as a sweet gherkin.

I jumped when a crash sounded from the stage area where Carlos and his crew worked.

I vowed to wait for Detective Ming to speak and was just about to tell him that when Leona returned carrying the Styrofoam star that had hit Ernesto.

She waggled it in Detective Ming's face. "I saw Charlee hide this murder weapon yesterday. That's why I called you."

"I didn't hide it! I found it!"

Leona scoffed. "Then why was it still in the basement, hidden behind a pile of puzzles and some trash?"

"That wasn't trash! Those were things I made for the Christmas store."

"Again, I'm wondering, if that's true, why was it all hidden in the basement?" She narrowed her eyes at me.

Detective Ming hadn't changed expression.

"Because I didn't know it was a murder weapon?"

"Aha! So you admit it's a murder weapon!" Leona jabbed one finger into the sky.

"I admit no such thing. I'm just making a leap of logic, since Detective Ming is here."

Leona jabbed her finger at me now. "Wait. Do you two know each other?"

The corners of Ming's mouth turned up the teensiest bit. "Our paths may have crossed once or twice." He gestured to Leona to place the star on a nearby chair. "Could you give us a minute, Ms McFalls?"

She turned on her heel and walked about eight feet away from us where she stood with her arms crossed.

From the stage Carlos yelled, "Watch out!" just before one of the flats fell over.

Detective Ming and I both started for the stage, but laughter and Carlos' wave stopped us. "Nothing to worry about! Just some wobbles." The crew righted the scenery and it fell over again, to much more laughter.

"What is going on up there?" Ming asked.

"Just our construction guy constructing," I said dismissively. I wanted to talk about the more immediate problem of Leona—and possibly Detective Ming—accusing me of … something.

"If he's in construction, why is everything so wobbly?"

I wasn't sure of that myself but said, "Because he wants to give kids autonomy so they can learn some skills and gain proficiency and self-esteem by doing this work themselves." But I didn't want to talk about Carlos. "Look, Detective, I was in the basement yesterday hiding these metal crafts I make. They're kind of cool and I—well never mind. Not germane to the story. But Leona must have seen me hiding my stuff in the same exact place where someone—not me—hid this star and she got the wrong idea. Jumped to the wrong conclusion."

"And what conclusion is that, Ms Russo?" He didn't say it like it was a question. He said it like he already knew the answer and was simply going through the motions of conversation.

"That this is a murder weapon and I had something to do with it. Or Ernesto. Or murder." Ming must delight in all the ways he flustered me. He probably kept a list. "And anyway, how can that be a murder weapon, anyway? It's just made of Styrofoam. The lightest, least dangerous thing on the planet."

Detective Ming stared at me. "It's not, you know."

"A murder weapon?"

"The lightest, least dangerous thing on the planet. What about a feather?"

"You could stab someone with the pokey end of a feather."

"A sheet of paper, then."

"You could roll it up and jab it at someone. Or give them ten thousand paper cuts."

Detective Ming thought for a moment. "A tissue."

"You could wad it up and stuff it down someone's throat and choke them to death."

"I often worry about you, Ms Russo." Detective Ming walked over to where the star balanced on the folding chair and picked it up. Now his expression did change. There was a flash of something, maybe worry, that passed quickly. He hefted the star, like he was weighing it. "I thought you said this was just Styrofoam."

"It is." I waved my hand vaguely above our heads. "All these are."

Ming turned the star this way and that, inspecting it. Squinting, he chipped away part of it with his fingernail and pulled out a piece of sheet metal.

Exactly like the ones I use in my crafts. A sudden chill ran through my body.

Bobby said, "Hey! That's the stuff you use, Charlee!"

I glanced toward him, barely registering his words. A small crowd had gathered near Leona. Along with Bobby, who was still pointing, there also Doug, Daisy, and Thelma.

I grabbed the star from Detective Ming. There was a deep slit where the piece of sheet metal slid right in. It was completely invisible in there. I carefully returned the star to the chair and backed slowly away from it. "I don't know anything about this. There's got to be some logical explanation." I couldn't guarantee those were the actual words that came out of my mouth, but it was what I wanted to say.

I stared at the sheet metal while Detective Ming stared at me. When I looked up I said, "It's been sabotaged." I wanted him to laugh and tell me how ridiculous that sounded.

He didn't. Instead, he just carried the star and the sheet metal out of the multi-purpose room, calling over his shoulder, "I'll be in touch."

Doug said, "Well, it was pretty clear Charlee had it in for Ernesto from the start."

Daisy said, "I'll be darned. My money was on Carlos."

TWELVE

The rest of Thursday went downhill from there. How that was possible, only the wisest sage might know.

In addition to having Stephanie stealing from the Christmas store, Don getting his senior center board seat taken away from him, and everyone thinking I'd sabotaged the star that hit Ernesto, rehearsal was terrible. Doug and Daisy hadn't even tried to learn their lines yet. The kids treated the stage like their playground. The seniors acting as their buddies couldn't figure out how to—or just didn't care to—wrangle them. And Peter O'Drool was living his best life, which just happened to always be under my feet and within tripping distance.

But the part that made my head really throb was that every single kid decided they wanted to change parts. Some more than once. Dogs wanted to be cats. Elves wanted to be dogs. Townspeople wanted to be elves. And one little boy wanted to be a tree and proudly showed me how he could hold his arms out like branches. I told him we had no parts for trees and he burst into tears, wailing until I hollered to Thelma, "Can you make a tree costume?" When she said yes, three more kids wanted to be trees, and one girl demanded to be snow.

"You'll get walked on," I reasoned with her.

"Then I'll melt."

"Then people will slip on you."

"Then I'll be a mop."

I lost the stare-down. I walked over to Thelma and whispered, "Can you make a mop costume?"

I lost that stare-down too.

Clomping back on stage I passed Doug and Daisy who I knew for a fact were gossiping about me. Maybe not a *fact* fact, but a pretty strong hypothesis.

I stopped everyone the only way I knew how—with two claps. Silence, blessed silence on the stage. I reveled in it as long as I thought I could get away with it. "Kids, here's the deal. We only have nine days—that's basically just one week—to get this play ready to show your parents and all the people who will come to watch. And what if the real Santa comes and wants to watch the play about him and his elves?" I didn't want to play the Santa card, but it had the effect I wanted. Big eyes, nervous faces. "We need to be ready just in case. And that means whatever part you had yesterday is the part you will have forever."

There was disappointed murmuring and shuffling of feet until Bobby said, "We don't want to disappoint Santa, do we?"

Bobby was a true leader and these kids clearly looked up to him, beginning to smile and nod their heads.

"I wanted to be a dog all along," said the ex-tree, dropping his branches to all fours.

"You can be *my* dog!" A girl in a long townsperson dress walked over and thumped him on his side.

Crisis averted. I considered buying Bobby a car.

We only made it a few pages through the play before I yelled, "Cut!" and then removed the bells from all the elves' ankles. I dropped them on Thelma's sewing table. "No. More. Bells."

After downing some ibuprofen for my pounding head, I made it through to the final curtain, at which time I clapped my hands twice and said, "Adults … please memorize your lines." I stretched the *please* from here to the North Pole, making all the kids laugh. I dismissed them just in time for lunch.

My head still hurt and I was starving. Maybe I'd be lucky and ibuprofen casserole would be on the menu.

Doug walked up to me while I was gathering up my papers. "Hey, Charlee, I'm sorry I haven't locked down my lines yet, but things have been a bit … crazy. In addition to my new job, I volunteered to organize the memorial for Ernesto at work."

My throat felt thick with guilt for forgetting that Ernesto was an esteemed colleague over at the hack factory. Ozzi had been moping around, but Doug was really in the thick of it.

I had to swallow twice before I could speak. "Are you sure you still want to do this silly play? I'm sure I could get one of the seniors to play Figgy instead of you." I had absolutely no confidence I could do that, but I was sympathetic to Doug's plight.

"Oh my gosh, no! I want to do it." He quirked his eyebrows and grabbed my forearm, just as quickly releasing it. "I'm sorry. It's just that I like being here with the kids and involved like this. It makes the other stuff easier to bear. And the memorial won't be until January."

"Are you sure?"

"Absolutely."

"Then I'm very much relieved because I can't quite picture getting anyone else up to speed in a week." I looked him in the eye. "I really appreciate everything, Doug. I know this has been a tough time for you. And Daisy." I glanced her way.

"Although I suspect she didn't know Ernesto nearly as long as you and Ozzi did."

"I guess technically Daisy has known Ernesto her whole life. He was her uncle." Doug made a noise then ran a jerky hand through his hair. He leaned close to me. "I shouldn't have told you that. It was in his personnel file. Confidential information. Forget I said anything. I'm not used to my new job yet." He glanced so furtively in Daisy's direction that I began to feel his distress in the pit of my own stomach.

I tried to remember that first day when everyone was being introduced. "They didn't act like they were related, but your secret is safe with me," I assured him.

Daisy walked over zipping up her coat. "I heard my name," she said scowling.

"That's because we were talking about you," Doug said with a nervous laugh.

"What about?" Her eyebrows knit together with suspicion.

Doug froze, unable to answer her.

"That you make a great elf," I said.

"Oh, that." She pulled a pair of gloves from her coat pocket. "You want to stop for lunch before we head back to the office?" she asked Doug.

"Sure." Doug put on his coat. "I promise we'll both get our lines memorized," he said to me then elbowed Daisy. "Right?"

"Whatever. Ho, ho, ho."

THIRTEEN

Ozzi had been busy with a project and we'd barely seen each other, but he called me late Thursday night and said he'd take the whole day off work Friday and come with me to the senior center. While we sipped coffee on the commute, quietly waking up, I was happy to spend some time with him even though he suggested that if he wasn't needed at the senior center, he might just sneak in the last of his Christmas shopping. I took the opportunity to remind him that if he drove my new Maserati into my parking space at the apartments, I'd politely turn my head so as not to ruin the surprise.

"That's very polite indeed." Ozzi removed his coat and it dropped to the floor. He stooped to retrieve it.

"You seem surprised. I can be polite when I set my mind —" Stephanie caught my eye because she tiptoed out of the Christmas store, looking every bit like a cartoon supervillain. She saw me staring and gave me a hard stare in return before fleeing in the opposite direction and down the stairs.

I elbowed Ozzi. "She's stealing from the store."

"Who?"

"Stephanie, Bobby's mom. Didn't you see her? She was right there."

"Sorry, babe. Didn't see a thing." He hung his coat on a hanger and helped me off with mine. A rolling coat rack had appeared in the last couple of days, a welcome addition to the lobby. "But are you sure? Don't go accusing anybody of anything until you're sure." He saw the look on my face. "Who'd you tell?"

"Just Don and Barb." At the look on *his* face I added, "They deserve to know if someone is stealing from them, Oz!"

"*If* being the operative word. Are you sure?"

I took my time hanging my coat on the coat rack. "Definitely. I saw her with my own two eyes."

"Do you want me to do anything?"

"No," I said glumly. "Don and Barb don't want to do anything because they don't want to upset Bobby or Carlos. They don't want me to say anything to anyone but Carlos."

"Then….?"

"Then that's what I'll do. Even though she's totally stealing from the store."

Ozzi pulled me in for a kiss. "You are a paragon of virtue."

"Oh, and speaking of Don, someone around here is ginning up enthusiasm for a recall election to remove him from his board seat."

"Why?"

"Because they think he had something to do with Ernesto's death. At least the ones who don't think I had something to do with Ernesto's death."

He raised his eyebrows so I told him the whole story about Detective Ming finding the same metal I use for my crafts inside the star that hit Ernesto. Then I launched into more details about Don, ending with how Barb had warned him about being too happy about getting Ernesto's Santa job.

When I finished, Ozzi said, "Barb was right, of course, but

it's a false equivalence to think the happiness of getting to play Santa outweighs the seriousness of Ernesto's death. It's just human nature. Like at work, Doug has stepped right into his new job with enthusiasm, but it doesn't diminish the fact he's also stepped into the job of planning Ernesto's memorial service. Just like Don stepped into those Santa boots."

"I have to figure out how to help Don keep his seat. You and I both know he didn't have anything to do with anything," I said.

"Is Ming serious about thinking you were involved? How'd that metal get in there?"

"I don't know, and I don't know. But I guess I have to figure that out too, along with what really happened to Ernesto," I said glumly. "This is not shaping up to be the holly jolliest of holidays. Where are my lords a-leaping or my dancing nutcrackers?"

Ozzi pointed toward the multi-purpose room. "I bet they're waiting inside with the maids a-milking." He took my hand. "You ready to go in?"

"As ready as I'll ever be."

We walked into the multi-purpose room holding hands and I immediately forgot all about Stephanie and her pilfering.

We greeted Barb and Thelma working furiously on dog costumes. Three kids in various states of dog-ness modeled for us. A boy wearing a headband adorned with brown droopy ears held up his paws when we neared. I gave him a pat on the head and lobbed a "Who's a good boy" in his direction. He barked in response, causing the Dalmatian and a pointy-eared mutt to join in.

I squeezed Ozzi's hand, happy they were having so much fun with this event, despite all the adult drama swirling around.

We passed Winston in his wheelchair talking to his buddy Javier. Again, they pored over the weather section of the newspaper while Winston explained barometric pressure to him.

Near the stage Doug, Daisy, Bobby, Carlos, and Don sat in folding chairs. All wore serious looks on their faces. I wondered how long they'd been in conversation. We stood near them, listening to Carlos.

"—third generation. My grandparents came from Guatemala. My parents were born and raised here, I was born and raised here. But last summer, Bobby, Stephanie, and I were at a street fair in Denver when a bunch of teenage thugs started following us and shouting, 'Go back where you came from.'"

Bobby interrupted Carlos, pride in his father evident. "He said, go back where? To Aurora? We plan to, just as soon as we have ice cream."

"I'm not gonna lie, I was scared," Carlos said, "but I couldn't bear to let Bobby see the bullies win." He shook his head. "I don't want the world to be color blind. I mean, it's obvious we're all different colors, even in my own house. I'm dark, Stephanie is so white she doesn't even tan, and Bobby here is a mix of us both. I just want it not to matter."

"But it does matter." Daisy puckered her forehead. "Santa is white."

Ohferpetesake. This again?

"Santa is whoever you want him to be," Bobby said patiently, like he's dealt with issues like this a hundred times in his twelve years. He nodded to a couple of younger kids who had wandered over. "Some kids even think Santa is their parents, which is cool."

"The fallacy of a white Santa has been debunked over and over again," Don said, a bit less patiently.

I wondered how long Doug and Daisy had been peddling their racism again. At least they were getting some push-back.

Don continued. "The idea of Santa has been traced back to Saint Nicholas, who was born in the third century in modern-day Turkey. He secretly delivered gold to a poor dad who needed a dowry for his daughters. The dad found out Nicholas was his benefactor, and word got around. After Nick's death, he was made a Catholic saint. Then in the twelfth century, inspired by Saint Nick, a group of French nuns secretly left fruit and nuts on the doorsteps of poor people's homes at night. A bunch of people got on that bandwagon and it spread across Europe, beginning the secret gift-giving we do today."

"What does that have to do with—" Daisy interrupted Don but he just kept talking.

"Forensic study of Saint Nick's bones determined he was a man of color, looking more Middle Eastern than our rosy-cheeked Santa."

"Then how did the rosy cheek guy get started?" Daisy asked irritably. "He had to come from somewhere."

"Advertising campaign," Don said. "No lie."

Javier pushed Winston in his wheelchair closer to see what was going on. The three costumed dogs scrambled over on all fours and sat up, panting.

"But who cares what Santa looks like?" Bobby said. "He's a symbol of joy and generosity. My teacher says humanity comes in all colors." He looked earnestly at Daisy and sounded much older than twelve. "So, when you guys say bad things about 'Mexican Santa' in front of little kids, well, you could ruin Christmas for them."

Daisy laughed. "You make me and Doug sound like racists. All I was saying is that kids could get confused if they didn't see a white Santa, like Don here."

"And that's exactly what makes you sound like a racist," I said. Ozzi squeezed my hand and I knew it was a warning to tread carefully and choose my words. I squeezed back acknowledgment that I had myself under control.

"White people can be discriminated against too, you know. I take it you've never heard of reverse racism?" Daisy's voice took on an edge I hadn't heard before. "I get profiled because I choose to express myself with tattoos." She pushed up both sleeves of her sweater to show them a butterfly on the inside of one forearm and a flower on the other. I was surprised to see it was a tulip instead of the obvious daisy. "And I didn't get one scholarship—not one—when I went to college because I'm white. Everybody knows that was why."

I started to speak but Bobby beat me to it. "But you can just wear a long-sleeved shirt and cover them up if you have to. I didn't even know you had tattoos until just now. But my dad can't change his clothes to make people not be racist at him. He's always had trouble getting a permanent job because of the way he looks."

"Maybe your dad has trouble because he's a crappy employee," she said with a shrug.

"And maybe you didn't get any scholarships because you had crappy grades," Don snapped.

Doug began to look uncomfortable with the conversation. He wasn't the only one. Ozzi and I held hands like a human vice grip.

But Bobby remained calm. "My dad isn't a crappy employee. He does anything anybody asks him to. My school needed somebody for this play and he volunteered."

Carlos reddened and he looked down at his boots.

"Same reason my mom is putting up flyers about the play all over town before she goes to work," said the Dalmatian.

"And why my *abuela* got everyone to make tamales to sell the night of the play." The floppy-eared dog stood and took off his headband. "People make fun because she doesn't speak English very good. That's all they see. They never see how hard she works or how she gives me everything I need."

"Some people have everything and still want more." The Dalmatian stood too. "But other people just want to have enough."

For once I was glad I kept my mouth shut. Everyone else

said everything so much more eloquently and with more agency than I ever could.

The crowd broke up, everyone going about their business.

I dragged Ozzi to a quiet corner. "I cannot believe how racist those two are!"

"Daisy and Doug?"

I gaped at him.

"Honestly, I've never heard either of them say anything like that before," he said. "Or what you told me about the read-through the other day. It doesn't make sense to me. Like they're two different people."

"They are two different people."

"You know what I mean. Like they both have alter egos, Jekylls and Hydes."

"You've never seen anything like that at work?" I knew he wouldn't lie to me, but it still made no sense.

"Never." He thought for a minute. "We don't really work together, though. I just see them at lunch sometimes. We're friendly, but we have different friends."

"I thought you said Doug was broken up about Ernesto's death."

"He was. We all are. I know you didn't really get to see the real Ernesto, but everyone at work really liked him."

I wondered if someone could still be a raging racist even if they technically liked the one Mexican man they worked for. I said out loud what I'd been thinking since Detective Ming's visit. "Do you think Doug or Daisy killed Ernesto in some racial incident?"

"What? How would they even do that?" Ozzi pressed both palms against his temples for a bit while he processed the idea. He looked like he was afraid his head might explode. "We were all standing right there. That's crazy talk, Charlee."

"I don't think it's crazy, Ozzi. I found out that Ernesto was Daisy's uncle, but she's never mentioned it. Did you know?"

Ozzi shook his head. "That's wild."

"I'm wondering if there's some long-lost rich uncle's will floating around that she wanted to get her hands on."

"Wow. Really? That's ... wild," he repeated, clearly at a loss for words.

We remained quiet, lost in our thoughts.

Suddenly, Ozzi's face softened and went a bit slack. "Uh oh. I just remembered something."

"About Daisy?" I asked hopefully.

"No, about Doug. There was this incident at work between him and a female programmer who subsequently quit."

"Harassment?"

Ozzi nodded. "She was Latina."

"Can you get her information? I'd like to talk to her about it."

"I'll try." He stepped away to make some calls.

I shook my head. I've never understood why people's skin colored mattered. But I had the privilege of only dealing with it on an academic level; it never touched me directly. I saw how some people changed their orders to to-go coffees at Lavar and Tuttle's Espresso Yourself. Was it because they were Black or gay or both? Or did those customers suddenly remember they had an appointment? I'd never know, but it never seemed to bother Lavar and Tuttle. I've seen them try to educate people, change hearts and minds, which they did on many occasions. Just like Bobby today. "Life's too short," Lavar would say. They had to live with discrimination and people telling them they're too sensitive every single day. I was exhausted from my few brushes with Doug and Daisy.

And I had the luxury of concentrating on this Christmas play, instead of the injustices of the world.

Lucky for me, the rehearsal went well. The scenery flats moved around the stage much easier. I mentioned it to Carlos and he beamed when he told me he replaced the casters to multi-directional ones.

Everyone had memorized most of their lines, or could at least offer quality ad-libs that were logical enough to keep us on track. The Buddy System worked great to keep everyone focused, and the idea to only have the extras in one scene was positively genius, if I did say so myself. And there were only two scenery mishaps.

When we broke for lunch, I congratulated everyone on a terrific run-through. The dogs barked at me and the cats tried weaving themselves through my legs. I had to hold on to Santa's throne to keep from getting knocked on my keister. Eventually they got hungry and dropped their costumes into Thelma's outstretched arms.

Ozzi had left long ago, and I wondered if he was going to be able to get me that Maserati on such short notice. I was giggling as I picked up a ham-and-cheese sandwich and a bag of chips from the buffet table at the front of the dining room and plopped myself down next to Barb and Don.

"You're sure in a good mood," Barb said.

"Because all her actors—present company excluded—have learned their lines," Don said.

"Aw, you're doing fine." I waved away his comment. "I'm starving, though." My sandwich was piled high with the lettuce, onions, and tomatoes I had embellished it with, and drooled the teensiest bit. Chef Joe was learning important lessons about children's palates. The basic sandwiches were, well, basic. Just the way kids liked them. I unfolded a paper napkin and draped it across my lap, leaving a second one nearby for inevitable splotches of mustard and mayo on my face.

I tore open my bag of chips and was ready to dig in when Detective Ming appeared next to me.

"Is there somewhere we can talk privately, Ms Russo?"

I looked forlornly at my sandwich and chips.

"It won't take long."

"Sure. The multi-purpose room is probably empty." I pointed at Don. "Do not eat my lunch. I'll be right back."

Don pretended to grab it, but I narrowed my eyes and he backed off, surrendering.

Barb said, "I'll keep an eye on him."

Detective Ming and I walked across the hall and found two seats on the far side of the multi-purpose room.

Before he could speak, I said, "I swear I didn't mess with that star."

"Were you in Ernesto Santiago's house last Saturday night?"

"No."

He scrutinized me with his inscrutable face. "Then why was there a bottle of ibuprofen on his kitchen table with only your fingerprints on it?"

"How do you know they're my fingerprints?"

He raised one eyebrow and I remembered my fingerprints were on file because of my agent's murder, the first time I met him.

"I had them at rehearsal that day. Ernesto must have taken them with him."

He flipped back through his notes. "You all said you told him not to take ibuprofen since he was on blood thinners for his atrial fibrillation."

"Maybe he wasn't really on blood thinners and didn't remember until he got home?"

"Then why would he have taken your bottle with him?"

I rubbed my temples. "I don't know, but I'd kill to have some ibuprofen right now." I wanted to claw the words back into my mouth.

Using both hands, Detective Ming smoothed his slicked-back hair but didn't take his eyes off me. "Why are you lying about being in Mr Santiago's house? I have a witness who saw—" He flipped some pages in his notebook again. "A hideous green car parked in front of his house." He turned the notebook so I could see how he'd underlined the word *hideous*.

"I'm not lying!"

Detective Ming checked his notes. "I asked if you were in Mr Santiago's house—"

"I wasn't IN his house! I was AT his house. I never crossed the threshold." I realized I was shouting at a police detective and notched my voice down a tad. "Words matter, Detective Ming. Words matter."

He regarded me with what seemed like amusement. At least as much as he was capable of. "Why were you *at* his house, then?"

"I found a wallet and looked inside to find a fifty-dollar bill and his ID. I figured he'd need it to drive the next day, so I took it over. I knew he had a headache so if his lights were on, I was going to return it to him. If his lights were off, I was going to give it to him when I saw him the next day at his costume fitting, or give it to Ozzi to give to him at work."

"Since words matter, Ms Russo, which of Mr Santiago's lights were on?"

Flustered, I waved my hands around. "I don't know! Living room lights. Kitchen lights."

"I thought you were never inside."

"But I know how houses work!"

Detective Ming stared at me through one squinted eye long enough that I had to look away. As he turned to leave, he added, Columbo-style, "Oh, by the way … we never found a wallet."

It was very clear to me he didn't believe anything I said. When he was out of sight, I moped back toward my sandwich, although I didn't think I could swallow even one bite.

Doug had joined Barb and Don who were now enjoying steaming mugs of coffee.

Don pushed my sandwich toward me. "Only had some nibbles."

"Actually, I lost my appetite. Detective Ming thinks I'm lying to him about Ernesto."

"Lying about what?" Doug took a bite of his sandwich.

I was suddenly very weary and didn't want to talk about it. "It's a long story. Just something about whatever Ming's case is." *I should have asked him to clarify if this was now a murder investigation. But of course it is. Why else would he be involved?* I couldn't help but wonder if Detective Ming would be involved in this if Leona hadn't called to accuse me.

"Ah, don't worry, Charlee." Barb patted my hand. "You'll crack this case just like all the others. Your agent's murder. Your friend's missing daughter. That terrible business with Lapaglia." She searched the room nervously for Peter O'Drool, still twitchy when she thought about it.

"Yeah, you're a pretty famous author. I've been reading the social media stuff about you," Doug said. "Too bad there's not as much written about your books."

"Well, I've gotta agree with you there." I pressed my index finger into the potato chips on my plate, one by one, metaphorically and melodramatically crushing them the same way my soul had been crushed. "I'll see you guys later."

Barb reached for my sandwich. "I'll get this wrapped up for you, dear. And I'll find you a couple of those chocolate chip cookies you like. You'll be hungry later."

I doubt it. "Thanks, Barb." I didn't really have any place to be, so I wandered through the curtain divider into the Christmas store. I shuffled past the merchandise, not seeing any of it.

I stepped on something which turned out to be Bobby's foot. "Oh. Sorry. You okay?"

He nodded. "What's the matter?"

"Detective Ming thinks I'm telling fibs."

"You'd fib to a cop?"

"No, of course not! But something disappeared—" Two things actually, if you counted the wallet and the star that Leona gleefully produced and said I'd hidden. "And he thinks maybe I had something to do with it."

"He said that?"

"No. But I'm sure that's how it looks." I sighed and ran my palm across a leather tooled purse.

Bobby sighed with me. "Something like that is happening to me too." He looked up. "All the stuff I've bought for my mom has been disappearing from my room." He leaned in and whispered. "I think she's selling them to buy drugs again."

Carlos was right when he told me Bobby was a smart kid and even though they didn't tell him about Stephanie, he did, in fact, know. You can't fool kids. *But geez, that Stephanie is a piece of work. Not only stealing from the charity, but stealing from her own son? That is low.*

"I'm sure that can't be true, Bobby. She's your mom, she'd never do that." He and I both knew that she absolutely could do that. "Maybe you just misplaced them. Or maybe your dad moved them. Did you put them in a hiding place?"

He nodded. "Lots of them. And I really don't even remember what all I've bought exactly. Maybe it's my imagination."

"That's probably it then. You've just forgotten where you hid them." I walked over to the ear cuffs I made. "Here. Pick out one of these. On me."

He studied each of them and we debated the merits of the unique designs on each. He asked how I had made them, and I told him a bit about the process—cutting the metal, using tiny tools to hammer in designs, bending them into shape. After a few minutes of careful deliberation, he chose one.

"That's pretty. I'm sure she'll love it." I spied a pretty emerald green lacquered box and dropped the ear cuff inside. I showed the box to Mrs Perez. "This is for Bobby's mom."

"Ooh, that's nice. You're going to spoil her!" She smiled and set aside her paperback to peek inside. "Your mom is going to have a lot of gifts to open on Christmas morning."

I opened my wallet and folded a ten-dollar bill so Bobby would think it was a single. "When you get home, you put that somewhere safe. And remember where you hid it!" I handed Mrs Perez the folded bill over the top of Bobby's head, then gave him a little shove to get him moving out of the store.

Mrs Perez winked at me and didn't unfold the money until Bobby was on his way.

I still felt uneasy about Detective Ming's visit, but it gave me warm fuzzies to do something nice for Bobby.

Now, if only Stephanie would get her act together.

FOURTEEN

I stumbled into the kitchen the next morning with only one thing on my mind. But there was no coffee in my apartment. Not even the emergency stash in the freezer.

Shaking Ozzi's shoulder to no avail, I leaned in right next to his ear. "Did you use the emergency coffee?"

He jolted awake. "Emergency? What's wrong?"

"It's bad. Real bad."

He saw my face and the realization dawned over him, despite the uncivilized awakening. "Ohmygawd. There's no coffee?"

"Not a single bean. What about at your apartment?"

He pulled a pillow over his head and began some fake sobbing.

I looked longingly out my window toward Espresso Yourself then gathered myself together. No time to stop over there. I had to redo the blocking for one of the scenes to keep everyone from crashing into each other all over the stage. The senior center would have the urn going by the time I got there.

I patted Ozzi on the pillow. "You're on your own, comrade."

I got to the senior center before anyone made the coffee and immediately threw myself into the task before I even removed my coat. I measured out the coffee and water, waiting impatiently for it to finish brewing. Finally able to pour myself a healthy dose, I carried it through the multi-purpose room and sat in Santa's throne to savor it. Today the throne was parked way offstage, in my favorite dark corner. I'd come to enjoy this small respite, curled up in a fantasy, before the clamor of rambunctious children and vigorous seniors invaded my peace. Not until my cup was empty did I get around to removing my coat.

A refill and a longer self-imposed time-out wouldn't be decadent, I convinced myself. As I untangled myself from Santa's throne, the curtain next to me swayed slowly in graceful waves, as if someone—or something—was walking on the other side. The lights weren't on back here yet, so everything was dim, shadowy. The rustling curtain caused a bit of concern. If the senior center had rats, I wasn't sure I could ever set foot in here again, Christmas pageant or not. I leaned to see around the scenery, able to discern Don's wispy gray hair bobbing toward me. He hurried past me with a grunt of greeting and a non-committal wave of his hand.

I didn't think Don was typically a grumpy morning person, but I allowed for the possibility today. It was just as well because I wanted a longer respite anyway. At least he'd be happy that I already made the coffee.

As I was heading back to my throne with my refill, movement near the bottom of the curtain caught my eye. If Don was here, Peter O'Drool was probably wandering around too. I knew how seriously Peter took his responsibility of patrolling the senior center. Mostly for wayward crumbs, but still, a patrol was a patrol.

The back door leading to the dumpster clanged in the distance.

I walked toward the curtain where it had rustled. I

dropped to one knee, lifted it from the bottom, and peered underneath. No wheezy little pug. Instead, ten feet away, Stephanie's unmistakable purple sheepskin boots.

I set my cup on the floor as I dropped to my belly to see what she was doing. More theft? There were no two ways about it—this woman was skulking. If you were to look up the word in the dictionary, you would see an illustration of Stephanie at this very moment. She was ducking behind scenery, hiding around corners, peering out with shifty, overly-eye-shadowed eyes.

Quietly angry voices. Arguing. Who was she talking to? Don? Some partner in crime? Her fence for stolen amateur scenery and used paintbrushes?

I belly-crawled under the curtain like I was in Marine Corps boot camp, mud and barbed wire notwithstanding. I slithered through the crowded scenery flats toward where she stood at the end of the curtain, trying to listen to her whispered conversation.

Suddenly Carlos loomed out of the area behind the rear curtain and grabbed her arm.

It startled me and I kicked one of the flats.

"What's that?" Carlos asked.

I heard footsteps coming near me, their argument paused. The only thing between us were two standing scenery flats, rolled haphazardly perpendicular to each other. They'd have to come around both of them to see me, which wasn't out of the realm of possibility. I didn't know how I'd explain crawling on my belly backstage, eavesdropping on their hissing argument. I wouldn't mind Don interrupting them, even if he was grumpy.

The flat nearest to them rolled about six inches.

"I don't see anything," Carlos said.

I wriggled backward but I soon heard their voices almost directly next to me on the other side of the rear curtain. If they were on the move, it wouldn't take much for them to clear the curtain and advance a few steps on to the stage. If they glanced my way, they'd see me.

If I could just get behind that scenery flat, I could stand and saunter out, pretending I'd just arrived. "Oh, hi, you two. Fancy meeting you here," I could casually say. "Just getting myself some coffee, not eavesdropping on your quarrel, lah di dah, lah di dah."

I heard more footsteps. They sounded in front of me, but I thought I heard them whispering behind me. Probably just a backstage trick. Sound travels funny up here, I'd found. I belly-crawled forward until I was between the two scenery flats. I was just beginning to gather my legs under me when one of the scenery flats crashed down on me.

My first insane thought was how fortunate it was that I broke its fall with my body since we didn't have much time for repairs before the performance.

My second insane thought was that if my stupid body damaged it, I hoped it wasn't the intricately painted town scene because that was a genuine work of folk art.

My third thought was less insane. *Breathe, Charlee!*

"Oof." The air exploded from my lungs and I gasped, but couldn't draw breath. I tried to slide out from under it, but the frame had pinned me all along my right side. I knew these flats were made from lightweight canvas stretched over two-by-fours, or was it one-by-threes? Didn't really matter since right now it felt like steel girders. But even though I probably wasn't in danger of being crushed, why couldn't I slide out from under it? I twisted and turned but that only seemed to make things worse. Tiny bits of gravel and debris from the unswept floor scratched my nose. When I panicked and tried to shake my head to clear it away, I inadvertently inhaled some.

I tried to call for help, but still couldn't gather enough lung capacity. I quit struggling and focused on breathing, not an easy task when you're flat on your belly. I panted until I could fill my chest with air, then let it out in a whoosh along with a yelp. I tried again and conjured a loud yell, despite the fact my face was smooshed into the filthy floor.

Carlos and Stephanie had just been there, why weren't they running toward the crash or my shouting? Where was Don? *Ugh. His broken hearing aid. He's not going to hear a thing.*

I continued to yell, but I stopped squirming as I assessed this contraption on top of me. I raised my head enough so I could rest my chin on the floor. The frame seemed to be on my head and down my entire right side. Because I'd been belly-crawling, my hands were both up by my shoulders. I tried raising my right palm to gently push on the canvas, but lost my nerve, worried I'd tear the canvas they'd worked on so diligently. I found a bit of purchase on the wooden frame itself and gave it a shove. It yanked my hair, which hurt, and pulled my face off the floor before dropping it back down. Which also hurt.

I stopped struggling and stopped yelling. Something was stuck in my hair. I maneuvered my hand along the side of my head, following the curve of my temple, over my ear, and to the back of my ponytail. My fingers found at least two nails protruding from the frame. My long hair was hopelessly wrapped around them both.

I started yelling again.

My fingers scrabbled against the hair twisted around the topmost nail. It seemed impossible. Like a knot in the waistband of your sweatpants when you've had too much coffee.

"Where is everyone?" I shouted.

This would never have happened if only I'd gone shopping for coffee. When we were growing up, my mom had an "open one, buy one" policy that I wish I had woven into the tapestry of my life. That way, I'd never run out of anything again. I could have enjoyed coffee at home with Ozzi, and never been distracted by that waving curtain or Carlos and Stephanie's argument. I could catastrophize with the best of them, but this precise scenario would not have made it to the top of my list of What Might Happen If I Didn't Buy Coffee.

I decided to save my energy and quit yelling, since it seemed to be wasted effort. Instead, I methodically tried to unwrap my hair from the nail heads. Unfortunately, because I was doing it without looking, I had no idea whether I was making it better or worse.

After concentrated effort, I succeeded in freeing my hair from the nails binding me to the scenery flat. Cautiously I reached toward the top of my head and grabbed the edge of the wooden frame. I lifted it an inch, two inches. No hair was being tugged. Four inches, six inches. I slithered out from under it, earning another mouthful of floor filth. I raised to hands and knees, spitting and blinking.

When I was able to stand, I assessed the damage. First to the flat, thankfully none that I could see. Second, to me. I ran my hands over my head. It throbbed and when I pulled my hands away, I saw a faint smear of blood on my palm. I rubbed my palm on my jeans, then felt my head again. Barely any this time. I poked and prodded with my index finger until I was satisfied my brains wouldn't leak out. But by then my back had tightened and was getting achy. I placed both hands on my low back and ran them down over my butt. Left side, no problem. Right side, ow.

Nothing seemed permanently damaged. Except my dignity.

I reached for the scenery flat to stand it upright again. It was embarrassingly easy to lift. If it hadn't attacked and pinned me with those nails, I probably could have lifted it right off. Maybe it was a good thing—at least for my pride—that nobody came to my rescue.

Turning it this way and that, I studied the flat more methodically and was relieved to confirm it hadn't been damaged. I pushed my finger on those two nails. What if it had fallen on a kid, or one of the seniors? Why did it fall, anyway? Carlos told me he had the sets figured out. I walked all the way around it, comparing it to the other flats.

The other flats all had sandbags on the frame to keep them from tipping. I searched the area. Where were the sandbags for this one? I spied a pile of townspeople costumes—long, heavy skirts and jackets—and heaped them on the frame to act as sandbags. As I was dropping them in place, my breath caught and a sour taste filled my mouth. Was this flat sabotaged the same way Ernesto's star had been? Was I the target … or was Don? I was virtually hidden, coiled on the throne in the dim light, but Don had been marching around all over backstage. Did someone have a thing against Santa Claus? Did it have anything to do with the nasty recall election against him?

I flipped on lights and performed a quick search backstage for Don, calling his name, but couldn't find him. I thought about hearing the back door clang earlier. I hadn't heard it clang again, leading me to believe he hadn't just emptied the trash. Where was he?

I raced through the senior center, but it appeared I was alone. No Don, no Barb, no Peter O'Drool. Not even Carlos or Stephanie seemed to be here.

A deep breath calmed me enough to wonder if my imagination was running away with me again. With senses still on alert, I found a hammer backstage to knock the nails in the rest of the way, then rolled the flat to the furthest wall, out of harm's way. As I was replacing the hammer, Carlos walked in the back door.

"Good morning, Charlee."

I leaped backward and let out a sharp scream. After I sufficiently recovered my wits, I said harshly, "Why didn't you come when I was yelling?"

"What?"

I pointed. "That flat that you and Stephanie were skulking behind just fell on me."

"Me … Stephanie … skulking?" Carlos glanced blankly in the direction I pointed.

"Yes!" He was proving himself a terrific actor.

"I was at the hardware store." Carlos raised a bag with a logo of a stylized hammer printed on it.

"You said you fixed the flats but that one didn't have any sandbags."

"I did fix them. They all had sandbags. I swear it!"

All the thoughts I'd had exploded. "Stephanie must have taken them. Why would she do that? What does she have against Don? Why would she want to hurt him?"

Carlos gawped at me, shaking his head. He must have stopped listening after my first question because all he said was, "She wouldn't have taken the sandbags off." He started looking around the area.

"Don't bother. They aren't here. She must have taken them with her after she shoved it over. Why else would it have toppled at the very moment I was behind them?"

"I don't know. I don't understand any of this."

Carlos seemed genuinely baffled to me, unless he was hiding his acting chops under a bushel.

I asked again, calmer this time. "What does Stephanie have against Don? Why would she try to hurt him?"

"She wouldn't!" Carlos lowered his voice, enunciating every word. "She would never hurt Don."

"Then what does she have against me? I heard her say something the other day about me not being Bobby's mother. Why would she say that?" Maybe they did know I was there earlier.

Carlos spoke even quieter and more distinctly. "She would never hurt you either. She wouldn't hurt anyone." He paused and looked into the distance. "Not on purpose anyway." He spoke so softly he might have thought he hadn't spoken at all.

I studied him while he stared into space. Did scenery falling on me have anything to do with the scenery that fell on Ernesto? I had inspected the flat every which way but didn't see any sabotage like the metal inserted into the star. But still. The coincidence was too great. Stephanie clearly had an issue with me. Perhaps Carlos had an issue with Ernesto. Married couples often join forces against enemies, right?

I tried a different tack. "Why didn't you want to drive Ernesto home after your star hit him?"

"My star?"

"You made it." I shrugged. "So why didn't you?"

"I don't remember …"

"Bobby asked if Ernesto's house was on your way and you just shut him down with a look."

Recognition dawned on Carlos' face. He spoke quietly. "That was the day Ernesto told me that everything I was doing was wrong and stupid. Why would I want to be in a closed up vehicle with him? He'd tell me everything that was wrong with my truck, and how I drove, and what if he started in on Bobby?"

We stared at each other. I didn't know what to think. Carlos sounded sincere about Ernesto, but that didn't explain Stephanie.

"Why would Stephanie want to hurt me?"

Carlos set the bag from the hardware store on a worktable. "I don't know, but I intend to find out." He strode across to the front of the stage and hopped down instead of using the stairs. Then he marched across the multi-purpose room and out the door.

I picked up my empty cup from where I left it on the floor then gingerly picked my way down the stage steps. At the bottom, pain shot through my low back and I held on to the stage for support. After a bit, the pain ebbed away and I let go of the stage. "Just a cramp," I said out loud, trying to convince myself.

"Excuse me?"

Doug's voice startled me and I turned toward him. "Geez, you scared me! Where'd you come from?"

"Oh, sorry. I just came up from the basement. I was doing a favor for Barb. She's been harping on someone to fill the bin with ice melt. I thought I'd surprise her by actually doing it." He grinned.

"Have you seen Don or Carlos or his wife this morning?"

"So early? Nope. Haven't seen anyone. Why? Do you need help with something?"

"Nah, I just wondered who all was here so far." I didn't want to advertise any of the earlier trouble. "Where is everyone today, anyway? Why aren't there kids and seniors all over the place?"

"It's Saturday, remember? Only half-day and rehearsal starts late?"

I made a combination snort and chuckle. I *had* forgotten. No wonder nobody heard me yelling. I massaged my lower back, resisting the urge to rub my butt cheek.

"What's wrong?" he asked while watching me knead it.

"It's nothing. Just a little mishap backstage. I'm fine." I did a few side-to-side twists. "Just going to get some more coffee. I like to take a few quiet minutes before rehearsal starts."

"Good idea. I came in early to nail down that bit of dialogue that keeps tripping me up."

"You'll get it. It's almost there."

"Between you and me, Charlee, I wasn't sure this was going to work out very well. All these kids and old folks. Amateur productions are hard. And then with Ernesto…"

"I know. I thought about pulling the plug a couple of times."

"I'm glad you didn't. I think it's going to be a great show and everyone seems to be having fun." He stepped away from me. "Well, I'll let you have your quiet time. See you later."

I let him leave the multi-purpose room before me so he

wouldn't see the extent of my limping. While it was still quiet, I snuck into the kitchen and filled a plastic bag with ice, then hobbled to the restroom. I lifted my shirt and pulled the waistband of my jeans down a bit. An ugly bruise was forming along the side of my back and butt. I closed myself in a stall and pressed the ice pack against my skin.

~

I didn't know if I was a little black cloud of stress and achiness over the rehearsal, or if it was destined to be bad regardless of my bruised tush, but things did not go well. Even when I was standing. I wrapped things up as soon as possible, the minute I saw parents start to wander in to pick up their kids after rehearsal.

I shooed everyone out, trying not to be rude, but probably failing, and waited until I was the last person in the building before locking the door behind me.

When I pulled into my parking space at my apartment complex, I saw Don and Barb's car in its place. As I walked across the lot, I glanced up at Don and Barb's apartment and saw their lights on. Barb's form walked in front of the curtains, looking like she carried the tea tray. All seemed well upstairs. I still wanted to know where he'd disappeared to this morning at the center, but it could wait until later. I was bone-tired and just wanted to get home.

The minute I opened the door of my apartment, I was greeted with the smell of roast pork. Good grief, I loved that man. Ozzi poked his head out of the kitchen. "Babe, just in time!"

"For what?" I dropped gingerly to the couch without taking my coat off.

"To tell me if you want brownies or blondies for dessert tonight."

"Brownies. Duh. Like that's even a valid choice."

"I got the urge to make green chile stew today." He came out wiping his hands on my favorite apron. The one that said *Don't make me poison you*. He took one look at me and asked, "What happened?"

He helped me remove my coat and boots while I chronicled the day's adventure.

Appropriate gestures were made to attend to my needs, which I appreciated. When we both realized he could do nothing further, short of switching bodies with me, he handed me a slip of paper that had been on the table. "I have something that might make you feel better."

I looked from his hand holding the paper to his face and back to the paper a few times. In the weakest, breathiest voice I could muster, I said, "What's that?"

He laughed and put the paper back on the table before sitting next to me. "I got Inez Trujillo's contact information for you." At my blank look he added, "The one with the harassment complaint against Doug?"

"Oh. Awesome."

"I called her and asked if she'd meet you at Espresso Yourself."

"Now?" I struggled to stand but Ozzi gently pushed me back down.

"Tomorrow. Relax." He nuzzled my neck. "Anything else I can do to make you feel better?"

"You mean in addition to making those brownies?"

FIFTEEN

I opened my front door to walk over to Espresso Yourself the next morning to meet Inez Trujillo and it was so cold it literally yanked the breath right out of my body.

Winston and Javier's polar vortex had arrived.

I stood on the threshold, gasping for breath through frozen lungs, when I heard scuffling above me at Barb and Don's apartment. "Don, is that you?" I called. When he didn't answer, I took the stairs two at a time.

"It's colder than a cast-iron commode out here!" he said when he saw me on the lower landing.

I breathed in through my nose to protect my lungs, only to find I'd frozen all my nose hairs, transforming them into sharp spikes stabbing my nasal cavity. "I know, right? Does Peter need to potty?" I called.

"Yes, but he's having second thoughts."

"Hang on." I bounded up the rest of the stairs where Don held Peter O'Drool in his arms, both their noses peeking out the two inches where he'd cracked open the door. "Let me do it. I'm already dressed like the abominable snowman." I took Peter from him and shut the door.

Peter tried to worm his way into the warmth of my coat. It

was all I could do to keep him from wiggling right out of my arms. I dropped him to his favorite patch of grass in an effort to speed things up. He was way ahead of me. He lifted his leg and hadn't technically finished before he began racing up the stairs toward home. Barb invited me inside for some coffee cake, but I told her I was on my way out.

"Where were you yesterday?" I asked her. "I didn't see you at the senior center."

"I had shopping to do," she said. "Did you see Don there?" She leaned closer and whispered. "He was fiddling with his good hearing aid and almost broke it. He was cranky because I needed the car so he had to go in early and look for one of those tiny screwdrivers. There are a million of them at the center, for emergency repairs to all our old people bifocals, but do you think we could find a single one here at home?"

I smiled. "I did see him early yesterday but was afraid to talk to him. Did he get it fixed?"

She nodded. "Guess what Santa will be bringing for his stocking, though?"

"Let me guess … a set of tiny screwdrivers?"

"Don't tell him."

"If I get the urge, I'll just whisper in his deaf ear."

"Oh, you!" She swatted me as I opened the door, closing it quickly behind me.

I shivered and tried to fill my lungs as I hurried across the street to Espresso Yourself. I flung open the door and fell inside like I was Pa Ingalls trying to get from the barn to the house in a blizzard.

Lavar wrapped me in a hug. "It ain't fit for man nor beast out there! I didn't even go to church today." He looked heavenward and crossed himself. "He understands, though."

While I assessed the crazy decorations on both sides of the shop, Tuttle scurried over with a steaming mug of coffee and a generous slice of blueberry butter braid.

"You have butter braid? This is my lucky day!" I chose a table as far away from the door as I could get. I didn't need an icy blast every time someone opened it.

"Not many customers today, it seems," Tuttle said. "Can't say as I blame them, though. What brings you out on a day like this?"

"I'm meeting someone."

I draped my coat over the back of a chair and squatted down to greet Nova, who hadn't moved from her toasty dog bed near the heat vent. Her golden tail with the little paint-dip white at the tip thumped a greeting, but her nose stayed tucked in her tail. I took no offense.

"Hey, you guys are coming to the play at the senior center on Saturday, right?"

"Wouldn't miss it!"

"With bells on!"

I told them about the bells on all the elves shoes. "So no bells, okay? But Peter O'Drool will be there, so go ahead and bring Nova with you. The kids love Peter so I know they'll really love a dog who doesn't fart all day. In fact, if my pretty girl plays her cards right, she could be one of my dog extras." I gave her one last rub on her velvety ear.

I saw the voting jars for the decorating contest were three-quarters of the way full, and they looked almost equal. "So who's winning?"

"Everyone who comes in here and gets a jolt of Christmas spirit!" Lavar said proudly.

I glanced around. It hadn't been toned down at all, in fact, quite the opposite. I think I even spied some new treasures. *Were those Magi dressed for an ugly sweater contest?*

Before I could ask, the door opened and a blast of frigid air shot through the room. Someone struggled to shut the door behind them and then began unwrapping a scarf that enshrouded them from the top of their head to their neck.

As the scarf peeled away, I saw a woman. "Are you Inez?"

She nodded but continued to unpeel. "I'm Charlee Russo." She nodded, finally removing her winter gear.

She stood with a mountain of cold-weather gear heaped in her arms. Tuttle and Lavar took it from her and began draping everything on the coatrack.

She shook off the chill, then smiled broadly and extended her hand. "Inez Trujillo, fresh from my expedition with Richard Peary to the North Pole."

Tuttle whistled then twirled her around. "Girl, you look divine! What is this gorgeousness?"

Inez wore black leggings, black stilettos, and a black tank, but over the top of everything was a magnificently intricate beaded and sequined lacy wrap that fell past her knees.

"Royal blue is your color!" Lavar fingered the delicate wrap.

"Isn't this fantastic?" she said. "We just got it in. I work at a little boutique in Cherry Creek."

"Stunning," I agreed.

"You should come in! I'll be your personal shopper. I know where they hide the good stuff," she said with a smile.

Lavar and Tuttle burst out laughing. They talked over each other, trying to get the words out through their laughter.

Inez looked at me, puzzled.

"They're pretty sure I can't wear anything like that," I explained dryly.

The men were draped all over each other, trying to draw breath.

"Ha, ha. Very funny," I said to them. "Now go get this nice lady some coffee. Bring the pot, actually."

Lavar and Tuttle took their histrionics behind the counter. Lavar hollered, "More butter braid?"

"Lots more!" I yelled back, directing Inez to the table near Nova. I gingerly took my seat, hoping not to exacerbate my injury. You'd think it would feel better since the whole world was one big ice pack today.

Inez ran a soft hand along Nova's face, ending at her ear. "What a pretty girl," she murmured before sitting down.

After we both had hot coffee and slices of blueberry pastry in front of us, I got down to business. "I don't know how much Ozzi told you—"

"Not much. Just that you were interested in hearing about that thing between me and Doug Beesley. Normally I wouldn't dredge up ancient history, but Ozzi said it was important. And I like Ozzi." She grinned at me. "You are a lucky lady."

I leaned forward and whispered, as if I didn't want to jinx anything. "He made me green chile stew and brownies yesterday. On a whim!"

Inez fanned herself. "Be still my heart." She stabbed a bite of butter braid, popped it in her mouth, then rolled her eyes back in ecstasy while she chewed. When she finished she said, "So what do you want to know?"

"Just tell me what happened. I don't really know anything."

"Hm, let's see, where to start." Inez took a sip of coffee, then stared into her cup as she organized her thoughts. "At the office, we had this group we called the Lunch Bunch. It was just a group of us who went out to eat. We took turns choosing the restaurants, and every time my day rolled around, Doug would make a big deal out of saying 'Yay, tacos!'"

I let my fork droop. *So he is a big fat racist.* "No wonder you complained about him."

"Oh, I didn't complain. But I think HR heard about it and *they* thought it sounded racist."

"Wasn't it?"

She shook her head. "No. I always pick the taco place, but Ernesto, he's the head of HR, heard about it and thought it sounded like Doug was harassing me. He calls me in for a meeting by myself and then both of us together. We explain it was just Ernesto misunderstanding, but he still writes Doug up for it. It was all so silly. I mean, who doesn't like tacos? It just seemed to me that management got nervous."

"About what?"

"Well, here I was, a new employee. Female. Latina. Programmer." She grinned again. "I scare people, I guess. Especially old white men, like the CEO. I always thought that he forced Ernesto to write up Doug—they're good friends, you know—maybe as a warning to other employees or something?"

"Did Doug get in a lot of trouble?"

"Not really. A written improvement plan"—she used air quotes—"is just a slap on the wrist. Less than a slap on the wrist." She took a sip of coffee. "I've never heard Doug say anything racist."

That was interesting and I almost told her about the cracks about kids of color getting all the scholarships, Mexican Santa and his low-rider sleigh and such. I decided against it, though. It felt too icky to say out loud. But I did feel like she deserved to know Ernesto was dead.

"That's a shame. He was really a nice guy." We both kept a respectful silence while we sipped coffee. She put her cup down and looked me in the eye. "Maybe I'm wrong about Doug, though. When I was in that meeting alone with Ernesto, he confided to me that he thought Doug had a pattern of racist harassment because every time Doug walked by Ernesto's office—Ernesto was Mexican—but every time Doug walked by, he'd whistle *La Cucaracha*. I didn't believe it at the time, thought maybe he was trying to railroad Doug or bait me or something."

"Is that why you quit?"

"No, not at all. I liked it there, just hated programming. A friend of mine owns this chain of clothing stores and needed a buyer for women's accessories. It's way more fun playing with hats and scarves and belts!"

❧

As I steeled myself against the polar vortex and walked back to my apartment, I mulled over everything Inez told me. Even though the harassment that got Doug a wrist slap from Ernesto appeared to be simply a misunderstanding, the thing about whistling *La Cucaracha* seemed more important.

I was convinced Doug and Daisy were raging racists, but would it catapult either of them into the category of murderer? What would they achieve by sabotaging that star with a piece of sheet metal and trying to frame me?

I shivered and wrapped my arms tighter around myself. Was that even what happened or was my imagination running away with me? I mean, yesterday I was convinced that Stephanie and Carlos knocked that scenery on me, and maybe were actually trying to hurt Don. With a little bit of distance, it all seemed far-fetched. Don's recall election was just a petty power play at a local senior center, and if someone was trying to hurt me, there were many other ways to do so. Unless someone was just sending some kind of warning to me—I shook my head. *Ridiculous!* I hurried across the parking lot.

After I burst into my apartment, teeth chattering, I sat down with Ozzi and a hot cup of coffee to tell him about my conversation with Inez.

Ozzi would help me focus on what was real and what was my imagination.

What I didn't expect was his laughter.

"Everyone sings, whistles, or hums *La Cucaracha* before they go in the break room. Ernesto's office is right next to it, so he must have misunderstood and thought it was directed at him."

"What? Do you do that?"

"I do."

"But why?"

"It has become a kind of a subconscious way to steel yourself against seeing creepy-crawlies in the break room. No matter how clean it is, or the fact they're harmless bugs, it's still kinda gross."

I stared at my otherwise sane and normal boyfriend for long enough that he drank half a cup of coffee and topped us both off.

"I don't buy it."

"But it's true." He paused and dropped his voice. "Well, not entirely."

I scooted forward, attentive.

"People don't always sing *La Cucaracha*."

"I knew it!"

"They also sing *Itsy Bitsy Spider*, anything by Adam Ant, and something called *Killa Beez*."

I threw up my hands in frustration and my back spasmed again. I tenderly pressed my bruise while he laughed some more. "Next you're going to tell me someone hires a full symphony orchestra to play the Goldbug Variations!"

"Do you mean Bach's Goldberg Variations?"

I flung myself backward on the couch, truly exasperated. And Ozzi knew it.

"Aw, I'm sorry." He squeezed my knee gently, rhythmically, until it tickled and I giggled. He leaned back on the couch and we both sipped our coffee for a bit. "But you know, now that I think about it, I'm pretty sure Doug started it."

SIXTEEN

The polar vortex had settled over Denver like that drunk guy at the bar who won't take no for an answer, unwelcome and all over you. When I tried to start my car to get to the senior center, it acted like a recalcitrant teenager and refused to wake. I hurried to Ozzi's apartment and was happy to see he hadn't left for work yet.

"Can you drop me at the senior center? My car has decided to hunker down for a while."

"It's got a case of the Mondays, eh? Yeah, I'll be ready in five."

"I'll meet you out front. I want to check on Don and Barb."

Bundled in her robe, Barb cracked open the door, then pulled me inside. "Brr."

Don looked like he just rolled out of bed too.

"I just came to tell you it's still freezing outside. My car won't even start."

Don was already up out of his recliner looking for his keys. "You need a ride somewhere?"

"Sit down. I came to see if *you* needed to go anywhere."

"No way." Barb shivered. "We were out yesterday and it was so cold I thought I was going to crack in half. We're

146

staying in today. Catch up on our Netflix. What's that murder show you like?"

I rattled off a dozen until she jabbed her finger in the air. "That's the one!"

"So you guys don't need anything? Ozzi's taking me to the senior center, but you call me if you need us to stop on the way home for anything. You're good for groceries? Medications all full?" I started toward the kitchen to check.

Barb stopped me. "We're fine, dear. It's not the Ice Age. We can stay in our apartment for a day."

Of course she was right. They were perfectly capable adults who didn't need my help. But as my surrogate grandparents, they were going to get doted on regardless. But for now, I let it drop. "It sure feels like the Ice Age."

"I bet most of the seniors will be staying in today, too. Rehearsal will probably be a bust." Don looked guilty. "I could come in, if you want."

"Don't be silly. You guys stay warm and safe today." I glanced over to Peter O'Drool's bed. He was cuddled up, wheezy nose to curly tail. "Hey, Pete. Need to go out?"

In response he shut his eyes tighter.

"I'll take that as a hard pass."

As I made my way down the wooden stairs from the second floor to the parking lot, I wondered if most of the kids would stay home too.

When Ozzi dropped me off, I was greeted by a swarm of hyperactive kids in the lobby of the senior center. I looked around for other seniors and only found a few, wearing dazed thousand-yard stares. *Egads. We're outnumbered.*

Some of the more cautious parents hovered around, waiting to make sure they weren't dumping their kids into a Lord of the Flies situation. Apparently, they took me for a responsible adult, ready to handle four thousand children who were all acting like they'd been on a three-week bender free-basing Pixie Stix. A thousand thoughts swirled through my brain, but the most important was whether Chef Joe was here today.

I ran down the hallway to the kitchen where I was thrilled to see lights on. "Oh, thank goodness you're here! I can't imagine how I'd go about feeding all those—" I saw Thelma scooping coffee into the big urn.

"Now you made me lose count," she scolded. She looked into the basket, then at her scoop. She scorched me with her eyes then dug in for more coffee with the scoop rigid in her gnarled fingers. "One, two, three ... four more." With narrowed eyes she said, "If this coffee is bad, it's your fault."

"Chef Joe's not here?" I already knew the answer.

"What do you think?" she snapped.

"What are we going to do about lunch?" I looked at her helplessly.

"We?" She turned on her heel and left me alone in the kitchen.

I'd work this problem over a nice warm cup of coffee. She'd forgotten to press the button to start the coffee brewing. Today was going to be bad, very bad.

By mid-morning, only about twenty-five percent of the seniors showed up, but it seemed like double the number of kids were here. I didn't even try to organize rehearsal, instead, I pulled all the seniors into a strategic huddle.

"Okay, who wants to do what?" I asked them.

There were volunteers for reading out loud, jigsaw puzzling, various craft activities, and Winston offered to lead a seminar about weather patterns, specifically the reasons and conditions behind a polar vortex. I nodded, murmured, "Thanks, that'll be great," but knew only Javier would be interested. "Hey, Winston. Do you think you could broaden your topic and mix in some Santa Claus, North Pole stuff? I bet a lot of kids would get a kick out of that."

"Sure. I'll enthrall them with the depth of my North Pole

knowledge." He winked at me and rolled away to get busy on his presentation.

I gathered everyone in the multi-purpose room and organized them into groups based on activities, promising they'd all switch later so they could cycle through all the activities. The kids were thrilled, but the adults already looked exhausted. Maybe the parents would pick up their children early today. Or maybe reinforcements would ride to our rescue.

After the groups trooped down to the classrooms in the basement, I had to figure out what to do about lunch. Maybe Chef Joe left instructions. Or at least a jar of peanut butter.

"Miss Charlee?" a girl said. "We're supposed to work with Mr Morales on the scenery this week." There were a group of six kids standing with her.

"I don't think he's here yet. Maybe he's not coming in at all. I think you'll have to wait until tomorrow to do that."

Her chin quivered. "I have to do it today. I can't come the rest of the week and he promised I could paint."

I stared at her and almost cried myself. I knew that stomach-churning end-of-the-world loss and betrayal you experience when things don't go your way through absolutely no fault of your own. Big stuff like death and little stuff like when your ice cream falls right off your cone and plops forlornly to the sidewalk. That doesn't change just because you get older.

I glanced toward the stage, hoping that Carlos had magically appeared. He had not. There was time to set these kids up painting before I had to worry about feeding everyone. I hoped.

"Okay, then. Let's go see what needs to be done."

They whooped and ran for the stage. The little girl grabbed my hand and swung it happily while we walked across the multi-purpose room.

I hadn't been involved in the nitty-gritty of the scenery,

unless you counted almost getting crushed by one. One of the kids rolled out the flat they'd been planning to work on.

"Be careful with that!" I rushed over to help him. "You don't want it to fall on anyone."

"It's light. It would only hurt an old person."

I resented the implication, but kind of had to agree. The flat rolled easily and two ten-year-olds were able to place it on the floor backstage with no trouble.

"We're going to paint Santa's workshop on this one," one of them said.

They all bustled around, acting like they knew exactly what to do. Since I didn't, I just watched while they gathered paints and brushes. Two of the older ones began sketching ideas on the blank canvas with a pencil, all of them pointing and shouting their opinions.

I wondered why Carlos had already placed the rolling casters on the flats if they hadn't been painted yet. It seemed to me it would be easier to paint backdrop scenes on canvas if the flat was, well, flat. Maybe if it wasn't even nailed to the frame yet. I almost suggested we pull out the nails holding the canvas to the frame, but the artists didn't seem to be hindered. Besides, Carlos knew what he was doing, and these kids seemed to as well.

"You guys are doing great. Don't spill paint everywhere and I'll be back in a minute." As I hurried toward the kitchen, I ran into Doug in the lobby just taking off his coat.

"Boy howdy, it's cold out there! Where is everyone?" He rubbed his hands together to warm them.

"Hiding from the polar vortex, it seems."

"I should have known."

"Is Daisy here?" Maybe we could at least work on their scenes today.

"Nope. Said her car wouldn't start."

"Sounds familiar." I almost asked why he didn't give her a ride, but then realized it was none of my beeswax. But that didn't stop me from wanting to ask about *La Cucaracha*. "Hey, I had coffee with Inez Trujillo yesterday." I watched carefully for his reaction.

"Inez!" Doug smiled. "How's she doing? I miss her. We used to eat a lot of tacos together."

He seemed perfectly at ease talking about her.

"She told me about your pattern of racism at work."

"My what?" Doug's open smile turned tight.

"How you sing *La Cucaracha* every time you passed Ernesto's office."

He frown turned into a grin. "She called it *a pattern of racism*? That's funny."

"No, it's not."

"No, I mean—First, it didn't have anything to do with Ernesto. And it certainly isn't racist." I started to speak but he continued. "I guess I can see why someone might think that, though. I mean, Ernesto's office was right next to the break room."

"So why—"

Doug gave a full-body shudder. "When I was a kid, during the summer we'd get earwigs in our kitchen, and in the winter the boxelder beetles. My brothers found out how much I hated them so they'd constantly torment me with them and made my phobia much worse." He closed his eyes against the memory before addressing me again. "In the break room they hide like little jerks and startle me. So I started whistling as a reminder to myself to be on the lookout for them."

"Then why whistle a Spanish song about cockroaches? I don't even think we have those here."

Doug stared at me like he was talking to one of Santa's boots. "Do you know any songs about boxelder bugs?"

"No, can't say that I do."

After a moment he cocked his head at me. "Did Inez really say Ernesto thought I was making fun of him or something?"

I nodded and immediately wished I hadn't. Doug's eyes filled with tears and he had to turn away from me.

"What must Ernesto have thought of me?" he murmured. "Why didn't he say anything?"

The anguish on his face seemed raw. The death of his friend was still fresh. My heart twisted and I changed the subject.

"Your brothers sure sound mean. Kids can be so cruel."

Doug swiped at his eyes and nose. "They didn't get much better as adults. Always made sure I knew *they* weren't afraid of bugs, and that they had the nicer cars and houses."

Lance and I had our tiffs when we were kids, but nothing like that, and certainly nothing that carried over into our adulthood. "They sound terrible."

Doug talked about his brothers some more, and began sniffling again when he said, "Ernesto was like the brother I never had combined with the father I never had. He was a good friend and mentor to me."

I watched him for a moment while he plucked a tissue from a nearby box in the lobby.

I spoke softly. "Then why did you and Daisy say such awful stuff about Mexican Santa and that the kids should leave out *cervezas* and tacos for him?"

"I didn't technically say any of that stuff." He had the good sense to look ashamed. "It was all Daisy. I just didn't want to get into it with her. She's a privileged twit, but harmless."

I reeled through my memory and saw that what he said was true. He hadn't said that stuff. And Daisy *was* a twit. But harmless? The jury was still out. "But you laughed, which must encourage her. Aren't you going to be the head of Human Resources now? You can't ignore comments like Daisy's anymore. And it's not harmless. What if more of those kids heard what she was saying and saw you condoning it?"

Doug covered his face with both hands. "I know. You're

right." He dropped his hands. "My first thought just now was to ask Ernesto how to handle it." He plucked another tissue.

"You'll figure it out. I know Ozzi has a calm, rational head. I'm sure if you wanted to bounce anything off him at work, he'd be happy to talk to you. Especially if you dangled Taco Tuesday in front of him because"—Doug said it in unison with me—"who doesn't like tacos?"

I didn't know what else to say so I gave him a choice to change gears. "So, the monkeys are running the zoo today and Chef Joe didn't come in. If you can stay a while, you can either go figure out what's for lunch, or you can go take over for Carlos and supervise scenery painting."

I barely got all the words out before he puts dibs on painting and hurried off.

Before heading to the kitchen, I snuck down to the basement to see if all was well down there. Everything was running like a dream. Kids listened to Thelma's story with rapt attention. She was smart to choose *Little House on the Prairie* over a shorter picture book. I heard her tell the children she had brought it from home.

Craft rooms were crafting, and even Winston's Weather Workshop seemed like it was well-received. I didn't want to jinx anything, so I did a quick and quiet head count before tiptoeing away.

In the kitchen I found what Chef Joe must have been planning for lunch, if not today, at least one of these days. And hot dogs seemed like something I could cook for a crowd. I found some potatoes, pickles, and celery and decided to make potato salad too.

While I cubed a mountain of potatoes, I thought about Doug. He had big Ernesto shoes to fill over at the hack factory if he couldn't even confront Daisy, dismissing her behavior as harmless. The two of them certainly weren't harmless, but the more I thought about his explanation of *La Cucaracha* and hearing about his brothers, I just couldn't picture him involved with some racist attack on Ernesto.

That star falling on Ernesto certainly wasn't a racist incident. But what was it? Simply an accident? If so, how did that sheet metal get shoved up inside? I thought maybe Carlos had done that to keep them from blowing around so hard when the furnace kicked on. But when I checked, none of the other stars had been similarly outfitted.

Regardless, I was positive that metal hadn't been in the star when it hit Ernesto. When it got kicked across the floor, it looked like an autumn leaf skittering across the sidewalk.

So who sabotaged it, and why?

Daisy? How did any of this fit into the fact she was related to Ernesto? Did she even know he was her uncle? Was that why she never mentioned it?

Stephanie? The same person who pushed the scenery over on me? What did she have against Ernesto to add metal to that star? She certainly had some beef with me, telling Carlos that I wasn't Bobby's mother. I couldn't even imagine where that ridiculous idea came from.

My mind had drifted from my chore. I nicked my finger when I thought about Carlos. He could have sabotaged the star *and* pushed the scenery on me. He said he was at the hardware store when the flat fell on me. But I knew he was lying. I heard him arguing with Stephanie. And didn't he come in after the star fell on Ernesto, asking what happened while claiming to have been at the hardware store? The hardware store seemed to be his alibi for everything.

I pressed hard on my finger and ran it under cold water until the bleeding stopped. None of it made sense. Ernesto didn't die because some Styrofoam star fell on him, whether it had the metal inside or not. He died because he was completely unhealthy and carelessly took ibuprofen on top of his prescribed blood thinner. And while I wouldn't say this to Barb or Don, Ernesto was old. Age, booze, and medical conditions were kind of the trifecta of poor health.

I hadn't heard from Detective Ming for a while either, so maybe Leona's finger-pointing, trying to get me in trouble over the hidden star, was all for naught. And my bottle of ibuprofen at Ernesto's house? He probably just scooped it up before he knew he shouldn't take it.

I dumped the potatoes into the huge pot and turned the burner to its highest setting. I watched until the water was boiling, angrily tossing the chunks of potato into each other, then turned it down.

It was sad that Ernesto died, but it didn't seem to be anyone's fault. I wondered about Ernesto's family. Had they been notified? What were they told? What did it mean that Daisy didn't know he was her uncle? Anything? Everything? Just a coincidence? Something nefarious? If so, on whose part … Ernesto's or Daisy's?

I jabbed at the potatoes, testing for doneness, while my mind churned with questions and scenarios. Soon enough they were cooked, and I had to focus on finishing lunch, something with decidedly fewer unanswerable questions. Using potholders I found in a nearby drawer, I warily tussled with the pot to pour the contents into the biggest colander I'd ever seen. I sprayed them down with cold water so they'd quit cooking. Nobody wanted mashed potato salad.

I used the same huge pot and dumped in all the hot dogs. I had absolutely no idea how many hot dogs a typical kid would eat. If there were leftovers, I was sure Chef Joe could figure out what to do with them, but if kids went hungry, I'd never hear the end of it.

As I waited for the water to boil, I set out bags of buns, jars of relish, and squirters of mustard and ketchup.

I turned it down to simmer while I mixed up the potato salad. I didn't measure anything, just started glopping everything together in a ginormous metal mixing bowl. When it looked right to me, I tasted it and surprised myself. "Not bad!" I said, licking the spoon.

I set it out, then drained the hot dogs and set them out.

I checked over everything one last time, then went to the multi-purpose room and called, "Doug! Lunch is ready. Will you send the kids in here then go get everyone up from the basement?"

As everyone came in, I directed them to line up. The kids were much more excited than the adults to see hot dogs on the menu.

Thelma even took the opportunity to scold me. "Don't you know hot dogs are the exact size of a child's throat? An extreme choking hazard."

I could have mentioned that Chef Joe was the one who bought all the hot dogs, but I held my tongue. I'd realized by now that Thelma wasn't happy unless she was complaining about something or someone. I watched as she bustled around slicing all the kids' hot dogs in half lengthwise. The ones that hadn't already been consumed anyway.

I waited until everyone had been served, then slathered mustard and relish on a bun of my own. I sat near the buffet in case anyone needed help with anything.

Not expecting praise for my culinary efforts, I was still pleased when many of the seniors and some of the kids said it was delicious. One lady even asked for my potato salad recipe.

I texted Ozzi to pick me up after all the kids had been collected by their parents. When he showed up and asked how my day went, I replied, "I didn't get any rehearsing done, but I may have found a new vocation."

"Daycare director?"

"Perish the thought. I'm thinking of starting a potato salad food truck." I started to put my coat on, but remembered something. "I want to check on the scenery the kids painted today."

I rolled all the scenery flats to where we could see them. Surprisingly, they all looked pretty good.

"Why are there so many for Santa's workshop?" Ozzi asked.

We rolled them all near each other on the stage. There were four. But none for the village scenes. "Oh no! They told me they wanted to paint the workshop scenes, but it never occurred to me to check to see if that's what they needed to paint!"

Ozzi handed me a paintbrush. "Scratch the food truck. You are now a stagehand."

SEVENTEEN

The next day dawned just as frigid and I kicked myself for not checking to see if my car would start before Ozzi left for work. We got home so late last night I just dropped into bed and barely remembered to set my alarm. I called Lance instead.

"Just stay home," he said.

"I can't!" I told him about yesterday. "I may have even fewer adults today. Everyone looked like they'd walked into Mordor by the time they left yesterday."

At my Tolkien reference, I heard him give a melodramatic sigh on the other end of the phone. "I'll be there in a while."

After we hung up I texted him the kissy-face emoji. He texted me the expected poop emoji. That's how I knew he loved me.

Normally the Colorado winter sky is crystalline, the brightest blue you'd ever seen. But this cold snap seemed to have dragged the gray sky down over us like a shroud. It was as dreary as it was frigid.

When we pulled into the senior center parking lot, I asked Lance if he had time to come in and play paper airplanes with the kids again. "They really loved it." I gave him the side-eye. "And I think you did too."

"I told you, I had some extra paper and a day off. No big deal." He tried to keep the smile from playing around the corners of his mouth, but he couldn't fool me.

Okay, I'll play. "So, you didn't enjoy it?"

"It was okay."

I leaned one inch from his cheek and stared until he grinned.

"I knew you had fun! Come in and do it again."

"Can't. Gotta get to work." He watched a group of kids and their parents walk toward the building. "There was a kid who reminded me so much of myself at that age." Before I could add something snarky, he said, "And one who reminded me of you." He glanced over at me. "She was annoying too."

"Ha!" I gathered my things but before I opened the door, I said, "You can come any time. They'll be doing daycare here until after the holidays and the kids go back to school. You were a big hit."

"I'll be here for the play and then I have a couple of days off after Christmas. I'll see if I can dig up some more paper somewhere around my house."

"You're fooling absolutely nobody, you know. See you later. Thanks for the ride."

"Need me to pick you up too, Space Case?"

"Thanks, but Ozzi is coming later."

As I crossed in front of the car, I wiggled my butt in his direction. He got the last laugh, though, by blasting his horn at me and making me jump.

Despite the Polar Vortex still gripping us in its fist, it seemed the hardy folks of the Leetsdale Senior Center couldn't stay away for two days in a row.

Barb, Don, and Peter O'Drool came in right behind me.

"Oh! If I thought you were coming out today, I would have had Lance bring you in too," I said.

"Or we could have brought you," Don said.

"Or that." It probably would have been more convenient, but it was nice to have an excuse to see Lance.

Thelma and Barb began organizing the kids and just beyond them, Chef Joe walked with purpose straight toward me, eyes trained on me like lasers.

"Uh oh."

"I hear you made lunch yesterday," he said.

"Um ... yes?"

"I just wanted to say you did a nice job. I was going to roast the hot dogs in the oven instead of boiling them, but whatever, right?"

I relaxed. "Thanks. I'm even more impressed by everything you do back there, now that I've had to do just a tiny bit of it."

Embarrassed, Chef Joe adjusted his apron. Without looking at me, he retied it and said, "That was the first day I've missed in seven years. I'm glad you were here."

"I'm glad I was too, but why didn't you call anyone to say you'd be out or to give instructions or something?"

"I did." He glanced around as if looking for someone. "I called Don. He said not to worry, that you'd be there."

It was my turn to be embarrassed. Don putting so much faith in me meant the world.

Chef Joe walked again with purpose back down the hallway and I went to find Don. When I did, I kissed him on the cheek. "You old coot," I said, then walked toward the multi-purpose room.

"Takes one to know one," he called after me.

Before I got there, however, the lobby doors whooshed open and a crowd of women carrying all manor of baskets, bags, and casserole dishes pushed their way into the lobby.

Ah, the tamale brigade. I'd been waiting for this chance to fill my freezer with homemade tamales. I didn't care what they cost, because I knew they'd be delicious and they were part of the school fundraiser.

A brace of frigid air came inside with the women, along with laughter, Spanish and English conversation, and Daisy.

"Tamale Brigade to the rescue!" one women sang out.

The bulk of the crowd went laughing and chattering down the hallway toward the kitchen, while Daisy veered toward me, muttering about "those people." She didn't say it in a way that made me think she was simply annoyed by a large group of people in her way. She said it in a way that made my skin crawl.

I had almost stepped in front of her when one of the women stepped in front of me, bobbling the two pans of tamales she carried. I quickly took one from her while she regained her balance, earning me a grateful smile, then followed her down the hall. It was just as well to wait to challenge Daisy. I needed time to formulate my thoughts.

I listened to the Tamale Brigade's easy camaraderie while they organized everything. The pan of tamales was whisked from my hands and I headed for the multi-purpose room, ready to confront Daisy about her comment.

She was alone on stage near Santa's throne. I was just about to call out to her when I saw her reach out and gently stroke the green velvet upholstery. She brushed back and forth with the same loving tenderness my parents used when they stroked my hair when I was sleepy or had the flu.

I watched Daisy from across the room, becoming uncomfortable at the intimacy of her private moment.

Suddenly she reared back and kicked the leg of the throne with the force worthy of a penalty shoot-out in a championship soccer game.

∽

T he only upside to the rest of Tuesday was that I didn't need to be responsible for anyone's lunch but my own. Oh, and that Ozzi came to pick me up and whisk me away to our favorite Italian place for dinner. Over a towering pile of lasagna, I told him—ie, whined—about my day. "Hardly any of the seniors came in. I mean, I get it. It's not their job or anything to come to the center, and this weather is dangerous, but ..."

"But you needed them."

"Yes." I twirled my fork around some stringy mozzarella. "And it makes me feel guilty. And Carlos' truck didn't start, so he wasn't there either, and I tried gathering just the kids for rehearsal, but without their buddies, it turned into a chaotic mess."

"They're just kids, you know, and this is their break from school. You remember what those couple of weeks were like before Christmas. I think you're expecting too much from them and from yourself." He pointed a breadstick at me. "*You've* never done this either."

"I know. You're right. It's all a bit overwhelming. First, finding out I'm directing this thing, then with Ernesto dying, and people thinking maybe Don or I had something to do with it—"

"That's so ridiculous. Ernesto died of natural causes. Or at least because that bump on his head exacerbated his poor health."

I told him about seeing Daisy kick Santa's throne, but as I did so, that niggly feeling came back. I mean, someone clearly had it in for Ernesto and if there was an estate of some kind involved, then Daisy was the likeliest suspect. People did crazy things when there was money at stake.

We finished eating in silence. Ozzi was probably thinking about Ernesto, but I had shifted gears into thinking about things I knew for certain. For instance, that this play was going to be a fiasco.

Only four more days and it would all be over. Then I could pretend it was just a bad dream, like Scrooge and his ghosts. But opposite, because there'd be no happy, uplifting ending.

EIGHTEEN

Wednesday was still incredibly arctic, but my car started. Maybe that meant this little weather phenomenon was coming to an end. I gave a little whoop and showed Ozzi a thumbs-up. He waved and drove away. I followed him out of the parking lot, but turned the opposite direction, toward the senior center.

I was beyond thankful to see Carlos wearing his toolbelt up on the stage when I got there. He was studying the scenery flats. When he saw me, he said proudly, "Look what the kids did!"

Pretending I didn't know what he was talking about, I studied them too. "Wow, the kids did a really good job with those village scenes."

Carlos nodded. "They're kind of primitive, clearly done by elementary school kids, but that's what makes them so great. This show really has a child-like look to it."

I decided to let Carlos continue to think his stage crew painted those scenes, but I smiled when I wondered if I should tell Ozzi our scenery had a primitive, child-like look to it.

While Carlos and I were having a moment, and it was still

quiet, I wanted to revisit something I'd been puzzling over. I gripped the side of one of the flats. It wobbled, but didn't fall down. I made a big show of looking for the reason, eventually pointing at the sandbags Ozzi and I made a point of placing on each one.

"I'm still wondering why that flat fell on me the other day. Why weren't there any sandbags on the frame?" I asked.

Carlos inhaled deeply. "I don't know. It's very worrisome."

Was he lying?

"It *is* very worrisome. It could have fallen on a child or a senior." He nodded and began to speak. I interrupted. "But we both know it didn't fall on its own." I removed both sandbags from the frame and it remained upright, unwavering. Then I pushed the frame. Carlos caught it as it began to topple. He righted it and I replaced the sandbags. "I heard you arguing with Stephanie. Was it because she was tampering with the set? I saw her back there. And you lied when you said you were at the hardware store when it fell on me."

Carlos took another deep breath. "I didn't lie. I did go to the hardware store after that argument. In fact, that's what we were arguing about."

"The hardware store?"

"Yes." Carlos wouldn't look at me.

"What?"

When he spoke, his voice was so quiet I could barely hear him. "I've been using my own money to buy this stuff, and Stephanie thinks I shouldn't do that. We're barely squeaking by with still paying off her rehab, my seasonal work, and the fact nobody will hire Stephanie with her track record."

"Then why are you using your own money at the hardware store? There's a budget for this. You just have to give the receipts to Don and he'll reimburse you. He told you that.

He'd even go with you to the hardware store and just pay for everything outright."

"I do that for some things, but I keep wasting and ruining things. They shouldn't have to pay for my mistakes."

"I'm confused. Why are you making so many mistakes? I thought you worked in construction."

"I do. But I'm no carpenter or anything." Carlos jammed his hands into the pockets of his fleece vest. "I lay pipe for new housing developments. Mostly I drive a bulldozer and dig trenches. Not much call for that here," he said ruefully.

"Why'd you volunteer to build sets then? Don't get me wrong, I volunteer for stuff I've never done before all the time. Just yesterday, in fact, I made lunch for our army here"—I grinned at him—"and painted some scenery. I hear it's primitive, like folk art."

"You painted—"

I waved his words away. "So you left for the hardware store right after your argument with Stephanie?"

"I was on my way out when Stephanie caught up with me. We must have been out at my truck when the flat fell on you. Otherwise I would have heard it. Or you. Did you yell?"

"I yelled like one of those screaming goats."

He looked at me blankly.

"Look it up. You can thank me later."

"But that doesn't explain how that flat fell on you," Carlos said.

I stared loudly at him. "That's what I've been trying to tell you. You keep telling me that Stephanie wouldn't do anything like that. But she was the only other person— besides you—around that morning. And you tell me you were at the hardware store." When he didn't reply, I said softly, "Why did she want to hurt me, Carlos?"

When Carlos looked up, his eyes blazed. "I told you before, she would never do anything like that."

"Was she trying to hurt Don? Did she mistake me for him?"

"No! That scenery fell on you by accident!" He stomped away, clenching and unclenching his fists.

"What was that all about? Scenery fell on you?" Daisy asked as she and Doug walked toward me.

"Yes, one of the flats fell over."

Daisy barked out a laugh. "Carlos tried to smother you with scenery? That's as cold as the weather!"

"He didn't try to smother me. It just ... fell."

"It fell *on* you?" Doug raised his eyebrows and I knew he didn't believe me.

"Yes, you were there," I said.

"I was?"

"Well, afterward."

He thought for a moment.

"That day you saw me limping?" I prompted.

"You said you had a cramp." His tone made me think he didn't believe me.

Daisy caught his tone, too and said suspiciously, "I never heard anything fell on anyone. And I heard a twenty-minute dissertation about Boyd's prostate problems the other day. There are no secrets at the Leetsdale Senior Center." She looked me over. "I don't see any bruises or anything." She steepled her fingers in front of her sternum. "Let me get this straight. Nobody saw this happen and you don't have any injuries." She rolled her eyes at Doug. "Are you sure that really happened?"

"Daisy, I don't think—"

I interrupted Doug and spoke to Daisy. "I have a big bruise on my butt. Wanna see?" I asked sarcastically. *There were a million secrets at the Leetsdale Senior Center—many of them Daisy's—but my life was an open book. Maybe I'd rub off on her.*

"I absolutely want to see," Daisy said.

I had no choice but to turn my butt toward her and yank the waistband of my jeans down.

"Oooh, ouchie." Daisy walked away, laughing.

I had never wished more fervently for someone to crash into a wall. Or choke on her own laughter. Or stumble down an abandoned well lined with razor wire where she'd land knee-deep in a tangle of vipers, alligators, and no cell service.

Doug again raised his eyebrows at me then followed Daisy.

"I didn't know mooning was still a thing, dear." Barb tried not to smile.

"I wasn't mooning anyone," I said crossly.

Barb immediately became worried. "What's the matter?"

"Daisy didn't believe the scenery flat fell on me so I was showing her my bruised butt."

"Scenery fell on you?"

I traveled a fine line here. I wanted my injury to be bad enough to convince Daisy, but not so bad that Barb would be concerned. "It's nothing." I pulled my waistband down again and jutted my hip toward her.

Barb bent close, lifted her glasses from where they hung on a chain around her neck, and peered at my exposed flank.

I glanced around to see who might need an explanation of this.

"I'm sorry, dear. I don't see anything."

"Oh, great." *Now both Daisy, Doug, and Barb think I'm lying about the set falling on me. Why would I lie about that?*

"Yes, it's great you're not injured." Barb dropped her glasses back to her chest where they dangled from the chain. "I actually came over to ask if you would be a dear and fill the bin of ice melt. Winston says now that the Polar Vortex is moving out, a storm might be coming in and we don't want anyone slipping on the sidewalk."

"Oh, Doug already did that. He told me so himself."

Barb clapped her hands and her nest of curls bopped

joyfully to the beat. "You kids and all your energy! What would we do without you?"

Calling Doug a kid made me smile. He was well into his forties. I guess if someone is half your age, it automatically makes them a kid.

Barb leaned toward me. "I just want to make sure everything is shipshape and that I do everything possible to help Don before the recall election."

"So do I. When is it?"

"We'll discuss it at the January board meeting, then set a date for the election. I'm not gonna lie, I'm a tad worried for him. This play has taken him away from some of his duties around here and combined with his … poorly-timed comments about being Santa, well, let's just say, getting that ice melt bin filled is one less nail in his coffin. We haven't even figured out who is behind the recall yet, but when I find out, I'm going to give them a piece of my mind!" She scurried away with a finger waggle wave.

I thought about how I could help Don keep his board seat. I settled on a good, old-fashioned whisper campaign then made my way to the kitchen to see if Chef Joe had put out any snacks yet because this kid was starving. A streusel-topped muffin and an individually wrapped string cheese hit the spot while I greeted and chatted with some of the parents dropping off their kids. When they left, I made my way over to a table where eight seniors sat drinking coffee and eating muffins.

I decided to put my plan in motion right then, but realized I had no idea how to wage a whisper campaign. Plus, I didn't have much time. So I simply dragged an empty chair over, plopped myself down and said, "You guys know that Don didn't have anything to do with Ernesto's injury, right? It was just an accident. This recall vote of no confidence, or whatever it is, is completely misguided. How would Don even know that Ernesto would happen to be under that star when it fell?"

The seniors were quiet while I spoke, but now looked around at each other, as if this had been the topic of many conversations amongst them.

Felix, the man who danced at the drop of a hat, said, "I heard you were right there when it happened and even moved Ernesto into position"— he lowered his voice in tone but not volume— "right under that star."

His comment seemed to open the floodgate from the others.

"Was it so you could give your buddy Don the coveted role of Santa?" Gloria Mae said.

"I don't know that the role of Santa is particularly cov—"

Muriel, in her caftan and beads interrupted me. "Maybe you didn't want him to die, but if he got hurt and bowed out, that would have been fine with you and Don, right?"

That hit home because that's exactly how I felt when that star hit Ernesto, but shouldn't septuagenarian hippies who walk around all day in a Pigpen-like haze of marijuana be gentler with my feelings?

"Muriel, I—"

"I looked you up on that internet," Boyd said, "and saw you got arrested for killing your agent and stealing a bunch of money from poor, innocent people who signed up to take a class from you." He shook a stubby finger at me. "There's blood on your hands, missy!"

"That's a bit dramatic, don't you think? None of what you read on the internet is true, Boyd. Besides, we're not talking about me. We were talking about Don."

Hazel, Boyd's wife, narrowed her eyes at me. "What about recipes? They're true."

"And my audiobooks," Lorraine said. "They're true."

"Except the fiction," Hazel said. "That's not true."

"I only go on the Facebook to see pictures of our great-grandkids," Vern said. He patted his wife Lorraine's hand. "And then I describe them to her."

Lorraine rolled her eyes. "And he doesn't do such a great

job at that, I'll have you know. The other day he told me about a picture of one of them and told me she was wearing a pink dress and her hair was cute." She looked at her tablemates. "What am I supposed to do with that?"

The conversation devolved to a discussion about the clothes their great grandchildren are allowed to wear these days and isn't it shameful to parade them all over the Facebook like that?

I took the opportunity to slip away, confident my whisper campaign was a rousing failure.

When I returned to the multi-purpose room to get ready for rehearsal, I was surprised to see Leona standing on a chair inspecting the stars hanging over the area where the audience would sit for the performance. On the floor next to her was a sandbag.

"Do you need any help?" I asked.

She didn't even look at me. "You can start by pointing out any other stars you sabotaged by sticking your metal into them."

"I didn't sabotage any stars!"

She stepped off the chair and stared at me. "Then who did?"

"I don't think anyone sabotaged anything." *Did I really think that?* "Maybe Carlos was trying to figure out how to keep them from blowing around in that hurricane of a furnace blast. Maybe Bobby told him about my metal crafts and that gave him an idea about giving them some extra weight."

Exactly on cue, the furnace kicked on. My long hair went over the top of my head, creating a set of bangs that went down past my throat. Leona's tight corkscrews bounced around but remained as stylish as ever. I finger-combed my hair back into place then gathered it in a probably messy ponytail with a scrunchy I wore on my wrist.

She watched me organize myself then said, "Let's ask him."

I followed her as she strode up the steps to the stage and called for Carlos.

"Hi, Ms McFalls. What can I help you with?" he asked.

"You can tell me if you added that metal piece to the star that hit Ernesto."

"Of course not!"

She looked at me with triumph. "See? I told you Carlos had nothing to do with it."

"Not even to give the Styrofoam some weight so the furnace wouldn't blow them around so hard?" I prompted.

He shook his head. "Do you want me to do that? That sounds like a really good idea." He glanced out at the stars dancing over the multi-purpose room.

Leona pointed to the sandbag out by the chair. "You can also explain that," she said to me.

"It's a sandbag."

"I found it in your hiding place in the basement. I'm guessing so you could pretend that piece of scenery fell on you."

"I'm not pretending! How did you hear about that, anyway?" I didn't actually care about the answer to that question. A prickly pain began at the base of my head. A headache was coming on and I was a bit surprised it took so long.

I walked away. That sheet metal was gnawing at me. I was almost positive it wasn't there when the star hit Ernesto. But if it wasn't in there, did the conk on his head really cause all this to happen? Ozzi was certain Ernesto's poor health was to blame, and I believed that at one time as well. But did I still think that? I decided to go right to the source and dialed Detective Ming.

"Ms Russo. What a pleasure."

"You don't mean that."

"No, not really. What can I do for you?"

"First, if you haven't yet, you should talk to Daisy, whose last name I don't know, but she works at Net Software, in Ernesto's department."

"Because …." Detective Ming prompted.

"I guess because she needs the money—oh, you mean why you should talk to her." *Why couldn't I talk to him without getting flustered or saying something stupid?* I thought for a minute but realized, a tad too late, that anything I said was likely to get Doug into trouble. I decided to stick with the facts. "Because she kicked a chair."

"A chair."

"Not just any chair. The Santa throne."

Detective Ming didn't respond so I reminded him, "And Ernesto was our Santa."

After a couple beats of silence he said, "Is that all you wanted to enlighten me about?"

"No." I took a deep breath. "I know it's none of my beeswax, even though it kind of is, but I wanted to know what the emergency room records said about Ernesto's injury."

"You're right, it's none of your … beeswax."

"But will you tell me anyway?"

"Remind me." He paused and I got poised to tell him the date of the accident, or Ernesto's full name or whatever it was he needed to get me the information I sought. "What section of the HIPAA privacy code does *beeswax* fall under?"

"But—"

"No ER records," he said before disconnecting.

I stared at the phone and took a deep breath while I redialed. "When you get them will you tell me?"

"No ER records," he repeated before disconnecting again.

Through the phone I heard his irritation with me and I suddenly wondered if he had any children. Was he this terse with them?

Because it seemed to be the day for terseness, Thelma

marched up and pointed a gnarled finger at me. "You happy with the play as is or are you gonna have rehearsal?" She marched away without waiting for an answer.

I dug my auxiliary bottle of aspirin from my bag while I gathered up my actors and crew, old and young. I herded them into the multi-purpose room like a mother duck, quacking to her ducklings. But instead of loud quacking, I was doing some silent worrying.

I popped the last two pain relievers in my mouth and washed them down with some coffee. We hadn't had a good rehearsal since last Friday, and watching all my actors—child and adult—hopped up on pre-Christmas anticipation and/or caffeine, I didn't have high hopes for today either. I couldn't remember the last time we ran through the whole thing without major glitches.

I rolled my shoulders and neck, trying to loosen up and put a positive spin on the day. At least all my principal actors were here.

I sat in the audience and we got started.

By the end of the day, I realized we all should have simply stayed in bed and watched cartoons.

NINETEEN

I couldn't be sure that my imagination wasn't playing tricks on me, but Thursday felt practically balmy when I braced myself to get my newspaper. I checked my weather app. It *was* balmy! The temperature had skyrocketed to thirty-one degrees. The polar vortex had broken, like a reverse fever.

I woke Ozzi with the good news while I handed him a cup of coffee and a plate of scrambled eggs and toast.

"You're not eating?" He nuzzled my neck while he took the plate.

"Already did. I need to stop at the twenty-four-hour pharmacy before I get to the senior center." At the alarm that registered on his face I hurriedly added that I just needed to restock my over-the-counter pharmaceuticals.

"It's still so early, though."

"I know. I also need to figure out how to get everyone to memorize their lines. I can kind of understand the seniors and the kids, but I'm beginning to wonder how Doug and Daisy can remember how to get home every night. It's like their memories are made from Swiss cheese." I had a horrible thought. "You don't think they're doing it on purpose to mess with me, do you?"

Ozzi laughed. "I wouldn't put it past them." When he saw my face, he nuzzled me again. "I'm joking. I'm sure they're not."

"Actually, I don't know which would be worse—whether they were messing with me, or whether they truly couldn't remember their lines." I took a sip from Ozzi's cup. "Either way, I'm going to do some research about mnemonic devices or something."

Ozzi gestured toward my laptop. "You can't do that here?"

I ogled him lasciviously. "If I stay here, that's absolutely not what I'd be doing."

~

Fifteen minutes later, in need of a cold shower, I pulled open the door to the pharmacy.

I picked out two different kinds of over-the-counter pain relief. Better be prepared for the rest of the week. Plopping it in front of the pharmacist's window I asked, "Can I pay for this here? I wanted to ask you something."

"Sure." She began to ring it up. "What do you want to know?"

"How bad is it to take ibuprofen if you're already on blood thinners?"

"Pretty bad." She stopped what she was doing and looked at me sharply. "Did you do that?"

"No, not me. A friend of mine got hit on the head and we were going to give him something, but we didn't when we found out he was taking something for his atrial fibrillation."

"He's very lucky, then. It doesn't take much over-the-counter stuff to give him a brain bleed."

"What's a brain bleed? Can that kill you?"

"Absolutely. Unless you get to the hospital. Then it's perfectly treatable."

"Would they give any over-the-counter stuff to him in the emergency room?"

"No way. Unless he didn't tell them the other medications he was on. People often bring in baggies of medications to show the nurses, just in case. If they did that, then no. ER folks know what drugs don't play well with each other. They're trained to look for stuff like that."

I paid and took my receipt. As I left the store I wondered if it was possible Ernesto didn't tell the hospital staff he was on blood thinners. I shook my head. That didn't matter. Doug was there. He probably brought a baggie of Ernesto's medications too, just like the pharmacist said.

Back at my car I dry swallowed two pills.

There were no other cars in the senior center parking lot when I got there. Ah, a blessed few minutes where I could try to figure out how to help my actors memorize their lines.

I looked down the hallway past the dining room toward the kitchen, but the lights were off. As I dropped my coat, I heard a noise coming from the darkened dining room. It was probably just a mouse or something, but I've learned in the past few months, one can't be too careful. I quietly slid an umbrella from the ubiquitous stand in the lobby. I had renewed appreciation for how well-prepared the members of the Leetsdale Senior Center were.

Creeping down the hallway, I slowly peeked in the open door of the dining room. I waited while my eyes adjusted to the darkness. I didn't see anything. I was just about to leave and let that mouse go on about its business without me, when I saw the curtain dividing the Christmas Store and the dining room flutter, alarmingly like the backstage curtain did right before the set piece tried to smoosh me.

I gripped my umbrella tighter and tiptoed past the tables and chairs.

I reached the partition with the Christmas store just in

time to see Stephanie skulking around again. For the third time I watched her steal items from the tables.

I'd had enough.

I stormed over to her and grabbed her arm with my left hand, waving the umbrella overhead with my right, surprising and scaring her. She tried to pull away but I held tight. I kept my voice down in case Bobby was around. "I didn't want to believe it, but how dare you steal from a charity and from that wonderful child of yours. Your desire to get high shouldn't supersede his needs."

I expected her to fight me, but instead, she went limp.

She leaned in and whispered. "I'm not stealing. Bobby is."

"Bobby? What?" I couldn't believe it. I dropped my grip on her.

"I know he has no money, but I keep finding expensive things hidden in his room so I'm bringing them back before anyone finds out. I don't want him to follow my same path in life."

I waved a hand around the tables. "None of this stuff is expensive. I mean it is, but it was donated and they're letting the kids buy it for hardly anything."

"We have less than *hardly anything*. We told Bobby that Santa will bring him something, but that we didn't have any extra money to spend on any other gifts, and that includes for me and Carlos."

I didn't know whether to believe her or not. I mean, this was the woman who tried to crush me under a cute picture of Santa's workshop. What was less charitable than that?

Stephanie scurried past me and dropped an emerald green lacquered box on the table. She opened it and plucked out an ear cuff and returned it to the display with the others.

I picked up the box and the ear cuff and cradled them, rubbing my thumb on the smooth box. "I actually bought these for Bobby."

Stephanie suddenly stiffened, muscles taut. "I knew you were up to something!"

"What are you talking about?"

"I've heard about women like you, insinuating your way into the heart of a child to get to the parent."

"Stephanie, I don't know what you're talking about." I raised my palms, not sure if she was completely unhinged or not. "I have a boyfriend. I have no designs on your family. I mean, I like Bobby, he's a really great kid, but he doesn't deserve to be treated this way."

She didn't seem to be listening. "Did you buy all those things for him?"

"No, just the box and the ear cuff. What did Carlos say when you told him you thought Bobby was stealing?"

"I didn't tell him. He has enough to worry about with me and I thought I could fix everything by myself. But I can't. I just make everything worse." Stephanie suddenly began weeping, covering her face with her hands.

Her sobs reminded me of my mother's, in the days after my dad was killed. Gut-wrenching sounds that bubbled up from the depths of grief. I placed my palm in the middle of her back and rubbed in small circles until she calmed.

"Why don't you talk to Bobby about all this?" I said quietly.

Stephanie roughly wiped her face with both hands. "Why would he listen to me? Everyone tells him I'm just a junkie and a petty thief."

Bobby hurried over and stepped between us. "But you're not! You haven't used since you got back from rehab—"

"You knew about that?" Stephanie's hand fluttered to her mouth.

"Of course I knew. I'm a kid, that doesn't make me stupid. You're just like in the play … sometimes naughty, sometimes nice. But you're my mom and you're trying and that's all that matters."

They hugged and when they pulled away, I pressed the lacquered box and the ear cuff into Bobby's hands. "Remember what you told me the other day?" He nodded. "Well, your mom thought you were stealing and she was putting everything back so you wouldn't get in trouble."

Bobby faced his mother. "And I was thinking you were stealing from me so you could buy drugs."

"Baby, why didn't you say anything?" Stephanie looked on the verge of tears again.

"And get you in trouble? You're my mom, I love you!"

I thought about how tight money was at their house. Carlos had mentioned it, and now Stephanie had. I bent at the waist to look him directly in the eyes. "Bobby … were you stealing?"

"No!"

"How'd you get the money?"

"I worked for it."

I narrowed my eyes. "Worked how?"

"I did jobs for people."

"When?" I asked. "You're always here."

"I worked here." He ticked them off on his fingers. "Don paid me to alphabetize books in the basement and sort the puzzles by number of pieces. Barb paid me to run the crumb catcher around after lunch. Thelma had me pick up every piece of snipped thread in her sewing area so it wouldn't be a tripping hazard for the seniors. Only she called them *old farts*." Bobby giggled. "And Ozzi paid me to wrap his Christmas gifts."

Stephanie pulled him into a hug. "I never should have doubted you."

"Me neither," I said. Nor should I have expected anything less from Don, Barb, and Ozzi. Thelma continued to surprise me, however. None of those chores needed to be done, but they recognized Bobby's need to earn money. I wondered how many other kids had been doing unnecessary chores around here to earn money to spend in the Christmas store. Geez, I loved these people.

I asked Bobby if his dad was here too.

"He's unloading some stuff from his truck out behind the stage door."

That explains why there were no cars in the parking lot. "I need you to do something for me. Go park yourself near the front door. Whenever any cast or crew member comes in, tell them we're having a dress rehearsal the minute everyone gets here. Then send them back to get their costumes on immediately. We're going to get through this play without interruption today, or … or … or … nobody gets any dessert today!"

Bobby's eyes widened. "That's the worst punishment ever!" he said before running off.

I turned toward Stephanie. "Now it's your turn to come clean." I winced at my word choice, but she didn't even flinch. "Why did you push that scenery over on me?"

"Why did I do what?"

"Push that scenery flat so it would land on top of me."

"When?"

"Saturday."

"I have no idea what you're talking about."

"You were skulking around, arguing with Carlos backstage…"

"I remember that, but you're crazy if you think I'd push scenery over."

Maybe she was one of those literal thinkers. "Okay, so you didn't push the scenery on purpose, but you removed the sandbags so an accidental shove would have the same result."

"You're crazy, I did no such thing. Something like that could ruin the canvas and wreck all the hard work from those stagehands."

We stared at each other until I said, "You don't like me. I heard you tell Carlos to keep me away from Bobby. Seems like you might want to hurt me just the teensiest bit."

Stephanie's face softened. "You're right. I didn't like you. You were always hanging around Bobby and I guess I just got … jealous."

"Jealous? You're his mom!"

She sighed. "I know. But I don't act like one all the time."

I thought about my mom after my dad died. She could barely take care of herself, much less two teenagers. "I don't think it's possible to be the perfect mom twenty-four hours a day."

"I don't even think I can claim twenty-four *minutes* a day," she said glumly.

I smiled at her. "I think you're wrong. Bobby is a great kid and you're his mom. Seems you're doing *something* right."

I felt good about our conversation and went off to take advantage of the remaining quiet time. Would my luck hold out long enough for me to find something to help Doug and Daisy memorize their lines?

By the time Doug walked into the multi-purpose room, I had something that might help.

"I found a website with advice about memorizing your lines. I want you to take the sections you're having trouble with and handwrite them as many times as you can. It's supposed to help."

"That might work," Doug said, nodding. "I don't know why I'm having so much trouble. It's possible I bit off more than I can chew. Back when I was a more serious actor, I didn't have a full-time job, especially a brand-new full-time job that took me by surprise. Plus, I was younger. It's amazing I can remember my own name." He chuckled.

"Speaking of remembering things, there's something that's been bugging me."

"Is it that scene at the end? I think I've figured out where I'm supposed to stand."

"No, it's not that. It's about Ernesto."

"What about him?"

"Which hospital did you take Ernesto to that night?"

He told me then asked why I wanted to know. "Did you find out something?"

"No, but something's bothering me. I just want to check it out. It's probably nothing."

"Let me know if I can do anything else."

"Just learn those lines!" I curled up in Santa's throne and looked up the number to the hospital while I still had a few minutes. I called and asked to speak with the ER Department.

"Is this an emergency?"

"No, I'm actually looking to find out something that happened to my friend when he had an ER visit."

"Oh, then you'll want Records. But unless you have a power-of-attorney they won't give you any information."

"Can you connect me anyway?"

She did and almost immediately a man's voice asked me if he could help me.

"I hope so, I'm trying to verify records for an ER visit Ernesto Santiago had late Saturday December eighth, or early Sunday December ninth."

"And you are?"

"A friend of his."

"Do you have his power-of-attorney?"

"I don't." I paused. "But he's dead. Does that matter?"

"To me or to him?"

"I don't—"

"Listen, unless you have standing to request records, they won't be released. If you do have standing, go to our website and download the request form. Fax both items to the number listed."

This was a dead end. "Thanks."

I called Lance, even though I knew what he was going to say. "Hey, can you get me somebody's ER records?"

"Sure, if I want to get fired. Who did you have in mind?"

I explained briefly what I was looking to find out.

"You're involved in another murder? What is *wrong* with you?"

"I'm not *involved* in another murder … I'm just … I guess … well, maybe."

"Oh, for Pete's—"

"I'm not doing it on purpose. I'm just cursed or something."

"I'm going to save you from yourself. No, I can't get you somebody's hospital records."

"Please?"

"No! I can't believe you're even asking me. I thought you watched TV. Surely that's crime drama rule number one. Nobody just waltzes in and willy-nilly gets medical records. Besides, I couldn't even if I wanted to. Not my case, not my jurisdiction."

"I knew you were going to say that."

"Then why'd you call me?"

"Just wanted to hear the dulcet tones of your voice. I love it when it gets all cranky and high-pitched like that."

Lance laughed even though I knew he was irked with me. I absolutely knew he wouldn't do it for me, but I also knew that sometimes if I planted a seed in his brain, that he'd come up with some alternative way for me to get what I wanted. Maybe this would be one of those times.

"Go soak your head," he said, offering one of our childhood insults.

"Love you."

"Love you too. Weirdo."

As I shoved my phone in my pocket, my hand brushed the soft velvet of Santa's throne. Rubbing my thumb back and forth, changing the nap of the fabric with each pass, I stared, mesmerized at how with only a gentle brush of a finger, I could make such a dramatic change. A profound metaphor swirled up in there that I couldn't quite land on, but in the case of the upholstery, it was literal: altering the color from

Kelly green to forest green. I wondered if Daisy had been equally mesmerized the other day as she did the same thing to the throne. At least up until the moment she hauled off and tried to punt it across the stage.

Recalling that day and her comment about "those people" made my blood boil again.

I went in search of her and found her coming out of the restroom. I stepped in front of her in the lobby. "What did you mean when you referred to the women of the Tamale Brigade as *those people*?"

I'd clearly caught her off guard because she stammered, "Those … people?"

"Yes," I said impatiently. "*Those people* who are working their butts off trying to deck the halls by making mounds of tamales to help their kids' school fundraiser be successful." I didn't wait for her to respond, but it didn't look like she was going to anyway. "What is the point of all your racist comments, anyway? What are you trying to accomplish? If it's anything other than making you look petty and foolish, you haven't succeeded." I stared at her and thought about her being related to Ernesto and kicking that throne so violently. "Did you slip Ernesto a lethal dose of ibuprofen so you could inherit his money?"

She gasped and stepped backward as if I'd slapped her.

"What? No! I was just getting to know him. I didn't want him dead!" She took a step away from me, incredulous. "You knew he was my uncle?"

And she knew Ernesto was her uncle. "You were listed as his next of kin or something," I said haltingly. I wondered how much trouble Doug would get into for revealing that information to me.

"He … knew who I was?" Daisy's words came out barely louder than a breath.

They both knew, but neither spoke of it? That's messed up. "Why all the secrecy?"

"Because that would change everything. I wanted to see for myself."

"See what?" I narrowed my eyes at her.

"If what my dad always said was true." Daisy's voice quavered.

"And what's that?"

Daisy blinked twice then took a deep breath. "Ernesto was married to my dad's older sister for a long time, until she died. I guess she ran off with him over the family's objections. Yes, because he wasn't white." She set her jaw, answering a question I hadn't asked. "Dad's family was rich, they had standing in the community. They thought they'd lose that." Daisy's face softened and she averted her eyes to study one of her fingernails. "You know that saying about being born on third base and thinking you hit a triple?" Her voice became stronger as she spoke.

I nodded.

"That's my dad. I've come to realize that Ernesto was really the more successful person. Dad ran Grandpa's business into the ground."

"So you decided to get your hands on some of Ernesto's estate? Worm your way into his life?" Her scheme was beginning to make more sense to me.

"It's not like that. The more I got to know him, the more I wanted to be part of his family, even if mine didn't want him."

I wondered if she was telling the truth. Had she already talked him into adding her to his will or something? His wife was dead, and I didn't think he had any children, so it would make sense she could wiggle into his good graces. "Did you and Ernesto talk about any of that?"

"No. I just wanted to meet him is all. But he'd never be welcomed back into our family. My dad blames him for everything. What difference would it make if Ernesto and I talked about it?"

"Then why are you so disparaging? All those awful comments." I wrinkled my nose.

Daisy looked surprised. "They were just jokes."

"Jokes are supposed to be funny. But not at the expense of someone else. Not to denigrate an entire group of people."

"I guess. My whole family talks like that. I never really thought about it before." She studied her fingernail again. "At least until I heard Bobby and Carlos tell that story about being yelled at to go home. I can totally see my dad doing something like that."

She raised her eyes but not her head to look at me. I didn't know what to say, though. It seemed I had no experience or wisdom to share. But I did have a question. "Why'd you kick the Santa throne?"

"I was angry."

"Clearly, but why specifically?" *Was she cut out of Ernesto's will? Did she learn her racist family had something to do with Ernesto's death? Did Detective Ming take my advice and talk to her?*

"Because now I'll never get any more time to get to know my uncle. He could be annoying as hell, but I liked him. I really did."

Gazing into her sad, pale face, I believed her. And felt guilty for siccing Detective Ming on her.

"Wanna know something funny?" she said. "My mom is from the Netherlands, moved here when she was in her twenties. I can almost guarantee she's never had anyone yell at her on the street and tell her to go back where she came from."

We were quiet for a moment, then I said, "You know, I think everyone has a book of their life. We fill our pages with everything that happens to us, everything we learn. I think you should underline this event and refer to it as often as you need to. You're an adult, Daisy. You get to decide if you really want to move through the world like your dad, sneering at anyone who is simply trying to move through their world too."

She chewed that over for a minute then said simply, "I guess."

I watched her wander away, passing Leona who seemed to be intent on moving through the world sneering at me. Except she was just standing there with her arms crossed, glaring at me.

~

I had high hopes for my morning dress rehearsal plans. But even though most of my actors and crew showed up mostly ready to work, thanks to Bobby making sure they knew about my threat about dessert, lunchtime came before Thelma, Barb, and I even managed to grapple with the wardrobe malfunctions.

Chef Joe stuck his head inside the multi-purpose room and told us lunch was ready.

The kids started to run for the door before one of them came to a crashing halt. "Do we get dessert?"

Everyone, old and young alike, began talking about dessert until I clapped my hands twice. The sound was drowned out by the rumble from the furnace. My hair swirled in front of my face and I batted it out of my mouth. I organized myself, expecting to see others doing the same. But nobody was. *Why was I the only one bothered by the furnace in here?* I looked at the ceiling, then at the clumps of seniors standing around. None of them were under the vents. Either by luck or design—probably design—they all knew where to stand so as not to be buffeted by the blast. And the kids clearly didn't care.

The rumble died down and I again clapped twice. This time I was heard. When everyone quieted, I narrowed my eyes and glanced around at them. They needed to see I meant business. "Here's the deal. You can have dessert if—and only if—you keep your costumes on and don't spill a drop of anything anywhere on them."

Don patted his stuffed Santa belly. "Uh oh," he said, to much laughter.

I tried not to smile. "After lunch, come straight back here. We are going to run through the entire play with no pauses. That means" —I looked pointedly at Doug and Daisy— "nobody gets any cues. Everyone *must* get their lines right, come in at the right time, and hit your marks. We only have this afternoon and tomorrow to nail this down before the performance on Saturday."

They all saw I meant business and sobered up, at least momentarily, when they heard how close show time was. But then they whooped and hollered and hurried to the dining room for lunch.

I let them leave before me while I jotted a list of names of the people who still needed some costume TLC before I headed to lunch.

While I filled a plate with tater tots and tuna casserole, my head began throbbing again. I thought about what the pharmacist told me. Searching for Doug, I slipped into a seat next to him.

He moved his plate to make a bit more room for me. He leaned close and asked quietly, "Did you find out what you needed from the hospital?"

"Not really. I wanted to ask you again about when you took Ernesto to the hospital. Are you sure you told them he was on blood thinners? Did you bring his medications with you?"

Doug thought for a moment. "I did. I gave them all of Ernesto's medications. I took them from his medicine chest. I didn't know what some of them were, but I gave them everything I found. Why? What's going on?"

"I don't know. I've just been thinking about all this. It

doesn't add up. How can someone get hit in the head with a piece of Styrofoam and just collapse the next day?"

"I know. I can't stop thinking about it. It's so sad and scary."

"I know Ernesto's wife died and they didn't have kids, but did he have a roommate? Anybody visiting him? He was alone that night?"

"As far as I know."

"So if he was treated for his headache in the emergency room, and nobody gave him any ibuprofen, then why did he die?" I pushed my tuna casserole around on my plate.

"Maybe the ER gave him something by mistake." Doug bit a tater tot off his fork.

"If they did, that's malpractice." I looked up at him. "Was Daisy Ernesto's next of kin, or just his emergency contact at work?"

Doug looked concerned. "Wouldn't the police or coroner or somebody have notified the next of kin already? Daisy hasn't mentioned anything."

I shrugged. "I'm pretty sure somebody would have been notified of his death, but his next of kin might want to look into the malpractice idea, if they're not already going down that road." Maybe that was why Detective Ming didn't want to talk about the emergency room records. Did police investigate medical malpractice? I had no idea. The pharmacist was pretty sure that the ER staff would check for any problems with mixing medications, though.

"Is it possible Ernesto took some of that ibuprofen anyway? Maybe before you got there?"

"What ibuprofen?" Doug asked.

I sighed. "It seems my bottle found its way to Ernesto's house that night. He probably just pocketed it without thinking. But if his head was hurting so bad when he called you, maybe he got desperate and took some. I know I've had some headaches that I thought were going to kill me if I didn't get some relief. Maybe the pain made him forget what we told him about the ibuprofen."

Doug stared at the far wall, tapping his fork on his plate while he mulled that over. When he turned to face me he said, "That's a definite possibility. He couldn't even work the seatbelt. I had to buckle him in my car myself. He couldn't even manage it. And then when I started the car I felt so bad that the boys left the radio on so loud. It must have really done a number on his head if he was in that much pain."

"That poor man."

We were almost the last ones to finish lunch. I picked up his empty plate with mine. "Can you go start gathering up everyone in the basement for rehearsal? I'll make a sweep up here."

Doug hurried off to round up the actors while I grabbed a couple of my extras still in the dining room.

It seemed my seriousness about the looming performance lit a fire under everyone. Costumes got arranged quickly. No food spilled on anything, at least none that couldn't be easily rubbed off. Scenery rolled easily and remained upright. Voices were loud and theatrical. Lines were spoken, often exactly as written. Dogs acted like dogs and cats like cats. Blocking was remembered. Nobody crashed into anyone.

Maybe we were going to pull off this performance after all.

TWENTY

Saturday, the day of the performance, dawned overcast, but I didn't care. We weren't in the grip of that awful polar vortex anymore and yesterday we had two—two!—perfect run-throughs of the play.

Ozzi and I slept in, woke up for a while, then went back to sleep. When we finally got up, we ate a leisurely and enormous breakfast of French toast, bacon, and eggs.

"Are you nervous about tonight?" he asked.

"Surprisingly, no. We've had three good rehearsals in a row, so I think everything will come off perfectly fine." I bit into my last piece of crispy bacon. "And I heard they sold all the tickets to the show, too."

"You've certainly done your part to make this event a rousing success."

I feigned shock and put my finger to my lips. "Don't say that! They might ask me to do it again." I cleared our plates. "You wash, I'll dry."

"I'll do both. But don't get used to it. Go take a long bubble bath and get ready for your debut. When do you have to be there?"

"I told everyone to be there at three o'clock, but I'm planning on being there by one. Just in case."

When I emerged from my ablutions at twelve-thirty, trailing the scents of lilac, vanilla, jasmine, cherry blossoms, and dentist-approved wintergreen, Ozzi was gone. He left me a note, though. *Barb asked me to help usher so I'll see you around six. Love you!*

"Love you too," I said to the note.

Before I left, I texted my critique group and Lavar and Tuttle that I left tickets for them at Will Call, which was really just an accordion file in the lobby. *If nobody is around, they're filed under my name. Just grab them. You probably won't get tased.*

There were several cars in the senior center parking lot when I got there. I even saw Winston's car in one of the handicapped spaces. A light dusting of snow covered it. Slow but steady icy pellets stung my face as I hurried in.

Winston and Javier had their noses together at a table in the lobby, studying an iPad.

"What's so interesting?" I pulled off my gloves while trying to sneak a peek.

"Weather app," Winston said.

"We're making sure about the weather," Javier added.

"Making sure?" I asked.

They both nodded.

"Storm might be headed this way, so we're just tracking it," Winston said. "Gotta be prepared." In unison, he and Javier said, "Like Boy Scouts!" They performed a soft high five before turning back to the iPad. "Stupid thing isn't showing us snow totals, though." I knew Winston was frustrated because he moved his wheelchair back and forth really fast a couple of times. "The only thing people care about."

"Maybe that means it's not going to snow much," I said hopefully.

"Fingers crossed," he said. "But I think the graupel is going to change over to real snow when the sun goes down."

I walked into the multi-purpose room humming "Silent Night." All *is* calm, I thought with a smile, despite the graupel.

I didn't see anyone on stage, but the curtain was definitely swaying. The hanging stars were still, however, so I knew it wasn't from the blast of the furnace. *Maybe Carlos came in early to check on everything.* I went backstage to see if he thought all the scenery was under control.

But Carlos wasn't there. I knew he typically unloaded things from his truck and brought them through the back door, so I started in that direction.

Suddenly I smelled smoke and panicked. I flung things out of the way, searching for any flames. I gave the stage curtains a good shake to peer under them all at once. Nothing.

In the very back, near the door, I knew were some containers of leftover paint and solvents. I hurried back there to check on them, just in time to see Leona open the door to the outside. I thought about what she said about doing everything in her power to make sure this event went well, how much she argued against having Ernesto involved and then he died, how she was the one who found the sabotaged star *and* the hidden sandbag.

Was she behind everything all along? Was she plotting some new trickery?

I crept down the passageway behind her, keeping an eye on her backlit form in the open door. As I drew closer, I saw she was leaning casually against the jamb.

Having a cigarette.

"Leona?"

She whirled around, stubbing out her cigarette with her shoe.

"What are you doing smoking in here?" I pointed to the solvents. "This is not a safe place to smoke."

Leona looked like she wanted to bolt out the door.

"Come in here and close that door," I snapped. Suddenly I had a revelation. "Wait. Is this why you're always skulking around? Were you looking for a place to smoke inside, out of the polar vortex, when you found my metal art, the snowflake, and that sandbag in the basement?"

"Fine." She surrendered, hands in the air. "You caught me. I'm an idiot and this is a filthy habit." Her voice had a sadness I hadn't heard before. "I figured you'd try to publicly out me." She tried to see behind me. She raised her voice. "You can come out now, kids. Miss Russo caught me."

I looked over my shoulder to see who she was talking to. Nobody was behind me. "Who are you talking to?"

"The kids. Everyone you told I was smoking that first day," she said bitterly.

"What in the world are you talking about? I didn't tell anyone you were smoking. I didn't even know you smoked until just now."

"You didn't rat me out?"

"Why would I do that?"

Leona looked confused. "I don't know, but the kids all seemed to know these last few days. How else would they know?"

"Because they're smart? Because they saw you?" I did not understand this conversation.

Leona tried to peer behind me again. She seemed surprised that an army of children from her school hadn't jumped out from the dark, point at her, and shout, "*J'accuse!*"

Suddenly, she turned back to face me. "I just processed what you said. You think I've been skulking?"

"I saw you stub out your cigarette. Of course I think you've been smoking."

"No. *Skulking.* You said I've been skulking around, finding the star, finding the sandbag." She got right in my face. "Are you accusing me of trying to sabotage this event when I very distinctly heard you tell Daisy you were going to *wreck McFalls* and *undermine this event*."

"What are you talking about?"

"Because I'll have you know, the last thing—the very last thing—I'd do is sabotage this event. If this doesn't go well tonight, I'm going to have to lay off half my staff."

"Is that why you accused *me* of sabotaging the star and hiding that sandbag? All I was doing was hiding things until I could decide what I wanted to give to Barb." Suddenly the conversation I had with Daisy came back to me and I began to laugh. "We weren't trying to *wreck McFalls*. We were watching the Tamale Brigade *deck the halls* with mounds of tamales. And I wasn't going to *undermine* this event. I wanted Daisy to *underline* it ... you know, remember it."

Leona didn't appear to have heard me. "And I can't believe I okayed a plan to sell Christmas gifts to children! Kids don't have any money! So what if all the items were donated? We haven't made any money from the store!" She again processed my words a bit late. She stared at me, then began to sing softly, rolling the words around in her mouth, testing them out. "Wreck McFalls with mounds of tamales. Fa la la la la, lalalala."

I joined in and sang, "Tis the season to adopt collies. Fa la la la la, lalalala."

"Don we now our major barrel, falala, lalala, lalala."

"Stroll the ancient lakeside peril."

We finished in unison with loud *fa la las*, then convulsed in laughter.

"Not only do I need to quit smoking, I need to get my hearing checked too."

"Or quit eavesdropping and jumping to conclusions."

"That too. I'm really sorry for all this, Charlee. And for tattling to Detective Ming about you."

"Oh, don't worry about that. He has a way of showing up out of the blue. It was only a matter of time."

She was quiet for a bit. "But if you didn't hide that star and the sandbag, then who did?"

"I wish I knew."

"And you're sure you didn't tell the kids I smoked?"

"Absolutely not. It's none of my business." I paused. "Even though it really sets a bad example."

"I know," she moaned. "But I'm so stressed out about money, I picked up the habit again. I'm so stupid. Quitting smoking was the hardest thing I ever did, and I just threw it all away."

Leona started to hyperventilate so I moved her to a chair and forced her head between her knees. "Just take some deep breaths," I urged.

She sat up. "I can't!" she wailed. "I'm a *smoker*!"

I chuckled and pushed her back down. "You're also a drama queen. Settle down."

Leona calmed down and began breathing normally after I convinced her there was nothing more she could have done, and that everything was going to come off without a hitch tonight. "We've had three perfect rehearsals and Thelma and her minions fixed all the little costume snafus. The performance will be perfect." Leona looked dubious, but I gave her some melodramatic and overzealous nodding until she bobbed her head the teensiest bit. "Atta girl!" I pulled her to her feet. "Now let's go get this show on the road!

TWENTY-ONE

As the actors and crew arrived, Leona and I shuttled them in the appropriate direction, sending them off with a cheery affirmation of some kind as they brushed the snow off their heads and shoulders. *You'll do great! This will be the most fun you've had in ages! When Santa sees your performance, he'll put you on the Nice List forever!* And other white lies.

After the crush of cast members slowed to a trickle, I left Leona to do the shuttling and affirming. I headed to the kitchen storage area.

I searched high and low until I found what I was looking for. I grabbed a marker and a sheet of paper and wrote HELP YOUR COMMUNITY! DONATE TO THE 56TH AVENUE SCHOOL! I taped it over a picture of a buzzing bee and the "Sun Tea" lettering on the front of a large jar.

Dragging a table into the center of the lobby, I placed the donation jar in front of the "Will Call" accordion file for tickets so nobody would miss it. Hopefully that would pull in some more donations for the school.

I hurried toward the dining room, which we designated as the actors' green room, and poked my head in. Thelma and her costume committee were frantically getting everyone in the right costume. The buzz of conversation was constant, but low, at least until one kid yelled, "Where are my Dalmatian ears? A Dalmatian can't have brown ears!" One of the adults scurried over with the correct ears and the crisis was averted.

Backing out of the green room before anyone saw me, I headed to the multi-purpose room. We didn't have a good way to keep the doors shut and the audience out, but decided we'd put out refreshments for sale before the show as well as afterward and perhaps fill the coffers with a bit more cash. I glanced at the refreshment area and saw the tables set up with festive tablecloths and centerpieces. Perfect.

Rows and rows of chairs had been placed across the multi-purpose room. Audience members were already beginning to arrive, but they milled around in the back of the room. Probably parents of kids in the play who didn't want to make two trips through the snow to the senior center.

As I reached the front of the room, I stood with my back to the stage and looked out. Uh oh. Like Blanche DuBois, I needed to rely on the kindness of strangers. I approached two couples standing together chatting.

One of the women said, "Are you involved with the play? The stage looks darling! We've been hearing so much about this, I'm glad it's finally here."

"Thanks, I am too. But can you guys do me a favor? When these chairs got set up, they forgot to leave a center aisle. Can you take two or three chairs from the center and move them to the other end? That'll make everything so much easier to maneuver around." They happily agreed to help and I thanked them profusely.

Another crisis averted. *This was going great!*

I took the steps up the stage, scanning to see that everything was ready on stage for the first act. Perfect.

I heard Daisy's voice backstage. I wanted to prod her to get moving into her costume so she could help out in the green room, wrestling kids into costumes. As I stepped around the curtain, though, I saw she was already in costume, talking to Carlos and Bobby.

"—sorry for those things I said and hope you can forgive me."

"Of course we can," Carlos said with a smile.

Bobby clearly needed more, however. "So why'd you say all that stuff then?"

"Because I'm dumb. Or I was, but you taught me some things I didn't know, things I never thought about." She looked at Carlos. "You should be proud of him."

"I'm proud of him every day." Carlos draped an arms across Bobby's shoulder.

Daisy turned and I scampered over to the prop table so she wouldn't know I'd been eavesdropping. She passed me without a word.

I checked over the props. Everything was there, but I switched a couple of items around to make them easier to grab in case the actors were in a hurry. As I was admiring the layout on the table, Barb rushed up behind me.

"Charlee! Paula forgot that she volunteered to be in charge of the treats we were going to sell to the audience!"

"Paula?" Barb and I met her at the pie-judging contest a while back. Her memory was like a sieve. I didn't say anything, but Barb must have read my face.

"I know, I know. She said she'd get her daughter to help, but she must have forgotten that too."

I put my arm around Barb. "This is not a problem. We have the tamales already packaged by the dozen in the freezer. Those need to come out. And for the sweets to eat tonight, you can run back to my apartment. I have all those goodies in my freezer. They'll thaw by the time the play is over. Oh, and grab the ones off my kitchen table. I was going to take those to Ozzi's office party tomorrow. We can sell those before the show. There's plenty of time. Let me just get you my apartment keys." I stopped short. "Wait. I don't want you driving in this snowstorm." I pushed her toward the kitchen. "You go make the coffee. I'll get Ozzi to run back for the cookies."

Barb hurried off to the kitchen and I stood on the stage and scanned the crowd until I saw Ozzi taking off his coat and draping it over a front row seat. I raced down to meet him.

"What's wrong?" he asked.

"I need you to go back to my apartment and grab all the Christmas cookies and treats you can find in my freezer. And the ones on the table."

"Charlee, the snow is piling up. My Prius barely made it here. I'm not sure it would do it a second time."

I frantically looked around to see who else could help. Maybe Carlos. I ran backstage with Ozzi close behind. When I found him, he was giving a pep talk to his crew.

"Carlos, is everything under control back here?"

"Surprisingly, yes."

Carlos was so calm and smiled so big I couldn't help but relax. Cookies were a tiny problem. I explained the situation.

He dug in his pocket and pulled out his keys. "Ozzi can take my truck. No worries."

Ozzi accepted the keys.

"You can drive a stick shift, right?" Carlos said.

"To my eternal shame, no I can't." He handed the keys back.

I searched for AmyJo. She grew up on a farm. She could drive anything. Too bad she wasn't here yet. "You can both go. Ozzi knows the way and—" I almost said *and you know how to drive* but I bit off the words just in time. I recovered by saying, "And it'll take both of you to carry all those cookies. There's plenty of time to get there and get back." They hurried off. "Be careful!" I shouted after them.

Another crisis averted. *I'm getting good at this.*

I texted Lavar and Tuttle. *Can you guys bring some butter braids to donate to the cause?* I didn't wait for a reply. They'd either get it before they arrived, or they wouldn't.

I went to the kitchen to start bringing out the tamales, leaving a dozen with my name on them in the freezer. I hand-wrote a cardboard placard offering a dozen tamales for twenty dollars. I threw it away and changed it to thirty bucks. This was a fundraiser, after all.

Barb was placing small pitchers of cream, sugar, spoons, cups, and a bowl stuffed with every type of artificial sweetener you could imagine next to the forty-cup coffee urn on the rolling cart. It was much too heavy to carry all the way from the kitchen to the refreshment area in the multi-purpose room. We loaded the tamales on the bottom of the cart and I helped her push it down the hall. I lifted the urn from the cart and set it on the table near the plug. I plugged it in and remembered to push the power button while Barb set everything else around it. As I got ready to return the cart to the kitchen, I glanced at the empty table that was supposed to be for the non-existent cookies and goodies. "Do you think we could sell each cup of coffee for fifty bucks?"

Barb glanced at the folded table cards she was just about to set out that read, *Donations Welcome for Refreshments.* "Or I could just have Don stand here with a bandana around his face saying 'Stick 'em up, you lonesome polecat' and hope people would empty their wallets."

"Sure, let's try that." I smirked and hurried away with the empty cart.

After I ditched it, I stepped into the dining room. The noise level reminded me of the one and only heavy metal concert I attended in college. There was less head thrashing, but even so, things did not look in control in here.

Thelma sat in the corner, a dazed look on her face.

Gloria Mae frantically tried to hand sew a ripped seam on Felix's trousers.

He kept squirming, saying, "If you jab me again, Gloria Mae, I swear I will drop trou right here in front of God and everyone!"

"For someone who has no compunction about grabbing unwilling dance partners wherever the spirit moves you, you sure are touchy about being grabbed yourself." Gloria Mae threatened him with her needle until he meekly acquiesced.

Another committee member was trying to console a sobbing boy with one hand, and with the other, trying to keep other kids—and Peter O'Drool—away from a pile of vomit on the floor in front of them.

I raced for the rolling bucket and mop and shooed them all away. I mopped with my eyes shut, in a valiant attempt to keep myself from sympathy barfing. I finished without incident, unless you count several dry heave false alarms.

After stashing the mop and bucket in the utility closet, offering up a fervent prayer that I remembered to rinse them out later, I crashed into Lance in the hallway.

He squinched his entire face. "What did you do, Space Case?"

"It wasn't me." At the dining room door, I pointed out the little boy, looking as weak and wan as poor Tiny Tim. "He barfed. Can you rinse out the mop in the closet and make sure he's okay?"

"On it." He crossed the room in three strides and took a knee in front of the boy.

I hurried back to Thelma and patted her on the shoulder. "Are you okay?"

She slowly looked up at me.

I asked her again and she nodded.

I hoped I didn't look as dubious as I felt. "Are you sure? You have to be on stage soon, and in your Mrs Claus costume."

She pointed a gnarled finger at her costume hanging over a wardrobe rack. "Getting it on now," she said, not moving.

"If you're not up to—"

"I'll be fine," she snapped. "Just as soon as I get away from all these … actors." She said it like a cotton farmer would say "boll weevil."

I handed her the Mrs Claus outfit. "Go get this on. Take a breath before we go on."

She stood and accepted the hanger from me.

Gloria Mae snipped a piece of thread from the seat of Felix's pants.

"Finally!" He hurried away, his hand feeling the new seam.

"What do you need me to do?" I asked her.

She stretched a kink from her shoulders. "I don't know what happened, except for Felix. He thought this was the perfect time to show the kids how to dance like a Cossack." She looked up at me, weariness covering her face. "It was not."

"So everything else is okay?"

She laughed. "Oh my goodness, no! All the elf costumes are falling apart. Thelma thought it would be a good idea to glue those costumes together, since they're mostly made of felt."

"You can't sew on felt?"

"You can most assuredly sew on felt."

"Then why—never mind. What do we need to do?"

"In the office, there's a drawer next to the file cabinet. In that drawer you will find a stapler and staples. Bring them here and we'll lock these kids into their costumes so tight, they'll be Easter elves too."

I raced down the hall and rummaged around the office until I found not one, but two staplers, a box of staples, and a roll of neon orange duct tape. As I juggled the items while trying to close the office door, I heard Lavar come up next to me. "Looks like somebody needs a hand."

I dumped my stash into his hands, then pulled the office

door closed. "I'm so glad to see you guys. You too, Nova, my love." I took ten seconds to rub my hands on either side of her muzzle and adjust the green-and-red plaid bow around her neck. Nova's serenity instantly calmed me. I straightened up and she leaned against my leg, calming me even further.

Tuttle pressed four butter braids into my hands. "Two blueberry and two strawberry."

"You guys are lifesavers! But I need your help. Follow me." I led them to the dining room. "Gloria Mae," I called. "This is Lavar and Tuttle. They have staplers and duct tape. Put them to work."

Peter O'Drool raced over to Nova, one of his besties. She watched imperiously while he bounced and wheezed around her feet, elf costume twisting on his fat little body.

Whisking away the butter braids, I left Lavar and Tuttle, trusting they could finish the job with Gloria Mae in plenty of time. Another crisis averted. In the kitchen I found two trays and arranged slices of the pastries over them, spacing them far apart to make it look like we had more than we did. I hoped Ozzi and Carlos made it back soon.

As I placed the trays on the refreshment table, Ozzi and Carlos hustled in, still stamping snow from their feet, juggling the bounty Barb gave me from her cookie exchange party a couple of weeks ago. "Oh, thank goodness!" I kissed Ozzi and took the bags from Carlos before sending him back to his stagehands. "You're a lifesaver, Carlos!"

"Anything to help the school!"

A crowd formed around us while Ozzi and I placed cookies on the table. Over my shoulder I said to them, "Those butter braids are primo and already thawed. I'd go for those if I were you." I dumped two kinds of cookies on a paper plate. On a different plate I wrote, DONATIONS WELCOME and placed it nearby.

The crowd surged to the other end of the table. Out of the corner of my eye I saw people dropping dollar bills on the plate. One man with a distinctive salt-and-pepper goatee dropped a twenty and handed a slice of butter braid to the next person in line. "On me," he said. "Merry Christmas."

That set off a round of philanthropy I couldn't have imagined. Everyone began mimicking and trying to one-up each other's generosity, laughing and jostling.

I almost wept.

"That's my boss," Ozzi whispered. "The owner of the company."

"I adore him," I whispered back.

Another crisis averted.

I checked the time and went to see if they'd stapled the elves into their costumes yet. "You guys almost ready?" I called from the doorway. Lavar flashed me his blindingly white grin and a thumbs-up.

I clapped twice and the room went silent.

"Dayum," Tuttle said, impressed.

"Okay everyone. It's almost go-time. Everyone hold hands with your buddy." I waited for the mad scramble to cease and everyone stood next to their buddy.

Lavar and Tuttle looked at each other, shrugged, and raised their clasped hands in the air too.

"You're going to stay in here—*quietly*—until it's time for your scene. Miss Gloria Mae or your buddy will tell you when it's time to go to the stage. For now, though, I want everyone in Scene One and Scene Two to follow me. Two by two, next to your buddy." I turned at the doorway and waited for everyone to line up. "I want to talk to my elves for a minute." When all the childrens' eyes were on me, I said, "Remember how we practiced? Most of you aren't on stage until Scene Two, but you need to be ready when it's your cue, so you'll wait backstage, absolutely silently like little mice. Adults, when your buddy is done with their scene, bring them back here, or you can watch the rest of the play from the very back of the audience. Everybody remember what to do?"

When I saw nods all around, I raised one finger to my lips. "Okay … let's do this thing!"

When I reached the door to the multi-purpose room, I stopped them and gestured that they scoot against the wall. "Wait here," I whispered.

I walked out to the lobby to round up any straggling audience members and direct them into their seats. I saw only Javier and Winston coming in, brushing snow off themselves.

"Just in time," I said with a smile. "Enjoy the show!"

"Now I'll be able to," Winston said.

I checked the Will Call tickets folder and grinned when I saw there weren't any left in there. I peeked in the doorway of the multi-purpose room. Ozzi and Lance were setting up more chairs anywhere they could find space.

Standing room only. Leona will be thrilled about that.

I put one finger to my lips again and led my actor train through the doors and across the back of the room until we got to the far side. As we turned the corner and headed for the stage, the audience began to notice us. Heads swiveled and more than a few "Awww"s were uttered. I had to admit my cast looked perfectly adorable. Kids dressed as elves, adults looking dapper in their old-fashioned villager clothes.

My critique group was sitting together on the aisle of the third row. As I passed, AmyJo gave a little squeal and squeezed my hand. They all gave me an encouraging smile or a thumbs-up. Except Einstein who simply took it all in with his typical lack of emotion. I didn't take it personally.

I hurried my actors up the steps of the stage and out of sight of the audience. I checked in with Carlos. "Everything ready?" I whispered.

He nodded.

Leona walked over to us. "Time to start?"

"Yep."

"Okay. I'll go give the introduction." Leona walked to center stage to loud applause. She blushed and cleared her throat, waving at them to quiet down. When they did, she said, "I'm Leona McFalls, the principal of the 56th Avenue School." She was interrupted by whoops and hollers, and I was reminded this was truly a community event. Waving them quiet again, she continued. "As I'm sure most of you know, this is our biggest fundraiser of the year. I was so pleased to be able to partner with the Leetsdale Senior Center for this fundraiser. I want to give them a huge round of applause for opening their doors to our students so they'd have someplace fun—and free—to go during the winter break."

"It's fun for us too!" yelled Winston from his wheelchair on the far side of the room. The seniors whooped and hollered this time.

"I'm delighted everyone has enjoyed their time together," Leona continued. "I know both generations have benefitted from this event, and please know that it strengthens our school community and our larger community. Just know that we couldn't have done any of this without the senior center governing board and members. So, from the bottom of my heart, please accept my deepest thanks." When the applause died down, she added. "And thank you so much for coming out tonight and braving this snowstorm. Looks like we might have a white Christmas this year!" Another cheer erupted from the crowd. "So now, without further ado, I'm pleased to present Charlee Russo's funny and charming Christmas play, *Santa's Middling List*."

As I waited for Leona to return to her seat, I saw Lance and Ozzi on the far side of the room, sitting with Lavar and Tuttle. Nova sat primly at the end of the row, waiting patiently for the play to begin. I caught Ozzi's eye and wiggled my fingers at him. He blew me a kiss in return. I took a deep breath and motioned for Carlos to dim the lights for a minute and then bring them up to begin the show.

TWENTY-TWO

When the lights came up, the audience had context for the set they'd been seeing on stage, the corporate offices of Santa's Information Technology Department at the North Pole. Doug's character Figgy the elf sat at his desk pretending to type frantically on his computer. Figgy's friend, Elfy, played by Daisy, walked onstage.

The play began.

After a few lines, I released the breath I'd been nervously holding. Everything was going well. With a few exceptions where they paraphrased the script, Doug and Daisy had their lines down pretty good.

The audience laughed in the right places, always gratifying to an author. And when Daisy's pointy left shoe spat fell off, she surreptitiously kicked it away, and even, by some miracle, got rid of the right one without me even noticing.

Don's Santa entered to wild applause, mainly because he hammed it up and did that thing where he waggled his hand to curry an ovation from the audience. They ate it up.

I relaxed some more. Still on alert, of course, just a tad more composed.

But I must have jinxed something.

At the end of Scene One, Carlos' stagehands scurried out in the semi-dark pushing the scenery flats for Scene Two, with the intention of putting them into place, then moving the Scene One flats off stage. But when they gave them the sturdy pushes they'd practiced, the flats sailed right past the back-stage area and thunked into the wall. Carlos and I caught them before they caromed backward and fell.

The wide-eyed team of stagehands did their best to move the set pieces to their marks, causing more than a few titters from the audience.

I raised questioning eyes to Carlos, but he looked as confused and panicky as I was. We did a cursory survey of the flats we held and realized, with horror, there were no sandbags adding weight to keep them steady.

Both of our mouths turned into capital Os.

As silently as I could, I peered at the scenery flats on stage. No sandbags on them either. I raced to where the upcoming scenes' scenery stood.

No sandbags on any of them.

Scene Two was set in Santa's corporate office conference room. Santa sat on his throne at one end of a long table that also had Mrs Claus, Figgy, Figgy's boss Cranberry, Figgy's mom Merry, and a whole passel of elf extras.

The dialogue began.

I held my breath again, as if that alone could keep the flats from falling over.

But when the cast had to get up from the table and cluster around Santa's throne, the set pieces wobbled like crazy.

Thelma as Mrs Claus remained at the table. I knew she was supposed to stand too, because, well, I wrote it and we'd rehearsed it a gajillion times. I hissed at her, trying to get her attention. She slowly turned toward me and I saw she had that same dazed look she'd worn earlier. But now it mani-fested as an extreme case of stage fright.

My horrified gaze bounced between Thelma, the wobbling

scenery, and the audience. I dashed on stage, trying to keep hidden behind the scenery flats. Squatting down behind the one closest to Thelma, I whispered to her. "Thelma … Thelma … THELMA!" until she looked my way. I gestured wildly at her to come to me. She began to snap out of her daze, glancing at the action on stage.

I thought she was going to get her head back in the game but just then the scene ended and the stage went semi-dark. Thelma's eyes widened and her face froze again. I crawled over and grabbed her hand, dragging her behind the scenery with me.

The stagehands needed to change the scenery from Santa's conference room back to his workshop. Flats began sailing across the stage at a velocity not seen since the last NASA launch. As one flew past me, I stuck out my hand to grab it, not at all confident it wouldn't rip my arm off at the shoulder. It careened in a semi-circle and wobbled, much to the surprise of the kid dressed all in black pushing it. He started to say something, but I put my finger to my lips and waved him off stage with the flat I'd been sitting on with Thelma.

He pulled that one away and I helped Thelma sit on the brace of the new scenery flat. "Just sit here out of sight," I whispered.

"No! I want out of here!" Thelma struggled to stand, but the lights had come up and Doug had already began speaking Figgy's lines. I held her in place.

He saw Thelma and me arguing in pantomime behind the set piece, but like the trained thespian he assured us he was— many, many times—he didn't break character or miss a line.

With my lips directly in Thelma's ear I said, "If you get up from here, this flat will fall over and the audience will see Mrs Claus hiding back here. Do you want that?"

She shook her head vigorously and clung to the wooden frame as if it were something she salvaged from the deck of the Titanic as it sunk.

I crawled behind the other scenery pieces to make my way backstage.

Thelma, however, held on a bit too vigorously and the movement of her sensible crepe-soled shoes on the stage began inching the flat across the stage.

It wasn't long before it threatened to pass in front of Doug on stage. He was in the middle of his dialogue and as if it were the most natural thing in the world to have Santa's workshop migrate in front of him, he simply gave it a gentle push with his pointy elf shoe and sent it wobbling back the other direction.

Frantic, I ran up to Carlos. "We have to get your crew out there to sit on the scenery flats to keep them from falling over!"

"Then who will move everything and hand out props and stuff?" If my face looked anything like his, then surely we'd both need to be taken to the ER before this night was over.

He was right, of course. We needed the stagehands to keep doing their job. But how to keep the scenery from falling over?

I heard Heinrich's distinctive phlegmy laugh and had an idea. Hunched over, I scurried down the steps into the audience and slid to the floor next to AmyJo's seat in the third row. I dove headfirst in front of her and whispered to my critique group. "Emergency. Follow me. Hurry."

They quickly, but not very quietly, followed me backstage where we huddled. I pointed to the scenery flats. "I need two of you on each of those so they don't fall over."

"Why don't you use sandbags?" Einstein said.

"Long story. Just do it."

"For how long?" Cordelia asked, smoothing her five-hundred-dollar skirt suit.

"Till the end of the play."

"How will we know when the scenery needs to change?" Kell asked.

"You'll know because—"

"Because of your stellar storytelling skills," Jenica interrupted.

I stared at her then began laughing hysterically. AmyJo clamped a hand over my mouth and everyone backstage regarded me with great concern.

I took huge gulping gasps of air. "The actors and stage-hands will make sure you know. Or … well, I guess we'll find out. Do your best." I pointed Heinrich and Einstein to the farthest piece of scenery, AmyJo and Jenica to the one in the middle. Before sending Cordelia and Kell to their assignment, I whispered, "When the lights go down again, help Thelma up and tell her to get over here."

After what seemed like an eternity, the lights came down on Scene Three. The stagehands entered with Scene Four scenery flats as light as feathers, sending them streaking across the stage, but when they tried to push the Scene Three flats, weighted down by full-grown and well-fed adults, they couldn't budge them.

Scene Four was a short, silent scene where Figgy and Elfy tiptoed around the stage in an exaggerated manner, searching for Santa's trunk of magic tinsel.

The audience was beginning to catch on that something was wonky onstage. Titters and chuckles began.

My critique group caught on that they needed to move from the old set pieces to the new. Kell helped Thelma to her feet and pointed her offstage.

My admonition to my cast throughout our long rehearsals about not missing their cues, unfortunately took that moment to click. Doug and Daisy, as Figgy and Elfy, immediately came to the stage, while Thelma was wandering off. She walked directly in front of them.

They stopped, frozen mid-tiptoe, and didn't start again until she was safely backstage. The audience howled.

I felt a tug on my sleeve.

"Miss Charlee," one of the elf extras said. "My pants broke."

I looked down and sure enough, her pants, so meticulously stapled and taped before the show began, had a trail of duct tape dragging behind her. The outside seam, starting at the waistband and ending halfway down her thigh, flapped open, showing her green-and-white striped tights. I hurried to retape it, but the tape had been dragging for so long, all the sticky had been taken up by dirt from the floor.

Apparently Tuttle and Lavar had already been alerted to the costume fiasco, or had intuitively known it was impending, because they were already backstage performing triage on the elf costumes. If I could travel back in time, I might revisit Thelma's decision not to actually sew the elf costumes. No, I'd go back further, to talk Thelma out of being in charge of costumes. No, even further than that. To when I met Don and Barb and told them I was a writer. Then, maybe none of this would have happened.

Nova had followed Lavar and Tuttle backstage and she came to offer her condolences by bopping my thigh with her nose. I rubbed her velvety ears and calmed, ever so slightly.

Scene Five was coming to a close. This was where I'd originally written that fog would swirl around Figgy and Elfy as they magically transported to the Village of Middling. With a fog machine inaccessible, we had decided that Doug and Daisy would simply do the old "Wayne's World" thing with their fingers to show propulsion through time and space.

The audience howled with laughter, truly enjoying the actual play.

Despite the costume failures and the scenery failures and all the other micro-failures, I had to admit, we were pulling off this production.

As Scene Five ended and Scene Six began, I realized another failure was imminent.

Scene Six was set in the village of Middling. It was an

outdoor scene, one of those scenes crawling with extras. Basically, anyone who wanted to be on stage, could be on stage, as townspeople—adults and children—and dogs and cats.

Backstage was packed with people trying to get to their places in between the flats weighted down by my critique group, and the non-weighted flats that flew around stage. The crew hadn't found the right balance between the light touch the new scenery needed, and the heavier shove the pieces needed when people were sitting on them. Of course, it didn't help that my critique group didn't ever stand up off the braces in time.

All the actors and set pieces were in place. With dismay, though, I realized the village scenery—bright colorful store-fronts depicting a bookstore, grocery, barbershop, ice cream parlor—had four pieces instead of the three that all the other scenes had.

I grabbed the stapler and duct tape from Lavar and Tuttle and shoved them out on stage, whispering frantically, and apparently too loudly, "Go sit on it!"

Some weisenheimer from the audience shouted, "Yeah, Potsie! You and Ralph Malph go sit on it!" Everyone who'd ever watched an episode of "Happy Days"—seemingly the entire audience—burst out laughing.

Since the lights were already up, Lavar and Tuttle couldn't be hidden in the slightest. Lavar took the opportunity to let his inner ham loose and did a sideways "Kilroy was here" on the scenery flat they needed to protect. Tuttle's yanking him away only made the audience laugh harder.

Nova wanted to see what all the commotion was, and wandered across the stage. She stopped and wagged her tail, receiving thunderous applause and laughter for her efforts. She shook her head, flapping her ears and causing her red-and-green plaid bow to twist cockeyed around her neck. She sat and scratched at it before moseying over to where Lavar and Tuttle sat behind the scenery, earning her more than a few cheers of "Bravo!"

Everyone on stage was looking at me to see if they should start the scene or not. I nodded.

The townspeople began wandering through their town, milling about, miming conversations with their friends, leafing through books, getting a haircut, picking out vegetables, paying for stuff. In the play, the village of Middling has lots of dogs and cats, but mostly dogs because it was pointed out to me that cats aren't particularly social like dogs are. Plus, turns out kids liked being dogs better. Therefore, most— if not all—kids were costumed as dogs in this scene. The villagers pretended to brush them, read them a book, offer a treat. It was completely charming to see the senior actors interacting with the child actors.

I breathed a relieved sigh.

The background action with the extras carried on while Doug and Daisy began their dialogue.

I relaxed even more.

Until Peter O'Drool, the only real dog acting in the scene, saw his old pal Nova sitting behind the scenery with Lavar and Tuttle. His short legs scuttled across the stage, nails clicking and clacking loud enough that Daisy had to raise her voice to speak her lines. Peter's momentum and lack of regard for the gravity of the situation caused him to slide around the slick stage.

Nova loped out to meet him mid-stage and they had a bit of the rough-and-tumble play they enjoyed, fake biting and growling, until Nova allowed Peter to pin her, winning the battle.

All the while, Doug and Daisy were trying to ignore the commotion of the rough-housing and the hisses and cajoling from Lavar and Tuttle, and me, trying to get Peter and Nova offstage. Finally Tuttle came out from behind the flat, waved to the audience, then scooped up Peter and held him on his lap on the brace. Nova sat primly next to them while she and Peter booped noses.

We made it through the rest of the play with no further calamities. Santa said his final "Ho, ho, ho!" The kids playing dogs started spontaneously barking. Peter and Nova joined in and broke free to take their bow.

The crowd, as they say, went wild, jumped to their feet, applauding and whistling. They clearly loved every minute of the performance, despite—or perhaps because of—all the mishaps.

I sent the actors out for three curtain calls, each more enthusiastic than the last. I had to wave my arms until they quieted enough for me to shout, "If you enjoyed that, be sure to show your appreciation by filling those donation jars to benefit these great kids and their school. There are treats to purchase in back, and you can meet-and-greet the cast while you enjoy the goodies." The noise level rose again as the audience pushed back chairs and stood. "Thanks so much for coming out tonight!"

Backstage there was much hugging and more than a few relieved tears before we all cleared out to the refreshment area. So many people came to tell me how much they enjoyed the show and shake my hand that I thought it might be in danger of falling off my wrist.

When the crowd around me dispersed enough that Ozzi could reach me, he said with a smile, "You look a bit shell-shocked. Are you okay?"

"I might be, as soon as I figure out who sabotaged the sets by stealing all the sandbags."

"I didn't steal them!"

I whirled around to see Winston behind me in his wheelchair. Javier was handing him a couple of cookies on a festive paper napkin.

"You took the sandbags?" I asked.

Winston stuffed part of a frosted sugar cookie in his

mouth. We waited impatiently while he chewed and swallowed. "The sidewalk was slick so we shoveled then used the sand to keep people from falling."

"I helped!" Javier beamed. "I sat on his lap with the snow shovel while he pushed us in his wheelchair. We were like a human snowplow. And then he rolled around and I poured the sand on the slick spots."

"We make an excellent team," Winston said.

"You took all those sandbags outside and emptied the sand on the sidewalk? Why didn't you use the ice melt in the bin?" I asked.

"What ice melt? The bin was empty. I assumed somebody forgot to order more. Didn't want to get anyone in trouble. Took matters into our own hands." Winston and Javier fist-bumped.

Wait until Barb finds out that Doug never actually filled the bin like he said.

I started laughing but stopped abruptly when I saw the look on Ozzi's face. I leaned in. "I sound hysterical, don't I?"

"Little bit," he said. "I'll grab you something to eat."

"Thanks. Anything with bourbon would be great," I called after him.

Stephanie and Bobby walked up and I blushed at my quip. She held a beribboned set of all my books that I'd donated to the Christmas store. She gave Bobby the side-eye.

"Yes, it's really her!" he said, tugging her sleeve to pull her closer to me.

"You're Charlemagne Russo? Seriously? I love your books! Will you sign these for me? One of your books literally saved my life."

I laughed. "Literally? I don't think so."

"Yes, quite literally. First, because it was the only thing I had to read in rehab so I wouldn't be bored to death, but also because I had to use it against the side of some guy's head in an alley once."

I blinked, then managed, "God bless hard covers, right?"

She cocked her head, assessing me. "You know, I read an interview with an author once who said that authors write for themselves. But I don't think that's true. Everything is all joined together in ways we don't even realize. Your books. You. Me. Bobby." She draped an arm over her son's shoulder. "Like I was being selfish, wanting to keep Bobby out of trouble, thinking he was stealing, following my path instead of Carlos'. But I was wrong. I couldn't see what was right in front of my face, blinded by my own thoughts. Of course Bobby wasn't stealing … he was buying stuff for me but I couldn't see that. Why would he want ear cuffs, scarves, a candle sconce, or any of those other 'mom' gifts?" She chuckled.

"But when I saw her looking at these, I knew exactly what to get her," Bobby said.

Just as I finished inscribing the last book for Stephanie, Carlos came out to tell them he'd warmed up the truck and was ready to go.

My critique group waited until the Morales family gathered their belongings and stepped away. Then AmyJo gave me a squeal and a huge hug.

"That was so much fun!" she said.

"Ja. I never went to a production like that before," Heinrich said.

"You wrote that?" Einstein asked with a shake of his head.

"Well, all except the parts that didn't go well. Those were ad-libs."

Cordelia placed my hand in hers. "It was lovely, Charlee. Those children were a delight."

"I have to agree." I looked around at them. "I'll deny I ever said this, but I really enjoyed working with them … despite everything."

Jenica said, "You know what they say, never work with children or animals. And you did both."

"I did." I wiped my brow melodramatically.

"And you lived to tell the tale." Kell gave me a hug. "The question is, would you do it again?"

"In a heartbeat," I said, surprising even myself.

I hugged each of them before they left. AmyJo hugged Lance as they passed.

"You outdid yourself, Space Case."

I beamed up at my big brother. Compliments from him were hard to come by. "Thank you."

"I meant you outdid yourself with the crazy." He laughed, hugged me, and walked away. "Oh, by the way, you owe me big time for that mop."

Little by little, the rest of the crowd melted away. It seemed nobody wanted the party to end.

Lavar and Tuttle huddled next to one of the donation buckets, debating something. When I walked over to see what the problem was, I saw one of their decorating contest jars on the table.

"What's up, guys?"

"We're trying to figure out whether to just leave all these pennies here, as a donation."

"Who won the contest?"

Lavar took a deep breath. "Tuttle did, for his gaudy secular display."

Tuttle took a theatrical bow. "I did have an unfair advantage. If only Lavar hadn't lit that candle and create that creepy angel. Pretty much everyone who dropped money in felt strongly that he should be punished for giving them nightmares."

"Ha! How much is in there?" I eyed the huge container.

"Dunno," Tuttle said. "I didn't want to gloat so we just commingled the votes tonight and decided to give it all to the school."

"Then what were you arguing about?"

"Whether it's fair to dump this many coins on anyone," Lavar said with a worried look.

"Dump away! It'll give the kids something to do, now that the play is over."

They also dropped a couple of twenties in the donations, and gave me hugs before leaving.

Eventually just me, Ozzi, Barb and Don were left. Ozzi and I convinced them to leave by telling them we'd pick them up and come back tomorrow to finish cleaning up.

"I'm taking this now, though." Don grabbed the various donation canisters and stuffed all the cash into one. He left the jar of coins, after I explained what it was. "I promised Leona I'd give her an estimate tomorrow."

Ozzi gave a low whistle when he saw the huge canister almost full of cash. I couldn't even imagine how much money it was, but I saw lots of tens and twenties in there. I guess my suggestion at the end of the play caught the audience at the right time, when they were still wrapped up in the fun they were having.

After I locked the door to the senior center behind us, Ozzi held my hand. "Be careful, it's slick."

"That's not possible. There's a thousand pounds of sand out here."

TWENTY-THREE

The next day after we'd reorganized the senior center and I'd come home to shower and get ready for Ozzi's office party, I thought about everything that had happened over the last couple of weeks. It seemed like an eternity ago since those paramedics had been working on Ernesto.

The entire episode still confounded me. I drummed my newly manicured nails on my kitchen table while I waited for Ozzi. How that metal ended up in that star. How the star and the sandbag ended up in the basement where I'd hidden those craft pieces I made. How my bottle of ibuprofen ended up in Ernesto's house. Who knocked the scenery over and who was the intended target. And why.

Stephanie's words from last night kept ringing in my head. *There's something right in front of my face that I'm just not seeing.*

Someone wanted Ernesto dead and seemed to want me or Don to take the fall for it.

Ozzi used his key in my front door. I stood to greet him, smoothing my red velvet halter dress. I couldn't stop myself from blushing when he whistled at me. "You look absolutely gorgeous," he said, taking my hand. He twirled me and the skirt flared around my knees.

"You're not so bad yourself," I told him when I came to a stop. Even though the party was at their office, it remained a dressy affair and Ozzi didn't disappoint. He wore a three-piece black suit with a muted red-and-green plaid vest and matching tie. Coupled with his perfect three-day stubble, which I quit trying to understand, he still had the ability to take my breath away.

We shared a tender kiss, trying not to muss each other.

"You ready to go?" he asked.

"I am." I glanced down at my strappy heels. "Is it still snowing?"

"No, it stopped a while ago. And maintenance looks like they cleared the sidewalks."

"Oh, good. I was afraid I'd have to call Winston and Javier."

∼

I hadn't been to Ozzi's office in a while, but I was always struck by what a lovely place it was. The building was a fascinating combination of classic and modern architecture. The grounds were meticulously landscaped with gently curving beds of native Colorado flowers, shrubs, and trees. Of course, under this blanket of snow, the only plants visible were the towering blue spruces.

The administrative offices were on the ground floor, surrounding an open lobby with an atrium, which was of no use right now, since it was already dark outside.

Ozzi and I plucked glasses of wine from one of the sharply dressed servers circulating with trays of drinks and hors d'oeuvres. We joined some of his co-workers, chatting in a circle. After introductions were made, they continued their discussion of this year's Christmas bonuses.

Ozzi kept glancing at me to make sure the chatter wasn't boring to me, but I found it fascinating. Never having worked for a large company before, I was intrigued by the backstage minutiae of something as seemingly innocuous as holiday bonus pay. As far as I could glean, everyone got varying amounts of cash every year, depending on how well the company did during the year, and on each employee's situation. There seemed to be a complicated formula to determine how much everyone received.

Based on what they were saying, I became lost in calculating what my bonus would be if I had a job here. But my attention was drawn back to the laughing conversation about the recent Lunch Bunch foray. Someone mentioned that Doug must have gotten his bonus early because he paid for his lunch with a fifty-dollar bill. "Pulled it right out of his wallet and waved it around."

"A fifty?" someone clarified. "That doesn't sound like Doug 'I-Can-Barely-Afford-College-Costs' Beesley. Maybe with his promotion he won't have to bum money off the rest of us anymore."

They laughed again, but it seemed to be in a good-natured way, like they'd say it directly to him if he'd been here. And knowing Doug like I did now, he'd probably be the first to laugh.

I remembered him lamenting college costs for his twins, but everybody must eat. You can't save every single nickel for your kids.

Ozzi said, "Man's gotta have some walkin' around money in his wallet."

I sipped my wine, but almost choked when I remembered that Ernesto's wallet had a fifty-dollar bill when I found it. But Detective Ming said they didn't find a wallet at all.

Could Doug have taken that money? He was at Ernesto's house that night when he took him to the emergency room.

Was he so worried about college costs that he stole cash from Ernesto?

I searched for him in the crowded lobby but didn't see him. It was just as well. I didn't know what I would have done … accuse him at a fancy holiday party in front of his co-workers of stealing fifty bucks? Not likely.

I murmured to Ozzi that I was going in search of food and told him I'd bring him some. He offered to go with me, but I told him to stay and chat with his friends. I'd be right back.

I found the buffet table across the room and took my time surveying all the options. When I reached the far end, planning to go back and fill plates with some Swedish meatballs, prosciutto-wrapped asparagus spears, stuffed dates, and rumaki, for starters, I saw Doug being irritated by his twins. The boys were both dressed in ill-fitting clothes, but one twin wore a suit at least two sizes too big, and the other at least two sizes too small.

As I picked up plates and silverware for me and Ozzi, I heard they were arguing about the car. I surmised the boys wanted the car keys so they could leave what they surely considered a snore of a party. It must be difficult to have three people sharing one car. The night Doug took Ernesto to the emergency room he said he'd felt bad that the boys had left the radio on so loud. There was probably a continuous disagreement about the radio stations, as well as the seat positions, looking at the difference in height between Doug and his boys.

I scooped some stuffed dates on my plate. Luckily Lance and I didn't have those teenage car arguments for very long, although, looking back, I would have liked to have them a bit longer. After Dad died and Lance graduated early and left, the car was all mine.

I reached for a chocolate-covered strawberry, freezing in mid-air. If Doug drove his car to Ernesto's house, he would have heard the too-loud radio when he started the car at his own house, not when he was already at Ernesto's and buckling him in the car.

Doug became exasperated with the boys and walked away from them.

I decided to clarify this car situation for myself and sauntered over to the twins. They eyed the plates hungrily and I handed one to each of them.

"I couldn't help but overhear. Your dad never lets you have the car, huh? I remember my—"

They interrupted with a diatribe, listing all the transgressions foisted upon them by their father. It was like they shared one brain, though. While one shoveled food in his mouth, the other spoke, and the minute he finished, the other jumped right in without missing a beat.

The only problem was they spoke in monotone, using very simple, declarative sentences, and every cliché and speech crutch imaginable.

"I haven't, like, driven in, like, a month," one said.

"Do you, like, know how hard it is to go, like, out on a date?" the other said.

"If you, like, ask a girl out and she says, like, yes—"

"Then you have to, like, ask her to drive."

"Word is, like, getting around—"

"So nobody says, like, yes anymore."

I could think of several more reasons why girls wouldn't want to date them. These kids were super boring, just like Ozzi said, and more than a little annoying.

"At least we get to, like, go away to, like, college next year."

"Which of you picked up your dad a couple of weekends ago, after rehearsal?" I asked.

"Rehearsal for, like, what?"

"We don't even, like, own a car anymore."

"It got, like, repossessed."

You could have led with that, I thought, collecting the empty plates from them.

I filled new plates for me and Ozzi, but I couldn't concentrate and accidentally put goat cheese puffs on them both.

Doug was whining at the run-through of the play that he couldn't afford college, and now both the twins were going? But their car had been repossessed all this time?

I remembered Doug crying and his Shakespeare in the Park story. I dropped both plates and they clattered to the buffet. "What a fool I've been!" I hurried to a quiet corner and dialed Detective Ming.

Afterward, I grabbed Ozzi on the run, dragging him away from his friends.

"Hey, where's my food?"

"No time. We have to go find Doug."

TWENTY-FOUR

I explained my suspicions to Ozzi as we hurried through the building, poking our heads in various rooms where knots of people stood chatting, balancing plates and cocktails.

We found Doug in his office with a crowd of people. He was gleefully showing off how he'd decorated his new office —Ernesto's old office—and what he still planned to do. I told everyone that we needed a minute with Doug and trundled them all out, trying not to cause any alarm.

Doug held up one finger as he finished a story extolling the virtues of the leather furniture his huge new salary could buy.

As everyone left the office, I was just about to whisper to Ozzi not to let on we knew that Doug had something to do with Ernesto's death. I'd learned my lesson about waiting for the police to arrive and not barging in to confront bad guys.

Ozzi, on the other hand, had not.

Before I could get out any words, Ozzi said, "You killed Ernesto, you slimy piece of—"

Doug must have been expecting something like this because he didn't even pretend to be confused or shocked by Ozzi's allegation.

We stood between Doug and the door. Doug came hurtling at Ozzi, knocking him to the floor. In the process, he fell himself. Probably not the grand getaway he'd envisioned.

I was trying to help Ozzi up, but he was flailing around, the wind knocked out of him. I knelt on the floor next to Ozzi, but I couldn't hoist him to his feet. I glanced at Doug, also struggling to get up. Movement caught my eye and I saw a boxelder bug crawling through a crack in the joint between the floor and the bottom of the wall. I watched as it scurried to join a swarm of its compatriots in a tall houseplant sitting on the floor near Doug.

Leaving Ozzi on the floor still trying to fill his lungs, I crawled toward the plant and let the beetles swarm my hand. I blanched, feeling them crawl all around, hard little bodies bumping into each other, tickling my hand. When I felt like there were enough, I flung them at Doug.

He screamed and dropped to his knees, batting hysterically at his face, neck, and arms.

Ozzi finally pulled himself to his feet. Breath ragged, he stepped over me and grabbed Doug's upper arms from behind. "Don't move or she'll shove those bugs down your pants."

Doug screamed again, but pressed himself closer to Ozzi, for protection from me and my boxelder friends, I guess. I held my fist closed, pretending it was full of bugs just waiting to be thrown on to him.

"Now talk, and talk fast," I said. I wanted to hear his story before Detective Ming came and read him his rights.

Doug's face crumpled. "I thought when that star fell and hurt Ernesto, he'd maybe have to be off work for a while. He was so unhealthy, I thought if I gave him a scare with that ibuprofen, maybe he'd decide to retire. Or maybe he'd be forced to by his doctor. I thought I was just putting my thumb on the scales. But when he came in and collapsed and the cops and paramedics showed up, I realized what I'd done. I couldn't let anyone know I was involved."

"You killed him!" Ozzi shouted. "Why shouldn't people know?"

"You don't have kids, Oz. You can't understand what it's like." Doug tried to crane his neck to look Ozzi in the face, but he held him tight. "When my wife died, it was all on me, everything. The twins were young and my daughter not much older. They needed their mom but they only had me. It was an emotional, financial, shocking loss but I had to learn to cook, buy their clothes, make time to go to PTA meetings. You can't imagine how many times I was up all night baking cupcakes. I had to do it all but I didn't know how. I could barely get out of bed myself most days. I didn't have time to wallow and I certainly didn't have enough money. One income barely covered the basics. And then day after day, year after year, there was Ernesto, nobody but himself to support, sitting in a job he'd already made a ton of money from. I realized he was never going to retire on his own so I could move up the ladder." Doug ran his hands through his hair. "I didn't want him to die, though, just retire!"

"But he did die," I said quietly.

"And now my kids won't have either of their parents," he said angrily. "They don't deserve that."

"No, they don't. And Ernesto didn't deserve getting murdered either," I said.

"But you don't understand!" Doug wailed. "The guy just wouldn't retire! He even got company policy changed so he could stay in his job forever, just like Vladimir Putin. He wanted to keep doing it because he thought it was fun." Doug looked me in the eyes, determined to make me understand. "But I *deserved* this job. I *needed* this job. I *wanted* this job. I have two kids in college and one getting married."

Barb's words rang in my ears. *People want what they want, Charlee.*

"Did you put that metal in the Styrofoam star?" I asked.

"Yes," Doug whimpered.

"You were trying to frame me?" I asked incredulously.

Ozzi gave him a hard shake.

"Ow! Either you or Carlos or Daisy. I didn't care. Nothing personal."

"Weird, but I'm taking that very personally."

Ozzi tightened his grip again and rasped in Doug's ear. "What is *wrong* with you?"

I stared at Doug and shoved my closed fist at him. It was scant satisfaction to see him flinch. "You took my ibuprofen to his house to frame me too." Realization dawned on me. "You were wearing your elf gloves! That's why only my fingerprints were on the bottle. How much did you give Ernesto that night?"

"None, I swear!"

"You wanted to kill him, but—"

"I didn't want to kill him! I just wanted him to die." Doug whimpered again.

I saw Ozzi's knuckles had turned white from gripping Doug's upper arms so hard.

"So you gave him that ibuprofen."

"I didn't. He took it himself. I didn't do it."

"But you knew the combo with his prescription would kill him, based on what you read online."

"But I didn't give it to him." Doug whimpered some more.

"How'd he take it, then?"

Doug dropped his head and looked at the floor. Ozzi yanked him by the hair until he was forced to look me in the face. "I just … told him … it wouldn't be bad for him."

I stared at Doug and let my hand go slack. He flinched, expecting bugs. "You never took him to the emergency room," I said quietly, the whole truth crashing over me. "That's why Ming didn't have any hospital records. You knew that a conk on his head like that, when he was already on blood thinners, could give him a brain bleed and the ibuprofen would guarantee more damage. You might believe you didn't kill him, but by withholding care, you surely did, just as much as if you would have stabbed or shot him."

Ozzi looked at me, stunned, as he also comprehended the terrible truth. "Do you mean Ernesto would still be alive if Doug had taken him to the ER like he told us he did?"

I nodded, remembering what the pharmacist said.

Ozzi shook with rage. He raised Doug to his feet and seemed like he was about to body slam him on the desk.

At that moment Detective Ming rushed in with two uniformed officers. Ming pointed to Doug. "That's him," and the officers wrenched Doug from Ozzi's grip.

Ozzi backed away.

"You took Ernesto's wallet and knocked that scenery over on me."

"That was just lucky," Doug said. "I saw Carlos and his wife arguing—"

"So you took advantage of another way to try to frame us. You grabbed the sandbag, gave a little push, then hid it downstairs, knowing someone would find it just like they found the star."

The police led Doug away to the noise of Ozzi's extensive and emotional torrent of cursing. He followed the police officers all the way out of the building, berating Doug the entire time.

When they were out of earshot I turned to Detective Ming. "When are you going to start believing I don't kill people?"

Detective Ming simply raised one inscrutable eyebrow and left the office.

TWENTY-FIVE

The next day was Christmas Eve. Ozzi and Lance and I were up in Barb and Don's apartment exchanging gifts after eating a delicious prime rib dinner with all the trimmings that Barb cooked for us.

"I know you kids would rather have your actual mom here, but we think of you as family," Barb said. "All of you."

They wore their Santa and Mrs Claus costumes and Peter O'Drool was in his elf costume.

"How'd you get that outfit away from Thelma?" I asked her.

"She wisely decided she wasn't cut out for the stage. Next year we have dibs on these roles."

"We'll store the costumes here, though, just in case," Don said with a wink.

After dinner we opened gifts. Everyone knew which ones Ozzi was giving, because of the newspaper wrapping paper Bobby had used on them. Each package utilized approximately one-and-a-half rolls of tape to hold the paper on. It was adorable.

Barb said, "I have a special gift for Don that I can't wrap up."

"Ooh la la," Don said. "Time for you kids to go."

She blushed. "Oh, you! No … well, maybe … but right now I wanted to tell you that Boyd has rescinded his request for the recall election."

"That's great!" I said.

"Indeed it is," Don said with a huge grin. "Did he have a visit from three ghosts?"

"Even better. His wife Hazel"—she looked at the three of us—"the one with all the wigs? She threatened him with having to cook for himself as punishment for being such a sore loser. Apparently, when he saw that Don got the Santa job he wanted, he thought *he* deserved the board job that *he* wanted. Hazel told him he lost that election last year fair and square and to quit whining about it. Everyone over at the senior center knows Don couldn't have had anything to do with Ernesto's death."

"They sure seemed adamant when I talked to them." I told them about my whisper campaign and how it backfired against me.

"This'll make you feel better." Lance tossed me a gift. When I tore the wrapping off, I saw a throw pillow adorned with his beloved poop emoji. He gave Don and Barb some expensive bottles of wine, and Ozzi a self-help book entitled, *How to Live with a Narcissist*. Ozzi thought it was much funnier than I did.

Ozzi redeemed himself by giving me an antique pen case, as well as a custom t-shirt that said "*Sister of an Awesome Cop*." He gave Lance one that said "*Brother of a Famous Author*." And he gave Barb and Don matching shirts that said "*Don't make me mad. The older I get, the less life in prison is a deterrent*." Don immediately donned his.

Barb gave us all handcrafted lacy things she called anti-macassars which we all admired until she realized she had to explain what they were. "In the olden days, you know, back when Don was a boy—"

Don cupped his ear. "Eh?"

"—men rubbed macassar oil into their hair. So these were made to protect furniture. Anti. Macassar. Get it?"

Ozzi ran a hand through his hair.

"Not that you guys do that," she said hurriedly. "I just thought it was a pretty pattern. You can use them as doilies, under flower vases or as a centerpiece on your table." When she saw Ozzi and Lance drape them over their heads she laughed. "Or wear them as hats. I won't judge."

I gave Don a complete set of signed Rodolfo Lapaglia books because Lapaglia *owed* me and despite everything he had put us through, Don still loved those books. I gave Barb a pug-shaped necklace and matching earrings, along with one of the jewelry holders I made. I gave Lance a solid chocolate gun and set of handcuffs, and Ozzi a telescope he could set up on his patio, along with a book about stargazing.

"Oh my gosh! That's the one I had my eye on." He flipped through the book and found a small envelope he began to open.

I stopped him. "Better if you open that later."

Don said, "Ooh la la" again.

Lance said, "Gross."

Don gave Ozzi and Lance both a couple of fat cigars, and me a framed photo of himself. When I saw him grinning, I turned it over to find a gift card to a nearby day spa.

"You old coot. I love them both." I hugged the photo to my heart.

"Okay, there's one more." Don looked at Peter O'Drool. "Go get Charlee's gift."

Peter's fat little legs carried him into the other room. When he returned, he was wheezing from the exertion but held an envelope in his mouth. Don handed the envelope to me after he rubbed the supplemental drool into his pant leg.

"You already gave me that glamorous photo of yourself."

"This isn't from us. It's payment from Leona for all your hard work."

I promptly handed it back without opening it. "I'm not taking money from a charity. Please give it back to her with my appreciation for her thoughtfulness, but I'm donating it back to the school."

"She's not going to like that." Don pointed the envelope at me. "The school made a ton of money—in no small part because of the enormous donations from your writing friends Kell and Cordelia—and she really thinks you should have been paid, at least for writing the play. She argued with the school board and everything."

"Regardless, I'm not taking money that those kids need. And that's that." I folded my arms.

Ozzi took an envelope from his jacket pocket. "You can tell Leona that Charlee *was* paid. The CEO of Net Software, my boss, saw how well Charlee handled all the problems during the play, and the entire week—"

"How'd he hear about that?" I asked sarcastically.

"A proud little birdie told him." He shot me a grin. "And he loved how funny and cool that play was and how our girl here thought fast on her feet." He fluttered the envelope. "This is a job offer. He wants you to handle all the company communication—website, ad copy, official emails."

"I won't have time to write."

"I told him you'd say that. He says you can work from home and make your own schedule. He hopes this is enough to make you say yes." Ozzi nudged the envelope toward me.

I opened it and saw a number larger than I could imagine. And I had a pretty good imagination.

"He wanted to talk to you at the party," Ozzi said, "but he got a little busy talking to the cops."

I was flabbergasted at this offer and didn't know what to say. I handed the letter to Lance. His eyes got big when he read it. He passed it to Barb and Don who both gasped.

There was a knock on the door and Peter went nuts.

"Must be Santa!" Don sang out.

"He has to knock because there's no chimney," Ozzi said.

Don opened the door.

"Mom?" I rushed to her.

"I was hoping you two were up here." She smothered me and Lance in a huge Mom hug. "My friend Doris' nephew stepped up to take care of her so I hot-footed it to Colorado to surprise you." She held us both at arm's length. "Surprise!"

"Come in, come in," Don boomed. "You're lucky you didn't get caught in that snowstorm."

Barb hurried forward and pulled Mom into the center of the room where she helped her out of her coat.

Don put his arm around me and whispered. "I knew you wouldn't end up on the Naughty List."

A NOTE FROM THE AUTHOR

Thank you so much for reading Police Navidad!

If you enjoyed it, I'd really appreciate if you posted a quick review. It doesn't have to be much, just what you liked about it so others might decide they'd like it too.

As a **SPECIAL BONUS**, you can download the script of "Santa's Middling List," the play they performed in the book. It's a free and fun PDF, about thirty pages. If your group stages it, I'd love to be invited to see it!

Grab it at BeckyClarkBooks.com under the Mystery Writer's Mysteries tab. Scroll to the cover of "Santa's Middling List" and follow the directions!

ACKNOWLEDGMENTS

I often say that it takes a village to raise me, and I'm not joking. I am, of course, a fully-formed human, but I continue to evolve as a writer. Each new manuscript changes me, teaches me, inspires, and frustrates me.

But thank goodness I have people in my corner!

There are always moments in the drafting phase where I need something relatively minor, but my brain refuses to cooperate, probably because it is so minor. An ancillary character's name. A punny business name. The name of that flower … you know … the purply kinda spiky one? With the petals? Used to grow in my grandma's yard?

In the case of Police Navidad, that moment came when I was trying to figure out what each of my main characters would give to each other at their Christmas party. I did the only sensible thing. I turned toward my street team, my readers—the members of Becky's Book Buddies. Within about thirty-eight seconds of asking, I got the perfect responses.

So THANK YOU to Tammy Barker, Tam Sesto, Kimberlee Fisher Sams, Pat Doyle, Emily Scudder, and Marsha Holtz for knowing my characters well enough to know how they'd complete their Christmas shopping.

Another thing I always need are a few extra eyeballs on my outline/synopsis and my full manuscript. Coincidentally, I had just taught my "Eight Weeks to a Complete Novel" workshop to my Sisters in Crime Colorado chapter where I explain how I write my outlines and synopses, at the same time I was putting the final touches on the outline and synopsis for Police Navidad. I asked if any of the participants wanted to see a real-life example of what I was talking about. Enormous thanks to Skye Griffith, Linda Solaya, Rosemary Berry, Karen Whalen, and Peg Brantley, the kind souls who took me up on the offer and responded with excellent feedback.

As I marvel about this village that has been raising me, I can't help but think back to my orientation at Chapman College in Orange, CA a million years ago. The very first person I met there was Patrick Brien. He was delightfully weird and wonderful, and we've been friends ever since. Now he's the Executive Director of the Riverside Arts Council so he was the first person I turned to when I realized I had to write the Christmas play that forms the backdrop of Police Navidad. In addition to reading my full manuscript to comment on my "stagecraft bits," he also read the complete play I'd written, even though I'd never written one before. He was generous, kind, and supportive, exactly as I expected. I owe him a huge debt.

My editor extraordinaire, Jessica Cornwell, works her magic on all of my manuscripts. I keep making stupid comma, tense, and POV errors so she won't think she's wasting her time. I hope she appreciates it. Any remaining mistakes I've probably slipped in after she signed off on it. I don't like things to be too perfect, after all.

My husband Wes continues to bolster me and my endeavors, despite the fact he has no freakin' idea what I do all day clacking away on my keyboard. It's probably best he doesn't know.

Nala, my greyhound mix canine companion, continues to be my hairy muse. She's actually come to fictional life as "Nova" in this Mystery Writer's series, but she's also contributed traits to every dog I've ever written, even Peter O'Drool the pug. (She asked me to clarify and make perfectly clear that she is not gassy like 'ol Peter, lest anyone think of her as less than ladylike.)

Lastly and most importantly, especially if you've stuck with me this far, I need to thank you, the reader. Writers without readers are just goofballs jabbing wildly at keyboards for absolutely no reason. Thank you for giving me a reason.

Seriously. Thank you.

ALSO BY BECKY CLARK

ABOUT THE AUTHOR

Becky Clark is the seventh of eight kids which explains both her insatiable need for attention and her atrocious table manners. She likes to read funny books so it felt natural to write them, too. She's a native of Colorado, which is where she lives with her indulgent husband and quirky dog, who looks and acts remarkably like Nova in this book.

Becky loves to present workshops to writing groups and is a founding member of the Colorado Chapter of Sisters in Crime. Visit her on Facebook and at BeckyClarkBooks.com for all sorts of shenanigans.

CPSIA information can be obtained
at www.ICGtesting.com
Printed in the USA
LVHW061005180422
716493LV00014B/208